Erika Nauck

The Easter Story Book

The Easter Story Book

Collected by Ineke Verschuren

Floris Books

Illustrated by Ronald Heuninck

This collection first published in Dutch in 1988 under the title
Laat mij het levenswater zoeken by Christofoor Publishers, Zeist
© 1988 Christofoor, Zeist

This collection first published in English in 1991 by Floris Books,
15 Harrison Gardens, Edinburgh EH11 1SH.
© 1991 Floris Books, Edinburgh.

British Library CIP Data available

ISBN 0-86315-118-3

Printed in Great Britain
by Billing & Sons, Worcester

Contents

FROM EASTER TO PENTECOST

MIDSUMMER, FEAST OF ST JOHN

The Entry into Jerusalem

From the Gospel of Matthew

When they drew near Jerusalem and came to Bethphage on the Mount of Olives, then Jesus sent out two disciples, saying to them: "Go into the village that is in front of you, and immediately you will find an ass tied up and a colt with her. Untie them and bring them to me; and if anyone says anything to you, say: The Lord needs them. And he will send them at once."

This happened, so that what was spoken through the prophets might be fulfilled when he said: Tell the daughters of Zion. See how your King comes to you, gentle, and mounted on an ass, on a colt, foal of a beast of burden.

The disciples went and did as Jesus had directed them. They brought the ass and the colt, putting on them their cloaks on which he sat. The large crowd spread out their cloaks on the road, and others cut branches from the trees and spread them on the road.

The crowds who went in front and those who followed, cried out: "Hosanna to the Son of David. Blest be the one who comes in the name of the Lord. Hosanna in the highest places."

As he entered Jerusalem, the whole city was in uproar, saying: "Who is this?" And the crowds said: "This is the prophet Jesus, from Nazareth in Galilee."

Jesus Washes His Disciples' Feet

From the Gospel of John

Before the festival of the Passover, when Jesus knew that the hour had come when he should pass from this world to the Father, he loved those who were his own in the world, and he loved them to the last.

During supper, when already the devil had put the intention to betray him into the heart of Judas Iscariot, the son of Simon, and when Jesus knew that everything had been given into his hands by the Father, and that he came forth from God and was going to God, he rose from supper, and when he had taken off his clothes, he took a towel and tied it round his waist. Then he poured water into a basin and began to wash the feet of the disciples, and to wipe them with the towel which he had tied round him.

He came to Simon Peter who said to him: "Lord, are you going to wash my feet?"

Jesus answered him: "Now you do not know what I am doing, but after this you will understand."

Peter said to him: "As long as this age shall last, you shall not wash my feet."

Jesus answered him: "Unless I wash you, you have no part with me."

Simon Peter said to him: "Lord, not only my feet, but also my hands and my head."

Jesus said to him: "Anyone who has taken a bath has no need to wash (except for his feet). You are clean, but not all of you." He said: "Not all of you are clean," because he knew who was going to betray him.

When he had washed their feet and had put on his clothes, he sat down again, and said to them: "Do you understand what I have done to you? You call me Teacher and the Lord, and that is right, for so I am. If I have myself washed your feet, who am Lord and Teacher, you too should wash one another's feet. Because I have given you an example, that as I have done to you, you yourselves should do also. Of a certainty I say to you: a servant is not greater than his master, nor a messenger greater than the one who has sent him. If you know this, blessings will be yours if you do it.

"I am not speaking about you all. Myself I know whom I have chosen in order that the Scripture may be fulfilled which says: He who eats my bread has lifted up his heel against me.

"From now on I shall be telling you before it takes place, so that when it does take place you may believe that I am he. Of a certainty I say to you, he who receives whomever I may send receives me. And he who receives me, receives the one who sent me."

Robin Redbreast

Selma Lagerlöf

It happened at the time when our Lord created the world, when he not only made heaven and earth, but all the animals and the plants as well, at the same time giving them their names.

There have been many histories concerning that time, and if we knew them all, we would have light upon everything in this world which we cannot now comprehend.

At that time it happened one day when our Lord sat in his paradise and painted the little birds, that the colours in our Lord's paint pot gave out, and the goldfinch would have been without colour if our Lord had not wiped all his paint brushes on its feathers.

It was then that the donkey got his long ears, because he could not remember the name that had been given him.

No sooner had he taken a few steps over the meadows of paradise than he forgot, and three times he came back to ask his name. At last our Lord grew somewhat impatient, took him by his two ears, and said:

"Your name is ass, ass, ass!" And while he thus spake our Lord pulled both of his ears that the ass might hear better, and remember what was said to him. It was on the same day, also, that the bee was punished.

Now, when the bee was created, she began immediately to gather honey, and the animals and human beings who caught the delicious odour of the honey came and wanted to taste of it. But the bee wanted to keep it all for herself and with her poisonous sting pursued every living creature that approached her hive. Our Lord saw this and at once called the bee to him and punished her.

"I gave you the gift of gathering honey, which is the sweetest thing in all creation," said our Lord, "but I did not give you the right to be cruel to your neighbour. Remember well that every time you sting any creature who desires to taste of your honey, you shall surely die!"

Ah, yes! It was at that time, too, that the cricket became blind and the ant missed her wings, so many strange things happened on that day!

Our Lord sat there, big and gentle, and planned and created all day long, and towards evening he conceived the idea of making a little grey bird.

"Remember your name is Robin Redbreast," said our Lord to the bird, as soon as it was finished. Then he held it in the palm of his open hand and let it fly.

After the bird had been testing his wings a while, and had seen something of the beautiful world in which he was destined to live, he became curious to see what he himself was like. He noticed that he was entirely grey, and that his breast was just as grey as all the rest of him. Robin Redbreast twisted and turned in all directions as he viewed himself in the mirror of a clear lake, but he couldn't find a single red feather. Then he flew back to our Lord.

Our Lord sat there on his throne, big and gentle. Out of his hands came butterflies that fluttered about his head; doves cooed on his shoulders; and out of the earth beneath him grew the rose, the lily, and the daisy.

The little bird's heart beat heavily with fright, but with easy curves he flew nearer and nearer our Lord, till at last he rested on our Lord's hand. Then our Lord asked what the little bird wanted.

"I only wish to ask you about one thing," said the little bird.

"What is it you wish to know?" said our Lord.

"Why should I be called Red Breast, when I am all grey, from my bill to the very end of my tail? Why am I called Red Breast when I do not possess one single red feather?"

The bird looked beseechingly on our Lord with his tiny black eyes — then turned his head. About him he saw pheasants all red under a sprinkle of gold dust, parrots with marvellous red neckbands, cocks with red combs, to say nothing about the butterflies, the gold–finches, and the roses! And naturally he thought how little he needed — just one tiny drop of colour on his breast and he, too, would be a beautiful bird, and his name would fit him.

"Why should I be called Red Breast when I am so entirely grey?" asked the bird once again, and waited for our Lord to say: "Ah, my friend, I see that I have forgotten to paint your breast feathers red, but wait a moment and it shall be done."

But our Lord only smiled a little and said: "I have called you Robin Redbreast, and Robin Redbreast shall your name be, but you must look to it that you yourself earn your red breast feathers."

Then our Lord lifted his hand and let the bird fly once more — out into the world.

The bird flew down into paradise, meditating deeply. What could a little bird like him do to earn for himself red feathers? The only thing he could think of was to make his nest in a brier bush. He built it in among the thorns in the close thicket. It looked as if he waited for a rose leaf to cling to his throat and give him colour.

Countless years had come and gone since that day, which was the happiest in all the world. Human beings had already advanced so far that they had learned to cultivate the earth and sail the seas. They had procured clothes and ornaments for themselves, and had long since learned to build big temples and great cities — such as Thebes, Rome and Jerusalem.

Then there dawned a new day, one that will long be remembered in the world's history. On the morning of this day Robin Redbreast sat upon a little naked hillock outside of Jerusalem's walls, and sang to his young ones, who rested in a tiny nest in a brier bush.

Robin Redbreast told the little ones all about that wonderful day of creation, and how the Lord had given names to everything, just as each Redbreast had told it ever since the first Redbreast had heard God's word, and gone out of God's hand. "And mark you," he ended sorrowfully, "so many years have gone, so many roses have bloomed, so many little birds have come out of their eggs since Creation Day, but Robin Redbreast is still a little grey bird. He has not yet succeeded in gaining his red feathers."

The little young ones opened wide their tiny bills and asked if their forbears had never tried to do any great thing to earn the priceless red colour.

"We have all done what we could," said the little bird, "but we have all gone amiss. Even the first Robin Redbreast met one day another bird exactly like himself, and he began immediately to love it with such a mighty love that he could feel his breast burn. 'Ah!' he thought then, ' now I understand! It was our Lord's meaning that I should love with so much ardour that my breast should grow red in colour from the very warmth of the love that lives in my heart.' But he missed it, as all those who came after him have missed it, and as even you shall miss it."

The little young ones twittered, utterly bewildered, and already began to mourn because the red colour would not come to beautify their little, downy grey breasts.

"We had also hoped that song would help us," said the grown–up bird, speaking long drawn–out tones — "the first Robin Redbreast sang until his heart swelled within him, he was so carried away, and he dared to hope anew. 'Ah!' he thought, 'it is the glow of the song which lives in my soul that will colour my breast feathers red.' But he missed it, as all the others have missed it and as even you shall miss it."

Again was heard a sad "peep" from the young ones' half–naked throats.

"We have also counted on our courage and our valour," said the bird. "The first Robin Redbreast fought bravely with other birds, until his breast flamed with the pride of conquest. 'Ah!' he thought, 'my breast feathers shall become red from the love of battle which burns in my heart.' He, too, missed it, as all those who came after him have missed it, and as even you shall miss it."

The little young ones peeped courageously that they still wished to try and win the much–sought–for prize, but the bird answered them sorrow- fully that it would be impossible. What could they do when so many splendid ancestors had missed the mark? What could they do more than love, sing and fight? What could — the little bird stopped short, for out of one of the gates of Jerusalem came a crowd of people marching, and the whole procession rushed toward the hillock, where the bird had its nest. There were riders on proud horses, soldiers with long spears, executioners with nails and hammers. There were judges and priests in the procession, weeping women, and above all a mob of mad, loose people running about — a filthy, howling mob of loiterers.

The little grey bird sat trembling on the edge of his nest. He feared each instant that the little brier bush would be trampled down and his young ones killed!

"Be careful!" he cried to the little defenceless young ones. "Creep together and remain quiet. Here comes a horse that will ride right over us! Here comes a warrior with iron–shod sandals! Here comes the whole wild, storming mob!" Immediately the bird ceased his cry of warning and grew calm and quiet. He almost forgot the danger hovering over him. Finally he hopped down into the nest and spread his wings over the young ones.

"Oh! this is too terrible," said he. "I don't wish you to witness this awful sight. There are three miscreants who are going to be cruci- fied!" And he spread his wings so that the little ones could see no- thing.

They caught only the sound of hammers, the cries of anguish, and the wild shrieks of the mob.

Robin Redbreast followed the whole spectacle with his eyes, which grew big with terror. He could not take his glance from the three unfortunates.

"How terrible human beings are!" said the bird after a little while. "It isn't enough that they nail these poor creatures to a cross, but they must place a crown of piercing thorns upon the head of one of them. I see that the thorns have wounded his brow so that the blood flows," he continued.

"And this man is so beautiful, and looks about him with such mild glances that every one ought to love him. I feel as if a arrow were shooting through my heart, when I see him suffer!"

The little bird began to feel a stronger and stronger pity for the thorn–crowned sufferer. "Oh, if I were only my brother the eagle," thought he, "I would draw the nails from his hands, and with my strong claws, I would drive away all those who torture him!" He saw how the blood trickled down from the brow of the Crucified One, and he could no longer remain quiet in his nest. "Even if I am little and weak, I can still do something for this poor tortured one," thought the bird. Then he left his nest and flew out into the air, striking wide circles around the Crucified One. He flew around him several times without daring to approach, for he was a shy little bird, who had never dared to go near a human being. But little by little he gained courage, flew close to him, and drew with his little bill a thorn that had become embedded in the brow of the Crucified One. And as he did this there fell on his breast a drop of blood from the face of the Crucified One; it spread quickly and floated out and coloured all the little fine breast feathers.

Then the Crucified One opened his lips and whispered to the bird: "Because of your compassion, you have won all that your kind have been striving after, even since the world was created."

As soon as the bird had returned to his nest, his young ones cried to him: "Your breast is red! Your breast feathers are redder than the roses!"

"It is only a drop of blood from the poor man's forehead," said the bird. "It will vanish as soon as I bathe in a pool or a clear well."

But no matter how much the little bird bathed, the red colour did not vanish — and when his little young ones grew up, the blood–red colour shone also on their breast feathers, just as it shines on every Robin Redbreast's throat and breast until this very day.

Saint Veronica

Selma Lagerlöf

I

During one of the latter years of Emperor Tiberius' reign, a poor vine–dresser and his wife came and settled in a solitary hut among the Sabine mountains. They were strangers, and lived in absolute solitude without ever receiving a visit from a human being. But one morning when the labourer opened his door, he found, to his astonishment, that an old woman sat huddled up on the threshold. She was wrapped in a plain grey mantle, and looked very poor. Nevertheless, she impressed him as being so respect–compelling, as she rose and came to meet him, that it made him think of what the legends had to say about goddesses who, in the form of old women, had visited mortals.

"My friend," said the old woman to the vine–dresser, "you must not wonder that I have slept this night on your threshold. My parents lived in this hut, and here I was born nearly ninety years ago. I expected to find it empty and deserted. I did not know that people still occupied it."

"I do not wonder that you thought a hut which lies so high up among these desolate hills should stand empty and deserted," said the vine–dresser. "But my wife and I come from a foreign land, and as poor strangers we have not been able to find a better dwelling–place. But to you, who must be tired and hungry after the long journey, which you at your extreme age have undertaken, it is perhaps more welcome that the hut is occupied by people than by Sabine mountain wolves. You will at least find a bed within to rest on, and a bowl of goat's milk, and a bread–cake, if you will accept them."

The old woman smiled a little, but this smile was so fleeting that it could not dispel the expression of deep sorrow which rested upon her countenance.

"I spent my entire youth up here among these mountains," she said. "I have not yet forgotten the trick of driving a wolf from his lair."

And she actually looked so strong and vigorous that the labourer didn't doubt that she still possessed strength enough, despite her great age, to fight with the wild beasts of the forest.

He repeated his invitation, and the old woman stepped into the cottage. She sat down to the frugal meal, and partook of it without hesitancy. Although she seemed to be well satisfied with the fare of coarse bread soaked in goat's milk, both the man and his wife thought: "Where can this old wanderer come from? She has certainly eaten pheasants served on silver plates oftener than she has drunk goat's milk from earthen bowls."

Now and then she raised her eyes from the food and looked around as if to try and realize that she was back in the hut. The poor old home with its bare clay walls and its earth floor was certainly not much changed. She pointed out to her hosts that on the walls there were still visible some traces of dogs and deer which her father had sketched there to amuse his little children. And on a shelf, high up, she thought she saw fragments of an earthen dish which she herself had used to measure milk in.

The man and his wife thought to themselves: "It must be true that she was born in this hut, but she has surely had much more to attend to in this life than milking goats and making butter and cheese."

They observed also that her thoughts were often far away, and that she sighed heavily and anxiously every time she came back to herself.

Finally she rose from the table. She thanked them graciously for the hospitality she had enjoyed, and walked toward the door.

But then it seemed to the vine–dresser that she was pitifully poor and lonely, and he exclaimed: "If I am not mistaken, it was not your intention when you dragged yourself up here last night, to leave this hut so soon. If you are actually as poor as you seem, it must have been your intention to remain here for the rest of your life. But now you wish to leave because my wife and I have taken possession of the hut."

The old woman did not deny that he had guessed rightly. "But this hut, which for many years has been deserted, belongs to you as much as to me," she said. "I have no right to drive you from it."

"It is still your parents' hut," said the labourer, "And you surely have a better right to it than we have. Besides, we are young and you are old; therefore, you shall remain and we will go."

When the old woman heard this, she was greatly astonished. She turned around on the threshold and stared at the man, as though she had not understood what he meant by his words.

But now the young wife joined in the conversation.

"If I might suggest," said she to her husband, "I should beg you to ask this old woman if she won't look upon us as her own children, and permit us to stay with her and take care of her. What service would we render her if we gave her this miserable hut and then left her? It would be terrible for her to live here in this wilderness alone! And what would she live on? It would be just like letting her starve to death."

The old woman went up to the man and his wife and regarded them carefully. "Why do you speak thus?" she asked. "Why are you so merciful to me? You are strangers."

Then the young wife answered: "It is because we ourselves once met with great mercy."

II

This is how the old woman came to live in the vine-dresser's hut. And she conceived a great friendship for the young people. But for all that she never told them whence she had come, or who she was, and they understood that she would not have taken it in good part had they questioned her.

But one evening, when the day's work was done, and all three sat on the big, flat rock which lay before the entrance, and partook of their evening meal, they saw an old man coming up the path.

He was a tall and powerfully built man, with shoulders as broad as a gladiator's. His face wore a cheerless and stern expression. The brows jutted far out over the deep-set eyes, and the lines around the mouth expressed bitterness and contempt. He walked with erect bearing and quick movements.

The man wore a simple dress, and the instant the vine-dresser saw him, he said: "He is an old soldier, one who has been discharged from service and is now on his way home."

When the stranger came directly before them he paused, as if in doubt. The labourer, who knew that the road terminated a short distance beyond the hut, laid down his spoon and called out to him: "Have you gone astray, stranger, since you come hither? Usually, no one takes the trouble to climb up here, unless he has an errand to one of us who live here."

When he questioned in this manner, the stranger came nearer. "It is as you say," said he. "I have taken the wrong road, and now I know not whither I shall direct my steps. If you will let me rest here a while, and then tell me which path I follow to get to some farm, I shall be grateful to you."

As he spoke he sat down upon one of the stones which lay before the hut. The young woman asked him if he wouldn't share their supper, but this he declined with a smile. On the other hand it was very evident that he was inclined to talk with them, while they ate. He asked the young folks about their manner of living, and their work, and they answered him frankly and cheerfully.

Suddenly the labourer turned toward the stranger and began to question him. "You see in what a lonely isolated way we live," said he. "It must be a year at least since I have talked with anyone except shepherds and vineyard labourers. Can you not, who must come from some camp, tell us something about Rome and the Emperor?"

Hardly had the man said this than the young wife noticed that the old woman gave him a warning glance and made with her hand the sign which means, "Have a care what you say."

The stranger, meanwhile, answered very affably: "I understand that you take me for a soldier, which is not untrue, although I have long since left the service. During Tiberius' reign there has not been much work for us soldiers. Yet he was once a great commander. Those were the days of his good fortune. Now he thinks of nothing except to guard himself against conspiracies. In Rome, every one is talking about how, last week, he let Senator Titius be seized and executed on the merest suspicion."

"The poor Emperor no longer knows what he does!" exclaimed the young woman; and shook her head in pity and surprise.

"You are perfectly right," said the stranger, as an expression of the deepest melancholy crossed his countenance. "Tiberius knows that everyone hates him, and this is driving him insane."

"What say you?" the woman retorted. "Why should we hate him? We only deplore the fact that he is no longer the great Emperor he was in the beginning of his reign."

"You are mistaken," said the stranger. "Everyone hates him and detests Tiberius. Why should they do otherwise? He is nothing but a cruel and merciless tyrant. In Rome they think that from now on he will become even more unreasonable than he has been."

"Has anything happened, then, which will turn him into a worse beast than he is already?" queried the vine-dresser.

When he said this, the wife noticed that the old woman gave him a new warning signal, but so stealthily that he could not see it.

The stranger answered him in a kindly manner, but at the same time a singular smile played about his lips.

"You have heard, perhaps, that until now Tiberius has had a friend in his household on whom he could rely, and who has always told him the truth. All the rest who live in his palace are fortune-hunters and hypocrites, who praise the Emperor's wicked and cunning acts just as much as his good and admirable ones. But there was, as we have said, one alone who never feared to let him know how his conduct was actually regarded.

This person, who was more courageous than senators and generals, was the Emperor's old nurse, Faustina."

"I have heard of her," said the labourer. "I've been told that the Emperor has always shown her great friendship."

"Yes, Tiberius knew how to prize her affection and loyalty. He treated this poor peasant woman, who came from a miserable hut in the Sabine mountains, as his second mother. As long as he stayed in Rome, he let her live in a mansion on the Palatine, that he might always have her near him. None of Rome's noble matrons has fared better than she. She was borne through the streets in a litter, and her dress was that of an empress. When the Emperor moved to Capri, she had to accompany him, and he bought a country estate for her there, and filled it with slaves and costly furnishings."

"She has certainly fared well," said the husband.

Now it was he who kept up the conversation with the stranger. The wife sat silent and observed with surprise the change which had come over the old woman. Since the stranger arrived, she had not spoken a word. She had lost her mild and friendly expression. She had pushed her food aside, and sat erect and rigid against the door–post, and stared straight ahead, with a severe and stony countenance.

"It was the Emperor's intention that she should have a happy life," said the stranger. "But, despite all his kindly acts, she too has deserted him."

The old woman gave a start at these words, but the young one laid her hand quietingly on her arm. Then she began to speak in her soft, sympathetic voice. "I cannot believe that Faustina has been as happy at court as you say," she said, as she turned toward the stranger. "I am sure that she has loved Tiberius as if he had been her own son. I can understand how proud she has been of his noble youth, and I can even understand how it must have grieved her to see him abandon himself in his old age to suspicion and cruelty. She has certainly warned and admonished him every day. It has been for her terrible always to plead in vain. At last she could no longer bear to see him sink lower and lower."

The stranger, astonished, leaned forward a bit when he heard this; but the young woman did not glance up at him. She kept her eyes lowered, and spoke very calmly and gently.

"Perhaps you are right in what you say of the old woman," he replied. "Faustina has really not been happy at court. It seems strange, nevertheless, that she has left the Emperor in his old age when she had endured him the span of a lifetime."

"What say you?" asked her husband. "Has old Faustina left the Emperor?"

"She has stolen away from Capri without anyone's knowledge," said the stranger. "She left just as poor as she came. She has not taken one of her treasures with her."

"And doesn't the Emperor really know where she has gone?" asked the wife.

"No! No one knows for certain what road the old woman has taken. Still, one takes it for granted that she has sought refuge among her native mountains."

"And the Emperor does not know, either, why she has gone away?" asked the young woman.

"No, the Emperor knows nothing of this. He cannot believe she left him because he once told her that she served him for money and gifts only, like all the rest. She knows, however, that he has never doubted her unselfishness. He has hoped all along that she would return to him voluntarily, for no one knows better than she that he is absolutely without friends."

"I do not know her," said the young woman, "but I think I can tell you why she has left the Emperor. The old woman was brought up among these mountains in simplicity and piety, and she has always longed to come back here again. Surely she never would have abandoned the Emperor if he had not insulted her. But I understand that, after this, she feels she has the right to think of herself, since her days are numbered. If I were a poor woman of the mountains, I certainly would have acted as she did. I would have thought that I had done enough when I had served my master during a whole lifetime. I would at last have abandoned luxury and royal favours to give my soul a taste of honour and integrity before it left me for the long journey."

The stranger glanced with a deep and tender sadness at the young woman. "You do not consider that the Emperor's propensities will become worse than ever. Now there is no one who can calm him when suspicion and misanthropy take possession of him. Think of this," he continued, as his melancholy gaze penetrated deeply into the eyes of the young woman, "in all the world there is no one now whom he does not hate; no one whom he does not despise — no one!"

As he uttered these words of bitter despair, the old woman made a sudden movement and turned toward him, but the young woman looked him straight in the eyes and answered: "Tiberius knows that Faustina will come back to him whenever he wishes it. But first she must know that her old eyes need never more behold vice and infamy at his court." They had all risen during this speech; but the vine-dresser and his wife placed themselves in front of the old woman, as if to shield her.

The stranger did not utter another syllable, but regarded the old woman with a questioning glance. Is this your last word also? he seemed to want to say. The old woman's lips quivered, but words would not pass them.

"If the Emperor has loved his old servant, then he can also let her live her last days in peace," said the young woman.

The stranger hesitated still, but suddenly his dark countenance brightened. "My friends," said he, "whatever one may say of Tiberius there is one thing which he has learned better than others; and that is renunciation. I have only one thing more to say to you: If this old woman, of whom we have spoken, should come to this hut, receive her well! The Emperor's favour rests upon anyone who succours her."

He wrapped his mantle about him and departed the same way that he had come.

III

After this, the vine–dresser and his wife never again spoke to the old woman about the Emperor. Between themselves they marvelled that she, at her great age, had had the strength to renounce all the wealth and power to which she had become accustomed. "I wonder if she will not soon go back to Tiberius?" they asked themselves. "It is certain that she still loves him. It is in the hope that it will awaken him to reason and enable him to repent of his low conduct, that she has left him."

"A man as old as the Emperor will never begin a new life," said the labourer. "How are you going to rid him of his great contempt for man-kind? Who could go to him and teach him to love his fellow man? Until this happens, he cannot be cured of suspicion and cruelty."

"You know that there is one who could actually do it," said the wife. "I often think of how it would turn out, if the two should meet. But God's ways are not our ways."

The old woman did not seem to miss her former life at all. After a time the young wife gave birth to a child. The old woman had the care of it; she seemed so content in consequence that one could have thought she had forgotten all her sorrows.

Once every half–year she used to wrap her long, grey mantle around her, and wander down to Rome. There she did not seek a soul, but went straight to the Forum. Here she stopped outside a little temple, which was erected on one side of the superbly decorated square.

All there was of this temple was an uncommonly large altar, which stood in a marble–paved court, under the open sky. On the top of the altar Fortuna, the goddess of happiness, was enthroned, and at its foot was a statue of Tiberius. Encircling the court were buildings for the priests, store-rooms for fuel, and stalls for the beasts of sacrifice.

Old Faustina's journeys never extended beyond this temple, where those who would pray for the welfare of Tiberius were wont to come. When she cast a glance in there and saw that both the goddess' and the Emperor's statues were wreathed in flowers; that the sacrificial fire burned; that throngs of reverent worshippers were assembled before the altar, and heard the priests' low chants sounding thereabouts, she turned around and went back to the mountains.

In this way she learned, without having to question a human being, that Tiberius was still among the living, and that all was well with him.

The third time she undertook this journey, she met with a surprise. When she reached the little temple, she found it empty and deserted. No fire burned before the statue, and not a worshipper was seen. A couple of dried garlands still hung on one side of the altar, but this was all that testified to its former glory. The priests were gone, and the Emperor's statue, which stood there unguarded, was damaged and mud-bespattered.

The old woman turned to the first passer-by. "What does this mean?" she asked. "Is Tiberius dead? Have we another Emperor?"

"No," replied the Roman. "Tiberius is still Emperor, but we have ceased to pray for him. Our prayers can no longer benefit him."

"My friend," said the old woman, "I live far away among the mountains, where one learns nothing of what happens out in the world. Won't you tell me what dreadful misfortune has overtaken the Emperor?"

"The most dreadful of all misfortunes! He has been stricken with a disease which has never before been known in Italy, but which seems to be common in the Orient. Since this evil has befallen the Emperor, his features are changed, his voice has become like an animal's grunt, and his toes and fingers are rotting away. And for this illness there appears to be no remedy. They believe that he will die within a few weeks. But if he does not die, he will be dethroned, for such an ill and wretched man can no longer conduct the affairs of State. You understand, of course that his fate is a foregone conclusion. It is useless to invoke the gods for his success, and it is not worthwhile," he added, with a faint smile. "No one has anything more either to fear or hope from him. Why, then, should we trouble ourselves on his account?"

He nodded and walked away; but the old woman stood there as if stunned.

For the first time in her life she collapsed and looked like one whom age has subdued. She stood with bent back and trembling head, and with hands that groped feebly in the air.

She longed to get away from the place, but she moved her feet slowly. She looked around to find something which she could use as a staff.

But after a few moments, by a tremendous effort of the will, she succeeded in conquering the faintness.

IV

A week later, old Faustina wandered up the steep inclines on the Island of Capri. It was a warm day and the dread consciousness of old age and feebleness came over her as she laboured up the winding roads and the hewn–out steps in the mountain, which led to Tiberius' villa.

This feeling increased when she observed how changed everything had become during the time she had been away. In truth, on and alongside these steps there had always been throngs of people. Here it used fairly to swarm with senators, borne by giant Libyans; with messengers from the provinces attended by long processions of slaves; with office–seekers; with noblemen invited to participate in the Emperor's feasts.

But today the steps and passages were entirely deserted. Grey–greenish lizards were the only living things which the old woman saw in her path.

She was amazed to see that already everything appeared to be going to ruin. At most, the Emperor's illness could not have progressed more than two months, and yet the grass had already taken root in the cracks between the marble stones. Rare shrubs, planted in beautiful vases, were already withered and here and there mischievous spoilers, whom no one had taken the trouble to stop, had broken down the balustrade.

But to her the most singular thing of all was the entire absence of people. Even if strangers were forbidden to appear on the island, attend–ants at least should still be found there: the endless crowds of soldiers and slaves; of dancers and musicians; of cooks and stewards; of palace–sentinels and gardeners; who belonged to the Emperor's household.

When Faustina reached the upper terrace, she caught sight of two slaves, who sat on the steps in front of the villa. As she approached, they rose and bowed to her.

"Be greeted, Faustina!" said one of them. "It is a god who sends thee to lighten our sorrows."

"What does this mean, Milo?" asked Faustina. "Why is it so deserted here? Yet they have told me that Tiberius still lives at Capri."

"The Emperor has driven away all his slaves because he suspects that one of us has given him poisoned wine to drink, and that this has brought on the illness. He would have driven even Tito and myself away, if we had not refused to obey him; yet, as you know, we have all our lives served the Emperor and his mother."

25

"I do not ask after slaves only," said Faustina. "Where are the senators and field marshals? Where are the Emperor's intimate friends, and all the fawning fortune–hunters?"

"Tiberius does not wish to show himself before strangers" said the slave. "Senator Lucius and Marco, Commander of the Life Guard, come here every day and receive orders. No one else may approach him."

Faustina had gone up the steps to enter the villa. The slave went before her, and on the way she asked: "What say the physicians of Tiberius' illness?"

"None of them understands how to treat this illness. They do not even know if it kills quickly or slowly. But this I can tell you, Faustina, Tiberius must die if he continues to refuse all food for fear it may be poisoned. And I know that a sick man cannot stay awake night and day, as the Emperor does, for fear he may be murdered in his sleep. If he will trust you as in former days, you might succeed in making him eat and sleep. Thereby you can prolong his life for many days."

The slave conducted Faustina through several passages and courts to a terrace which Tiberius used to frequent to enjoy the view of the beautiful bays and proud Vesuvius.

When Faustina stepped out upon the terrace, she saw a hideous creature with a swollen face and animal–like features. His hands and feet were swathed in white bandages, but through the bandages protruded half–rotted fingers and toes. And this being's clothes were soiled and dusty. It was evident he could not walk erect, but had been obliged to crawl out upon the terrace. He lay with closed eyes near the balustrade at the farthest end, and did not move when the slave and Faustina came.

Faustina whispered to the slave, who walked before her: "But, Milo, how can such a creature be found here on the Emperor's private terrace? Make haste, and take him away!"

But she had scarcely said this when she saw the slave bow to the ground before the miserable creature who lay there.

"Caesar Tiberius," said he, "at last I have glad tidings to bring thee."

At the same time the slave turned towards Faustina, but he shrank back, aghast, and could not speak another word.

He did not behold the proud matron who had looked so strong that one might have expected that she would live to the age of a sibyl. In this moment, she had drooped into impotent age, and the slave saw before him a bent old woman with misty eyes and fumbling hands.

Faustina had certainly heard that the Emperor was terribly changed, yet never for a moment had she ceased to think of him as the strong man he was when she last saw him. She had also heard someone say that this ill–

ness progressed slowly, and that it took years to transform a human being. But here it had advanced with such virulence that it had made the Emperor unrecognizable in just two months.

She tottered up to the Emperor. She could not speak, but stood silent beside him, and wept.

"Have you come now, Faustina?" he said, without opening his eyes. "I lay and fancied that you stood here and wept over me. I dare not look up for fear I will find that it was only an illusion."

Then the old woman sat down beside him. She raised his head and placed it on her knee.

But Tiberius lay still, without looking at her. A sense of sweet repose enfolded him, and the next moment he sank into a peaceful slumber.

V

A few weeks later, one of the Emperor's slaves came to the lonely hut in the Sabine mountains. It drew on toward evening, and the vine–dresser and his wife stood in the doorway and saw the sun set in the distant west. The slave turned out of the path, and came up and greeted them. Thereupon he took a heavy purse, which he carried in his girdle, and laid it in the husband's hand.

"This, Faustina, the old woman to whom you have shown compassion, sends you," said the slave. "She begs that with this money you will purchase a vineyard of your own, and build a house that does not lie as high in the air as the eagles' nests."

"Old Faustina still lives, then?" said the husband. "We have searched for her in cleft and morass. When she did not come back to us, I thought that she had met her death in these wretched mountains."

"Don't you remember," the wife interposed, "that I would not believe that she was dead? Did I not say to you that she had gone back to the Emperor?"

This the husband admitted. "And I am glad," he added, "that you were right, not only because Faustina has become rich enough to help us out of our poverty, but also on the poor Emperor's account."

The slave wanted to say farewell at once, in order to reach densely–settled quarters before dark, but this the couple would not permit. "You must stop with us until morning," said they. "We cannot let you go before you have told us all that has happened to Faustina. Why has she returned to the Emperor? What was their meeting like? Are they glad to be together again?"

The slave yielded to those solicitations. He followed them into the hut, and during the evening meal he told them all about the Emperor's illness and Faustina's return.

When the slave had finished his narrative, he saw that both the man and the woman sat motionless — dumb with amazement. Their gaze was fixed on the ground, as though not to betray the emotion which affected them.

Finally, the man looked up and said to his wife: "Don't you believe God has decreed this?"

"Yes," said the wife, "surely it was for this that our Lord sent us across the sea to this lonely hut. Surely this was his purpose when he sent the old woman to our door."

As soon as the wife had spoken these words, the vine–dresser turned again to the slave.

"Friend!" he said to him. "You shall carry a message from me to Faustina. Tell her this word for word: Thus your friend the vineyard labourer from the Sabine mountains greets you. You have seen the young woman, my wife. Did she not appear fair to you, and blooming with health? And yet this young woman once suffered from the same disease which now has stricken Tiberius."

The slave made a gesture of surprise, but the vine–dresser continued with greater emphasis on his words.

"If Faustina refuses to believe my word, tell her that my wife and I came from Palestine, in Asia, a land where this disease is common. There the law is such that the lepers are driven from the cities and towns, and must live in tombs and mountain grottoes. Tell Faustina that my wife was born of diseased parents in a mountain grotto. As long as she was a child she was healthy, but when she grew up into young maidenhood she was stricken with the disease."

The slave bowed, smiled pleasantly, and said: "How can you expect that Faustina will believe this? She has seen your wife in her beauty and health. And she must know that there is no remedy for this illness."

The man replied: "It were best for her that she believed me. But I am not without witnesses. She can send inquiries over to Nazareth, in Galilee. There everyone will confirm my statement."

"Is it perchance through a miracle of some god that your wife has been cured?" asked the slave.

"Yes, it is as you say," answered the labourer. "One day a rumour reached the sick who lived in the wilderness: 'Behold, a great Prophet has arisen in Nazareth of Galilee. He is filled with the power of God's Spirit, and he can cure your illness just by laying his hand upon your forehead!' But the sick who lay in their misery would not believe that this rumour was the truth. 'No one can heal us,' they said. 'Since the days of the great prophets no one has been able to save one of us from this misfortune.'

"But there was one amongst them who believed, and that was a young maiden. She left the others to seek her way to the city of Nazareth, where the Prophet lived. One day, when she wandered over wide plains, she met a man tall of stature, with a pale face and hair which lay in even, black curls. His dark eyes shone like stars and drew her toward him. But before they met, she called out to him: 'Come not near me, for I am unclean, but tell me where I can find the Prophet from Nazareth!'

"But the man continued to walk towards her, and when he stood directly in front of her, he said: 'Why do you seek the Prophet of Nazareth?'

" 'I seek him that he may lay his hand on my forehead and heal me of my illness.'

"Then the man went up and laid his hand upon her brow. But she said to him: 'What doth it avail me that you lay your hand upon my forehead? You surely are no prophet?'

"Then he smiled on her and said: 'Go now into the city which lies yonder at the foot of the mountain, and show thyself before the priests!'

"The sick maiden thought to herself: 'He mocks me because I believe I can be healed. From him I cannot learn what I would know.' And she went farther. Soon thereafter she saw a man, who was going out to hunt, riding across the wide field. When he came so near that he could hear her, she called to him: 'Come not close to me, I am unclean! But tell me where I can find the Prophet of Nazareth!'

" 'What do you want of the Prophet?' asked the man, riding slowly toward her.

" 'I wish only that he might lay his hand on my forehead and heal me of my illness.'

"The man rode still nearer. 'Of what illness do you wish to be healed?' said he. 'Surely you need no physician!'

" 'Can't you see that I am a leper?' said she. 'I was born of diseased parents in a mountain grotto.'

"But the man continued to approach, for she was beautiful and fair, like a new–blown rose. 'You are the most beautiful maiden in Judea!' he exclaimed.

" 'Ah, taunt me not — you, too!' said she. 'I know that my features are destroyed, and that my voice is like a wild beast's growl.'

"He looked deep into her eyes and said to her: 'Your voice is as resonant as the spring brook's when it ripples over pebbles, and your face is as smooth as a coverlet of soft satin.'

"That moment he rode so close to her that she could see her face in the shining mountings which decorated his saddle.

" 'You shall look at yourself here,' said he. She did so, and saw a face smooth and soft as a newly–formed butterfly wing.

" 'What is this that I see?' she said. 'This is not my face!'

" 'Yes, it is your face,' said the rider.

" 'But my voice, is it not rough? Does it not sound as when wagons are drawn over a stony road?'

" 'No! It sounds like a zither player's sweetest songs,' said the rider.

"She turned and pointed toward the road. 'Do you know who that man is just disappearing behind the two oaks?' she asked.

" 'It is he whom you lately asked after; it is the Prophet from Nazareth,' said the man. Then she clasped her hands in astonishment and tears filled her eyes.

" 'Oh, thou Holy One! Oh, thou Messenger of God's power!' she cried. 'Thou hast healed me!'

"Then the rider lifted her into the saddle and bore her to the city at the foot of the mountain and went with her to the priests and elders, and told them how he had found her. They questioned her carefully; but when they heard that the maiden was born in the wilderness, of diseased parents, they would not believe that she was healed. 'Go back thither whence you came!' said they. 'If you have been ill, you must remain so as long as you live. You must not come here to the city, to infect the rest of us with your disease.'

"She said to them, 'I know that I am well, for the Prophet from Nazareth hath laid his hand upon my forehead.'

"When they heard this they exclaimed: 'Who is he, that he should be able to make clean the unclean? All this is but a delusion of the evil spirits. Go back to your own, that you may not bring destruction upon all of us!'

"They would not declare her healed, and they forbade her to remain in the city. They decreed that each and every one who gave her shelter should also be adjudged unclean.

"When the priests had pronounced this judgment, the young maiden turned to the man who had found her in the field: 'Whither shall I go now? Must I go back again to the lepers in the wilderness?'

"But the man lifted her once more upon his horse, and said to her: ' No, under no conditions shall you go out to the lepers in their mountain caves, but we shall travel across the sea to another land, where there are no laws for clean and unclean.' And they —"

But when the vineyard labourer had got thus far in his narrative, the slave arose and interrupted him. "You need not tell any more," said he. "Stand up rather and follow me on the way, you who know the mountains, so that I can begin my home journey tonight, and not wait until morning. The Emperor and Faustina cannot hear your tidings a moment too soon."

When the vine–dresser had accompanied the slave, and come home again to the hut, he found his wife still awake.

"I cannot sleep," said she. "I am thinking that these two will meet: he who loves all mankind, and he who hates them. Such a meeting would be enough to sweep the earth out of existence!"

VI

Old Faustina was in distant Palestine, on her way to Jerusalem. She had not desired that the mission to seek the Prophet and bring him to the Emperor should be entrusted to anyone but herself. She said to herself: "That which we demand of this stranger, is something which we cannot coax from him either by force or bribes. But perhaps he will grant it us if someone falls at his feet and tells him in what dire need the Emperor is. Who can make an honest plea for Tiberius, but the one who suffers from his misfortune as much as he does?"

The hope of possibly saving Tiberius had renewed the old woman's youth. She withstood without difficulty the long sea trip to Joppa and on the journey to Jerusalem she made no use of a litter, but rode a horse. She appeared to stand the difficult ride as easily as the Roman nobles, the soldiers, and the slaves who made up the retinue.

The journey from Joppa to Jerusalem filled the old woman's heart with joy and bright hopes. It was springtime, and Sharon's plain, over which they had ridden during the first day's travel, had been a brilliant carpet of flowers. Even during the second day's journey, when they came to the hills of Judea, they were not abandoned by the flowers. All the multi-formed hills between which the road wound were planted with fruit trees, which stood in full bloom. And when the travellers wearied of looking at the white and red blossoms of the apricots and persimmons, they could rest their eyes by observing the young vine–leaves, which pushed their way through the dark brown branches, and their growth was so rapid that one could almost follow it with the eye.

It was not only flowers and spring green that made the journey pleasant, but the pleasure was enhanced by watching the throngs of people who were on their way to Jerusalem this morning. From all the roads and by–paths, from lonely heights, and from the most remote corners of the plain came travellers. When they had reached the road to

Jerusalem, those who travelled alone formed themselves into companies and marched forward with glad shouts. Round an elderly man, who rode on a jogging camel, walked his sons and daughters, his sons–in–law and daughters–in–law, and all his grandchildren. It was such a large family that it made up an entire little village. An old grandmother who was too feeble to walk her sons had taken in their arms, and with pride she let herself be borne among the crowds, who respectfully stepped aside.

In truth, it was a morning to inspire joy even in the most disconsolate. To be sure the sky was not clear, but was overcast with a thin greyish–white mist, but none of the wayfarers thought of grumbling because the sun's piercing brilliancy was dampened. Under this veiled sky the perfume of the budding leaves and blossoms did not penetrate the air as usual, but lingered over roads and fields. And this beautiful day, with its faint mist and hushed winds, which reminded one of night's rest and calm, seemed to communicate to the hastening crowds somewhat of itself, so that they went forward happy — yet with solemnity — singing in subdued voices ancient hymns, or playing upon peculiar old–fashioned instruments, from which came tones like the buzzing of gnats, or grass–hoppers' piping.

When old Faustina rode forward among all the people, she became infected with their joy and excitement. She prodded her horse to quicker speed, as she said to a young Roman who rode beside her: "I dreamt last night that I saw Tiberius, and he implored me not to postpone the journey, but to ride to Jerusalem today. It appears as if the gods had wished to send me a warning not to neglect to go there this beautiful morning."

Just as she said this, she came to the top of a long mountain ridge, and there she was obliged to halt. Before her lay a large, deep valley–basin, surrounded by pretty hills, and from the dark, shadowy depths of the vale rose the massive mountain which held on its head the city of Jerusalem.

But the narrow mountain city, with its walls and towers, which lay like a jewelled coronet upon the cliff's smooth height, was this day magnified a thousandfold. All the hills which encircled the valley were bedecked with gay tents, and with a swarm of human beings.

It was evident to Faustina that all the inhabitants were on their way to Jerusalem to celebrate some great holiday. Those from a distance had already come, and had managed to put their tents in order. On the other hand those who lived near the city were still on their way. Along all the shining rock–heights one saw them come streaming in like an unbroken sea of white robes, of songs, of holiday cheer.

For some time the old woman surveyed these seething throngs of people and the long rows of tent–poles. Thereupon she said to the young

Roman who rode beside her: "Truly, Sulpicius, the whole nation must have come to Jerusalem."

"It really appears like it," replied the Roman, who had been chosen by Tiberius to accompany Faustina because he had, during a number of years, lived in Judea. "They celebrate now the great Spring Festival, and at this time all the people, both old and young, come to Jerusalem."

Faustina reflected a moment. "I am glad that we came to this city on the day that the people celebrate their festival," said she. "It cannot signify anything else than that the gods protect our journey. Do you think it likely that he whom we seek, the Prophet of Nazareth, has also come to Jerusalem to participate in the festivities?"

"You are surely right, Faustina," said the Roman. "He must be here in Jerusalem. This is indeed a decree of the gods. Strong and vigorous though you be, you may consider yourself fortunate if you escape making the long and troublesome journey up to Galilee."

At once he rode over to a couple of wayfarers and asked them if they thought the Prophet of Nazareth was in Jerusalem.

"We have seen him here every day at this season," answered one. "Surely he must be here even this year, for he is a holy and righteous man."

A woman stretched forth her hand and pointed towards a hill, which lay east of the city. "Do you see the foot of that mountain, which is covered with olive trees?" she said. "It is there that the Galileans usually raise their tents, and there you will get the most reliable information about him whom you seek."

They journeyed farther, and travelled on a winding path all the way down to the bottom of the valley, and then they began to ride up toward Zion's hill, to reach the city on its heights. The woman who had spoken went along the same way.

The steep ascending road was encompassed here by low walls, and upon these countless beggars and cripples sat or lolled. "Look," said the woman who had spoken, pointing to one of the beggars who sat on the wall, "there is a Galilean! I recollect that I have seen him among the Prophet's disciples. He can tell you where you will find him you seek."

Faustina and Sulpicius rode up to the man who had been pointed out to her. He was a poor old man with a heavy iron–grey beard. His face was bronzed by heat and sunshine. He asked no alms; on the contrary, he was so engrossed in anxious thought that he did not even glance at the passers–by.

Nor did he hear that Sulpicius addressed him and the latter had to repeat his question several times.

"My friend, I've been told that you are Galilean. I beg you, therefore, to tell me where I shall find the Prophet from Nazareth!"

The Galilean gave a sudden start and looked around him, confused. But when he finally comprehended what was wanted of him, he was seized with rage mixed with terror. "What are you talking about?" he burst out. "Why do you ask me about that man? I know nothing of him. I'm not a Galilean."

The Hebrew woman now joined in the conversation. "Still I have seen you in his company," she protested. "Do not fear, but tell this noble Roman lady, who is the Emperor's friend, where she is most likely to find him."

But the terrified disciple grew more and more irascible. "Have all the people gone mad today?" said he. "Are they possessed by an evil spirit, since they come again and again and ask me about that man? Why will no one believe me when I say that I do not know the Prophet? I do not come from his country. I have never seen him."

His irritability attracted attention, and a couple of beggars who sat on the wall beside him also began to dispute his word.

"Certainly you were among his disciples," said one. "We all know that you came with him from Galilee."

Then the man raised his arms toward heaven and cried: "I could not endure it in Jerusalem today on that man's account, and now they will not even leave me in peace out here among the beggars! Why don't you believe me when I say to you that I have never seen him?"

Faustina turned away with a shrug. "Let us go farther!" said she. "The man is mad. From him we will learn nothing."

They went farther up the mountain. Faustina was not more than two steps from the city gate, when the Hebrew woman who had wished to help her find the Prophet called to her to be careful. She pulled in her reins and saw that a man lay in the road, just in front of the horse's feet, where the crush was greatest. It was a miracle that he had not already been trampled to death by animals or people.

The man lay upon his back and stared upward with lustreless eyes. He did not move, although the camels placed their heavy feet close beside him. He was poorly clad, and besides he was covered with dust and dirt. In fact, he had thrown so much gravel over himself that it looked as if he tried to hide himself, to be more easily over–ridden and trampled down.

"What does this mean? Why does this man lie here on the road?" asked Faustina.

Instantly the man began shouting to the passers–by: "In mercy, brothers and sisters, drive your horses and camels over me! Do not turn aside for me! Trample me to dust! I have betrayed innocent blood. Trample me to dust!"

Sulpicius caught Faustina's horse by the bridle and turned it to one side. "It is a sinner who wants to do penance," said he. "Do not let this delay your journey. These people are peculiar and one must let them follow their own bent."

The man in the road continued to shout: "Set your heels on my heart! Let the camels crush my breast and the asses dig their hoofs into my eyes!"

But Faustina seemed loath to ride past the miserable man without trying to make him rise. She remained all the while beside him.

The Hebrew woman who had wished to serve her once before, pushed her way forward again. "This man also belonged to the Prophet's disciples", said she. "Do you wish me to ask him about his Master?"

Faustina nodded affirmatively, and the woman bent down over the man.

"What have you Galileans done this day with your Master?" she asked. "I meet you scattered on highways and byways, but him I see nowhere."

But when she questioned in this manner, the man who lay in the dust rose to his knees. "What evil spirit has possessed you to ask me about him?" he said, in a voice that was filled with despair. "You see, surely, that I have lain down in the road to be trampled to death. Is not that enough for you? Shall you come also and ask me what I have done with him?"

When she repeated the question, the man staggered to his feet and put both hands to his ears.

"Woe unto you, that you cannot let me die in peace!" he cried. He forced his way through the crowds that thronged in front of the gate, and rushed away shrieking with terror, while his torn robe fluttered around him like dark wings.

"It appears to me as though we had come to a nation of madmen," said Faustina, when she saw the man flee. She had become depressed by seeing these disciples of the Prophet. Could the man who numbered such fools among his followers do anything for the Emperor?

Even the Hebrew woman looked distressed, and she said very earnestly to Faustina: "Mistress, do not delay in your search for him whom you wish to find! I fear some evil has befallen him, since his disciples are beside themselves and cannot bear to hear him spoken of."

Faustina and her retinue finally rode through the gate archway and came in on the narrow and dark streets, which were alive with people. It seemed well-nigh impossible to get through the city. The riders time and again had to stand still. Slaves and soldiers tried in vain to clear the way. The people continued to rush on in a compact, irresistible stream.

"Truly," said the old woman, "the streets of Rome are peaceful pleasure gardens compared with these!"

Sulpicius soon saw that almost insurmountable difficulties awaited them.

"On these overcrowded streets it is easier to walk than to ride," said he. "If you are not too fatigued, I should advise you to walk to the Governor's palace. It is good distance away, but if we ride we certainly will not get there until after midnight."

Faustina accepted the suggestion at once. She dismounted and left her horse with one of the slaves. Thereupon the Roman travellers began to walk through the city.

This was much better. They pushed their way quickly toward the heart of the city, and Sulpicius showed Faustina a rather wide street which they were nearing.

"Look, Faustina," he said, "if we take this street, we will soon be there. It leads directly down to our quarters."

But just as they were about to turn into the street, the worst obstacle met them.

It happened that the very moment when Faustina reached the street which extended from the Governor's palace to Righteousness' Gate and Golgotha, they brought through it a prisoner, who was to be taken out and crucified. Before him ran a crowd of wild youths who wanted to witness the execution. They raced up the street, waved their arms in rapture towards the hill, and emitted unintelligible howls — in their delight at being allowed to view something which they did not see every day.

Behind them came companies of men in silken robes, who appeared to belong to the city's elite and foremost. Then came women, many of whom had tear-stained faces. A gathering of poor and maimed staggered forward, uttering shrieks that pierced the ears.

"O God!" they cried, "Save him! Send Thine angel and save him! Send a deliverer in his direst need!"

Finally there came a few Roman soldiers on great horses. They kept guard so that none of the people could dash up to the prisoner and try to rescue him.

Directly behind them followed the executioners, whose task it was to lead forward the man that was to be crucified. They had laid a heavy wooden cross over his shoulder, but he was too weak for this burden. It weighed him down so that his body was almost bent to the ground. He held his head down so far that no one could see his face.

Faustina stood at the opening of the little by–street and saw the doomed man's heavy tread. She noticed, with surprise, that he wore a purple mantle, and that a crown of thorns was pressed down upon his head.

"Who is this man?" she asked.

One of the bystanders answered her: "It is one who wished to make himself Emperor."

"And must he suffer death for a thing which is scarcely worth striving after?" said the old woman sadly.

The doomed man staggered under the cross. He dragged himself forward more and more slowly. The executioners had tied a rope around his waist, and they began to pull on it to hasten the speed. But as they pulled the rope the man fell, and lay there with the cross over him.

There was a terrible uproar. The Roman soldiers had all they could do to hold the crowds back. They drew their swords on a couple of women who tried to rush forward to help the fallen man. The executioners attempted to force him up with cuffs and lashes, but he could not move because of the cross. Finally two of them took hold of the cross to remove it.

Then he raised his head, and old Faustina could see his face. The cheeks were streaked by lashes from a whip, and from his brow, which was wounded by the thorn–crown, trickled some drops of blood. His hair hung in knotted tangles, clotted with sweat and blood. His jaw was firm set, but his lips trembled, as if they struggled to suppress a cry. His eyes, tear–filled and almost blinded from torture and fatigue, stared straight ahead.

But behind this half–dead person's face, the old woman saw — as in a vision — a pale and beautiful One with glorious, majestic eyes and gentle features, and she was seized with sudden grief — touched by the unknown man's misfortune and degradation.

"Oh, what have they done with you, you poor soul!" she burst out, and moved a step nearer him, while her eyes filled with tears. She forgot her own sorrow and anxiety for this tortured man's distress. She thought her heart would burst from pity. She, like the other women, wanted to rush forward and tear him away from the executioners!

The fallen man saw how she came toward him, and he crept closer to her. It was as though he had expected to find protection with her against all those who persecuted and tortured him. He embraced her knees. He pressed himself against her, like a child who clings close to his mother for safety.

The old woman bent over him, and as the tears streamed down her

cheeks, she felt the most blissful joy because he had come and sought protection with her. She placed one arm around his neck, and as a mother first of all wipes away the tears from her child's eyes, she laid her kerchief of sheer fine linen over his face, to wipe away the tears and the blood.

But now the executioners were ready with the cross. They came now and snatched away the prisoner. Impatient over the delay, they dragged him off in wild haste. The condemned man uttered a groan when he was led away from the refuge he had found, but he offered no resistance.

Faustina embraced him to hold him back, and when her feeble old hands were powerless and she saw him borne away, she felt as if some-one had torn her own child from her, and she cried: "No, no! Do not take him from me! He must not die! He shall not die!"

She felt the most intense grief and indignation because he was being led away. She wanted to rush after him. She wanted to fight with the executioners and tear him from them.

But with the first step she took, she was seized with weakness and dizziness. Sulpicius made haste to place his arm around her, to prevent her from falling.

On one side of the street he saw a little shop, and carried her in. There was neither bench nor chair inside, but the shopkeeper was a kindly man. He helped her over to a rug, and arranged a bed for her on the stone floor.

She was not unconscious, but such a great dizziness had seized her that she could not sit up, but was forced to lie down.

"She has made a long journey today, and the noise and crush in the city have been too much for her," said Sulpicius to the merchant. "She is very old, and no one is so strong as not to be conquered by age."

"This is a trying day, even for one who is not old," said the merchant. "The air is almost too heavy to breathe. It would not surprise me if a severe storm were in store for us."

Sulpicius bent over the old woman. She had fallen asleep, and she slept with calm, regular respirations after all the excitement and fatigue.

He walked over to the shop door, stood there, and looked at the crowds while he awaited her waking.

VII

The Roman governor at Jerusalem had a young wife, and she had had a dream during the night preceding the day when Faustina entered the city.

She dreamed that she stood on the roof of her house and looked down upon the beautiful court, which according to the Oriental custom, was paved with marble, and planted with rare shrubs.

But in the court she saw assembled all the sick and blind and lame there were in the world. She saw before her the pest–ridden, with bodies swollen with boils; lepers with disfigured faces; the paralytics, who could not move, but lay helpless upon the ground; and all the wretched creatures who writhed in torment and pain.

They all crowded up towards the entrance, to get into the house; and a number of those who walked foremost pounded on the palace door.

At last she saw that a slave opened the door and came out on the threshold, and she heard him ask what they wanted.

Then they answered him saying: "We seek the great Prophet whom God has sent to the world. Where is the Prophet of Nazareth, he who is master of all suffering? Where is he who can deliver us from all our torment?"

Then the slave answered them in an arrogant and indifferent tone — as palace servants do when they turn away the poor stranger:

"It will profit you nothing to seek the great Prophet. Pilate has killed him."

Then there arose among all the sick a grief and a moaning and a gnashing of teeth which she could not bear to hear. Her heart was wrung with compassion, and tears streamed from her eyes. But when she had begun to weep, she awakened.

Again she fell asleep; and again she dreamed that she stood on the roof of her house and looked down upon the big court, which was as broad as a square.

And behold, the court was filled with all the insane and soul–sick and those possessed of evil spirits. And she saw those who were naked; and those who were covered with their long hair, and those who had braided themselves crowns of straw and mantles of grass and believed they were kings, and those who crawled on the ground and thought themselves beasts, and those who came dragging heavy stones, which they believed to be gold, and those who thought that the evil spirits spoke through their mouths.

She saw all these crowd up toward the palace gate. And the ones who stood nearest to it knocked and pounded to get in.

At last the door opened, and a slave stepped out on the threshold and asked: "What do you want?"

Then all began to cry aloud, saying: "Where is the great Prophet of Nazareth, he who was sent of God, and who shall restore to us our souls and our wits?"

She heard the slave answer them in the most indifferent tone: "It is useless for you to seek the great Prophet. Pilate has killed him."

When this was said, they uttered a shriek as wild as a beast's howl, and in their despair they began to lacerate themselves until the blood ran down on the stones. And when she that dreamed saw their distress, she wrung her hands and moaned. And her own moans awakened her.

But again she fell asleep, and again, in her dream, she was on the roof of her house. Round about her sat her slaves, who played for her upon cymbals and zithers, and the almond trees shook their white blossoms over her, and clambering rose-vines exhaled their perfume.

As she sat there a voice spoke to her: "Go over to the balustrade which encloses the roof, and see who they are that stand and wait in your court!"

But in the dream she declined, and said: "I do not care to see any more of those who throng my court tonight."

Just then she heard a clanking of chains and a pounding of heavy hammers, and the pounding of wood against wood. Her slaves ceased their singing and playing and hurried over to the railing and looked down. Nor could she herself remain seated, but walked thither and looked down on the court.

Then she saw that the court was filled with all the poor prisoners in the world. She saw those who must lie in dark prison dungeons, fettered with heavy chains; she saw those who laboured in the dark mines come dragging their heavy planks, and those who were rowers on war galleys come with their heavy iron-bound oars. And those who were condemned to be crucified came dragging their crosses, and those who were to be beheaded came with their broad-axes. She saw those who were sent into slavery to foreign lands and whose eyes burned with homesickness. She saw those who must serve as beasts of burden, and whose backs were bleeding from lashes.

All these unfortunates cried as with one voice: "Open, open!"

Then the slave who guarded the entrance stepped to the door and asked: "What is it that you wish?"

And these answered like the others: "We seek the great Prophet of Nazareth, who has come to the world to give the prisoners their freedom and the slaves their lost happiness."

The slave answered them in a tired and indifferent tone: "You cannot find him here. Pilate has killed him."

When this was said, she who dreamed thought that among all the unhappy there arose such an outburst of scorn and blasphemy that heaven and earth trembled. She was ice-cold with fright, and her body shook so that she awoke.

When she was thoroughly awake, she sat up in bed and thought to herself: "I would not dream more. Now I want to remain awake all night, that I may escape seeing more of this horror."

And even whilst she was thinking thus, drowsiness crept in upon her anew, and she laid her head on the pillow and fell asleep.

Again she dreamed that she sat on the roof of her house, and now her little son ran back and forth up there, and played with a ball.

Then she heard a voice that said to her: "Go over to the balustrade, which encloses the roof, and see who they are that stand and wait in your court!" But she who dreamed said to herself: "I have seen enough misery this night. I cannot endure any more. I would remain where I am."

At that moment her son threw his ball so that it dropped outside the balustrade, and the child ran forward and clambered up on the railing. Then she was frightened. She rushed over and seized hold of the child.

But with that she happened to cast her eyes downward and once more she saw that the court was full of people.

In the court were all the peoples of earth who had been wounded in battle. They came with severed bodies, with cut–off limbs, and with big open wounds from which the blood oozed, so that the whole court was drenched with it.

And beside these, came all the people in the world who had lost their loved ones on the battlefield. They were the fatherless who mourned their protectors, and the young maidens who cried for their lovers, and the aged who sighed for their sons.

The foremost among them pushed against the door, and the watchman came out as before, and opened it.

He asked all these, who had been wounded in battles and skirmishes: "What do you seek in this house?"

And they answered: "We seek the great Prophet of Nazareth, who shall prohibit wars and rumours of wars and bring peace to the earth. We seek him who shall convert spears into scythes and swords into pruning hooks."

Then answered the slave somewhat impatiently: "Let no more come to pester me! I have already said it often enough. The great Prophet is not here. Pilate has killed him."

Thereupon he closed the gate. But she who dreamed thought of all the lamentation which would come now. "I do not wish to hear it," said she, and rushed away from the balustrade. That instant she awoke. Then she discovered that in her terror she had jumped out of her bed and down on the cold stone floor.

Again she thought she did not want to sleep more that night, and again sleep overpowered her, and she closed her eyes and began to dream.

She sat once more on the roof of her house, and beside her stood her husband. She told him of her dreams, and he ridiculed her.

Again she heard a voice, which said to her: "Go and see the people who wait in your court!"

But she thought: "I would not see them. I have seen enough misery tonight"

Just then she heard three loud raps on the gate, and her husband walked over to the balustrade to see who it was that asked admittance to his house.

But no sooner had he leaned over the railing, than he beckoned to his wife to come over to him.

"Know you not this man?" said he, and pointed down.

When she looked down on the court, she found that it was filled with horses and riders; slaves were busy unloading asses and camels. It looked as though a distinguished traveller might have arrived.

At the entrance gate stood the traveller. He was a large elderly man with broad shoulders and a heavy and gloomy appearance.

The dreamer recognized the stranger instantly, and whispered to her husband: "It is Caesar Tiberius, who is here in Jerusalem. It cannot be any one else."

"I also seem to recognize him," said her husband; at the same time he placed his finger on his mouth, as a signal that they should be quiet and listen to what was said down in the court.

They saw that the doorkeeper came out and asked the stranger: "Whom do you seek?"

And the traveller answered: "I seek the great Prophet of Nazareth, who is endowed with God's power to perform miracles. It is Emperor Tiberius who calls him, that he may liberate him from a terrible disease, which no other physician can cure."

When he had spoken, the slave bowed very humbly and said: "My lord, be not wroth! but your wish cannot be fulfilled."

Then the Emperor turned toward his slaves; who waited below in the court, and gave them a command.

Then the slaves hastened forward — some with handfuls of ornaments, others carried goblets studded with pearls, others again dragged sacks filled with gold coin.

The Emperor turned to the slave who guarded the gate, and said: "All this shall be his, if he helps Tiberius. With this he can give riches to all the world's poor."

But the doorkeeper bowed still lower and said: "Master, be not wroth with your servant, but your request cannot be fulfilled."

Then the Emperor beckoned again to his slaves, and a pair of them hurried forward with a richly embroidered robe, upon which glittered a breast–piece of jewels.

And the Emperor said to the slave: "See! This which I offer him is the power over Judea. He shall rule his people like the highest judge, if he will only come and heal Tiberius!"

The slave bowed still nearer the earth, and said: "Master, it is not within my power to help you."

Then the Emperor beckoned once again, and his slaves rushed up with a golden coronet and a purple mantle.

"See," he said, "this is the Emperor's will: He promises to appoint the Prophet his successor, and give him dominion over the world. He shall have power to rule the world according to his God's will, if he will only stretch forth his hand and heal Tiberius!"

Then the slave fell at the Emperor's feet and said in an imploring tone: "Master, it does not lie in my power to attend to your command. He whom you seek is no longer here. Pilate has killed him."

VIII

When the young woman awoke, it was already full, clear day and her female slaves stood and waited so that they might help her dress.

She was very silent while she dressed, but finally she asked the slave who arranged her hair, if her husband was up. She learned that he had been called out to pass judgment on a criminal. "I should have liked to talk with him," said the young woman.

"Mistress," said the slave, "it will be difficult to do so during the trial. We will let you know as soon as it is over."

She sat silent now until her toilet was completed. Then she asked: "Has any among you heard of the Prophet of Nazareth?"

"The Prophet of Nazareth is a Jewish miracle–performer," answered one of the slaves instantly.

"It is strange, Mistress, that you should ask after him today," said another slave. "It is just he whom the Jews have brought here to the palace, to let him be tried by the Governor."

She bade them go at once and ascertain for what cause he was arraigned, and one of the slaves withdrew. When she returned she said: "They accuse him of wanting to make himself King over this land, and they entreat the Governor to let him be crucified."

When the Governor's wife heard this, she grew terrified and said: "I must speak with my husband, otherwise a terrible calamity will happen here this day."

When the slaves said once again that this was impossible, she began to weep and shudder. And one among them was touched, so she said: "If you will send a written message to the Governor, I will try and take it to him."

Immediately she took a stylus and wrote a few words on a wax tablet, and this was given to Pilate.

But she did not meet him alone the whole day; for when he had dismissed the Jews, and the condemned man was taken to the place of execution, the hour for repast had come, and to this Pilate had invited a few of the Romans who visited Jerusalem at this season. They were the commander of the troops and a young instructor in oratory, and several others besides.

This repast was not very gay, for the Governor's wife sat all the while silent and dejected, and took no part in the conversation.

When the guests asked if she was ill or distraught, the Governor laughingly related about the message she had sent him in the morning. He chaffed her because she had believed that a Roman governor would let himself be guided in his judgments by a woman's dreams.

She answered gently and sadly: "In truth, it was no dream, but a warning sent by the gods. You should at least have let the man live through this one day."

They saw that she was seriously distressed. She would not be comforted, no matter how much the guests exerted themselves, by keeping up the conversation to make her forget these empty fancies.

But after a while one of them raised his head and exclaimed: "What is this? Have we sat so long at table that the day is already gone?"

All looked up now, and they observed that a dim twilight settled down over nature. Above all, it was remarkable to see how the whole variegated play of colour which it spread over all creatures and objects, faded away slowly, so that all looked a uniform grey.

Like everything else, even their own faces lost their colour. "We actually look like the dead," said the young orator with a shudder. "Our cheeks are grey and our lips black."

As this darkness grew more intense, the woman's fear increased. "Oh, my friend!" she burst out at last. "Can't you perceive even now that the Immortals warn you? They are incensed because you condemned a holy and innocent man. I am thinking that although he may already be on the cross, he is surely not dead yet. Let him be taken down from the cross!

I would with my own hands nurse his wounds. Only grant that he be called back to life!"

But Pilate answered laughingly: "You are surely right in that this is a sign from the gods. But they do not let the sun lose its lustre because a Jewish heretic has been condemned to the cross. On the contrary, we may expect that important matters shall appear, which concern the whole kingdom. Who can tell how long old Tiberius —"

He did not finish the sentence, for the darkness had become so profound he could not see even the wine goblet standing in front of him. He broke off, therefore, to order the slaves to fetch some lamps instantly.

When it had become so light that he could see the faces of his guests, it was impossible for him not to notice the depression which had come over them. "Mark you!" he said half–angrily to his wife. "Now it is apparent to me that you have succeeded with your dreams in driving away the joys of the table. But if it must needs be that you cannot think of anything else today, then let us hear what you have dreamed. Tell it to us and we will try to interpret its meaning!"

For this the young wife was ready at once. And while she related vision after vision, the guests grew more and more serious. They ceased emptying their goblets, and they sat with brows knit. The only on who continued to laugh and to call the whole thing madness, was the Governor himself.

When the narrative had ended, the young rhetorician said: "Truly, this is something more than a dream, for I have seen this day not the Emperor, but his old friend Faustina, march into the city. Only it surprises me that she has not already appeared in the Governor's palace."

"There is actually a rumour abroad to the effect that the Emperor has been stricken with a terrible illness," observed the leader of the troops. "It also seems very possible to me that your wife's dream may be a godsent warning."

"There's nothing incredible in this, that Tiberius has sent messengers after the Prophet to summon him to his sick–bed," agreed the young rhetorician.

The Commander turned with profound seriousness toward Pilate. "If the Emperor has actually taken it into his head to let this miracle–worker be summoned, it were better for you and for all of us that he found him alive."

Pilate answered irritably: "Is it the darkness that has turned you into children? One would think that you had all been transformed into dream–interpreters and prophets."

But the courtier continued his argument: "It may not be impossible, perhaps, to save the man's life, if you sent a swift messenger."

"You want to make a laughing-stock of me," answered the Governor. "Tell me, what would become of law and order in this land, if they learned that the Governor pardoned a criminal because his wife has dreamed a bad dream?"

"It is the truth, however, and not a dream, that I have seen Faustina in Jerusalem," said the young orator.

"I shall take the responsibility of defending my actions before the Emperor," said Pilate. "He will understand that this visionary, who let himself be misused by my soldiers without resistance, would not have had the power to help him."

As he was speaking, the house was shaken by a noise like a powerful rolling thunder, and an earthquake shook the ground. The Governor's palace stood intact, but during some minutes just after the earthquake, a terrific crash of crumbling houses and falling pillars was heard.

As soon as a human voice could make itself heard, the Governor called a slave.

"Run out to the place of execution and command in my name that the Prophet of Nazareth shall be taken down from the cross!"

The slave hurried away. The guests filed from the dining-hall out on the peristyle, to be under the open sky in case the earthquake should be repeated. No-one dared to utter a word, while they awaited the slave's return.

He came back very shortly. He stopped before the Governor.

"You found him alive?" said he.

"Master, he was dead, and on the very second that he gave up the ghost, the earthquake occurred."

The words were hardly spoken when two loud knocks sounded against the outer gate. When these knocks were heard, they all staggered back and leaped up, as though it had been a new earthquake.

Immediately afterwards a slave came up.

"It is the noble Faustina and the Emperor's kinsman Sulpicius. They have come to beg you help them find the Prophet from Nazareth."

A low murmur passed through the peristyle, and soft footfalls were heard. When the Governor looked around, he noticed that his friends had withdrawn from him, as from one upon whom misfortune has fallen.

IX

Old Faustina had returned to Capri and had sought out the Emperor. She told him her story, and while she spoke she hardly dared look at him.

During her absence the illness had made frightful ravages, and she thought to herself: "If there had been any pity among the Celestials, they would have let me die before being forced to tell this poor, tortured man that all hope is gone."

To her astonishment, Tiberius listened to her with the utmost indifference. When she related how the great miracle–performer had been crucified the same day that she had arrived in Jerusalem, and how near she had been to saving him, she began to weep under the weight of her failure. But Tiberius only remarked: "You actually grieve over this? Ah, Faustina! A whole lifetime in Rome has not weaned you then of faith in sorcerers and miracle–workers, which you imbibed during your childhood in the Sabine mountains!"

Then the old woman perceived that Tiberius had never expected any help from the Prophet of Nazareth.

"Why did you let me make the journey to that distant land, if you believed all the while that it was useless?"

"You are the only friend I have," said the Emperor. "Why should I deny your prayer, so long as I still have the power to grant it." But the old woman did not like it that the Emperor had taken her for a fool.

"Ah! this is your usual cunning," she burst out. "This is just what I can tolerate least in you."

"You should not have come back to me," said Tiberius. "You should have remained in the mountains."

It looked for a moment as if these two, who had clashed so often, would again fall into a war of words, but the old woman's anger subsided immediately. The times were past when she could quarrel in earnest with the Emperor. She lowered her voice again; but she could not altogether relinquish every effort to obtain justice.

"But this man was really a prophet," she said. "I have seen him. When his eyes met mine, I thought he was a god. I was mad to allow him to go to his death."

"I am glad you let him die," said Tiberius. "He was a traitor and a dangerous agitator."

Faustina was about to burst into another passion — then checked herself.

"I have spoken with many of his friends in Jerusalem about him," said she. "He had not committed the crimes for which he was arraigned."

"Even if he had not committed these crimes, he was surely no better than anyone else," said the Emperor wearily. "Where will you find the person who during his lifetime has not a thousand times deserved death?"

But these remarks of the Emperor decided Faustina to undertake something which she had until now hesitated about. "I will show you a proof of his power," said she. "I said to you just now that I laid my kerchief over his face. It is the same kerchief which I hold in my hand. Will you look at it a moment?"

She spread the kerchief out before the Emperor, and he saw delineated thereon the shadowy likeness of a human face.

The old woman's voice shook with emotion as she continued: "This man saw that I loved him. I know not by what power he was enabled to leave me his portrait. But my eyes fill up with tears when I see it."

The Emperor leaned forward and regarded the picture, which appeared to be made up of blood and tears and the dark shadows of grief. Gradually the whole face stood out before him, exactly as it had been imprinted upon the kerchief. He saw the blood–drops on the forehead, the piercing thorn–crown, the hair, which was matted with blood, and the mouth whose lips seemed to quiver with agony.

He bent down closer and closer to the picture. The face stood out clearer and clearer. From out the shadow–like outlines, all at once, he saw the eyes sparkle as with hidden life. And while they spoke to him of the most terrible suffering, they also revealed a purity and sublimity which he had never seen before.

He lay upon his couch and drank in the picture with his eyes. "Is this a mortal?" he said softly and slowly. "Is this a mortal?" Again he lay still and regarded the picture. The tears began to stream down his cheeks. "I mourn over thy death, thou Unknown!" he whispered. "Faustina!" he cried out at last. "Why did you let this man die? He would have healed me."

And again he was lost in the picture. "O Man!" he said, after a moment, "if I cannot gain my health from thee, I can still avenge thy murder. My hand shall rest heavily upon those who have robbed me of thee!"

Again he lay still a long time; then he let himself glide down to the floor — and he knelt before the picture.

"Thou art Man!" said he. "Thou art that which I never dreamed I should see." And he pointed to his disfigured face and destroyed hands. "I and all others are wild beasts and monsters, but thou art Man."

He bowed his head so low before the picture that it touched the floor. "Have pity on me, thou Unknown!" he sobbed, and his tears watered the stones.

"If thou hadst lived, thy glance alone would have healed me," he said.

The poor old woman was terror–stricken over what she had done. It would have been wiser not to show the Emperor the picture, thought she.

From the start she had been afraid that if he should see it his grief would be too overwhelming.

And in her despair over the Emperor's grief, she snatched the picture away, as if to remove it from his sight.

Then the Emperor looked up. And, lo! his features were transformed, and he was as he had been before the illness. It was as if the illness had had its root and sustenance in the contempt and hatred of mankind which had lived in his heart; and it had been forced to flee the very moment he had felt love and compassion.

The following day Tiberius despatched three messengers.

The first messenger travelled to Rome with the command that the Senate should institute investigations as to how the governor of Palestine administered his official duties and punish him, should it appear that he oppressed the people and condemned the innocent to death.

The second messenger went to the vineyard–labourer and his wife, to thank them and reward them for the counsel they had given the Emperor, and also to tell them how everything had turned out. When they had heard all, they wept silently, and the man said: "I know that all my life I shall ponder what would have happened if these two had met." But the woman answered: "It could not happen in any other way. It was too great a thought that these two should meet. God knew that the world could not support it."

The third messenger travelled to Palestine and brought back with him to Capri some of Jesus' disciples, and these began to teach there the doctrine that had been preached by the Crucified One.

When the disciples landed in Capri, old Faustina lay upon her death–bed. Still they had time before her death to make of her a follower of the great Prophet, and to baptize her. And in the baptism she was called VERONICA, because to her it had been granted to give to mankind the true likeness of their Saviour.

The Student

Anton Chekhov

At first the weather was fine and calm. Thrushes sang and in the marshes close by some living creature hummed plaintively, as if blowing into an empty bottle. A woodcock flew over and a shot rang out, echoing cheerfully in the spring air. But when darkness fell on the forest, an unwelcome, bitingly cold wind blew up from the east and everything became quiet. Ice needles formed on puddles and the forest became uninviting, bleak and empty. It smelt of winter.

Ivan Velikopolsky, a theology student and parish priest's son, was returning home along the path across the water meadows after a shooting expedition. His fingers were numb and his face burned in the wind. It seemed that this sudden onset of cold had destroyed order and harmony in all things, putting Nature herself in fear and making the evening shadows thicken faster than was necessary. All was deserted and somehow particularly gloomy. Only in the widow's vegetable plots by the river did a light gleam. Far around, though, where the village stood about three miles away, everything was completely submerged in the chill evening mists. The student remembered that when he left home his mother had been sitting barefoot on the floor of the hall, cleaning the samovar, while his father lay coughing on the stove. As it was Good Friday no cooking was done at home and he felt starving. Shrinking from the cold, the student thought of similar winds blowing in the time of Ryurlk, Ivan the Terrible and Peter the Great — during their reigns there had been the same grinding poverty and hunger. There had been the same thatched roofs with holes in them, the same ignorance and suffering, the same wilderness all around, the same gloom and feeling of oppression. All these horrors had been, existed now and would continue to do so. The passing of another thousand years would bring no improvement. He didn't feel like going home.

The vegetable plots were called "widows" because they were kept by two widows, mother and daughter. A bonfire was burning fiercely, crackling and lighting up the ploughed land far around. Widow Vasilisa, a tall, plump old woman in a man's sheepskin coat, was standing gazing pensively at the fire. Her short, pock-marked, stupid-faced daughter Lukerya was sitting on the ground washing a copper pot and some spoons. Clearly they had just finished supper. Men's voices could be heard — some local farm–workers were watering their horses at the river.

"So winter's here again," the student said as he approached the bonfire. "Good evening."

Vasilisa shuddered, but then she recognized the student and gave him a welcoming smile.

"Heavens, I didn't know it was you," she said. "That means you'll be a rich man one day."

They started talking, Vasilisa, a woman of the world, once a wet–nurse to some gentry and then a nanny, had a delicate way of speaking and she always smiled gently, demurely. But her daughter Lukerya, a peasant woman who had been beaten by her husband, only screwed up her eyes at the student and said nothing. She had a strange expression, as if she were a deafmute.

"It was on a cold night like this that the Apostle Peter warmed himself by a fire," the student said, stretching his hands towards the flames. "That is to say, it was cold then as well. Oh, what a terrible night that was, Grandma! A dreadfully sad, never–ending night!"

He peered into the surrounding darkness, violently jerked his head and asked, "I suppose you were at the Twelve Readings from the Gospels yesterday?"

"Yes," Vasilisa replied.

"You'll remember, during the Last Supper, Peter said to Jesus, 'I am ready to go with Thee, both into prison and to death.' And the Lord replied, 'I say unto thee, Peter, before the cock crow twice thou shalt deny me thrice.' After the Supper, Jesus prayed in the garden, in mortal agony, while poor Peter was down–hearted and his eyes grew heavy. He couldn't fight off sleep, and he slept. Then, as you know, Judas kissed Jesus on that night and betrayed Him to the torturers. They led Him bound to the High Priest and they beat Him, while Peter, exhausted and sorely troubled by anguish and fear — he didn't have enough sleep, you understand — and in expectation of something dreadful taking place on earth at any moment, followed them. He loved Jesus passionately, to distraction, and now, from afar, he could see them beating Him."

Lukerya put the spoons down and stared intently at the student.

"They went to the High Priest," he continued, "they started questioning Jesus and meanwhile the workmen, as it was so cold, had made a fire in the middle of the hall and were warning themselves. Peter stood with them by the fire, warming himself as well, as I am now. One woman who saw him said: 'This man was also with Jesus.' So she really meant that this man too had to be led away for questioning. And all the workmen around the fire must have looked at him suspiciously and sternly, as he was taken aback and said, 'I know him not.' Soon afterwards someone recognized him as one of Jesus's disciples and said: 'Thou also wast with Him.' But again he denied it and for the third time someone turned to him and asked: 'Did I not see you in the garden with Him this day?' He denied Him for the third time. And straight after that a cock crowed and as he looked on Jesus from afar Peter remembered the words He had spoken to him at supper. He remembered, his eyes were opened, he left the hall and wept bitterly. As it is said in the Gospels: 'And he went out and wept bitterly.' I can imagine that quiet, terribly dark garden, those dull sobs, barely audible in the silence ..."

The student sighed and became deeply pensive. Still smiling. Vasilisa suddenly broke into sobs and large, copious tears streamed down her cheeks. She shielded her face from the fire with her sleeve as if ashamed of her tears, while Lukerya stared at the student and blushed. Her face became anguished and tense, like someone stifling a dreadful pain.

The workmen were returning from the river and one of them on horseback, was quite near and the light from the bonfire flickered on him. The student wished the widows goodnight and moved on. Again darkness descended and his hands began to freeze. A cruel wind was blowing — winter had really returned with a vengeance and it did not seem as if Easter Sunday was only the day after tomorrow.

Now the student thought of Vasilisa: she had wept, so everything that had happened to Peter on that terrible night must have had some special significance for her.

He glanced back. The solitary fire calmly flickered in the darkness and no one was visible near it. Once again the student reflected that, since Vasilisa had wept and her daughter had been deeply touched, then obviously what he had just been telling them about events centuries ago had some significance for the present, for both women, for this village, for himself and for all people. That old woman had wept, but not at his moving narrative: it was because Peter was close to her and because she was concerned, from the bottom of her heart, with his most intimate feelings.

His heart suddenly thrilled with joy and he even stopped for a moment to catch his breath. "The past," he thought, "is linked to the present by an unbroken chain of events, each flowing from the other." He felt that he had just witnessed both ends of this chain. When he touched one end, the other started shaking.

After crossing the river by ferry and climbing the hill, he looked at his native village and towards the west, where a narrow strip of cold crimson sunset was glimmering. And he reflected how truth and beauty, which had guided human life there in the garden and the High Priest's palace and had continued unbroken to the present, were the most important parts of the life of man, and of the whole of terrestrial life. A feeling of youthfulness, health, strength — he was only twenty–two — and an inexpressibly sweet anticipation of happiness, of a mysterious unfamiliar happiness, gradually took possession of him. And life seemed entrancing, wonderful and endowed with sublime meaning.

The Juniper Tree

Brothers Grimm

It is now long ago, quite two thousand years, since there was a rich man who had a beautiful and pious wife, and they loved each other dearly. They had, however, no children, though they wished for them very much, and the woman prayed for them day and night, but still they had none. Now there was a courtyard in front of their house in which was a juniper tree, and one day in winter the woman was standing beneath it, paring herself an apple, and while she was paring herself the apple she cut her finger, and the blood fell on the snow.

"Ah," said the woman, and sighed right heavily, and looked at the blood before her, and was most unhappy, "if I had but a child as red as blood and as white as snow!" And while she thus spoke, she became quite happy in her mind, and felt just as if that were going to happen.

Then she went into the house, and a month went by and the snow was gone; and two months, and then everything was green; and three months, and then all the flowers came out of the earth; and four months, and then all the trees in the wood grew thicker, and the green branches were all closely entwined, and the birds sang until the wood resounded and the blossoms fell from the trees; then the fifth month passed away and she stood under the juniper tree, which smelt so sweetly that her heart leapt, and she fell on her knees and was beside herself with joy; and when the sixth month was over the fruit was large and fine, and then she was quite still; and the seventh month she snatched at the juniper–berries and ate them greedily, then she grew sick and sorrowful; then the eighth month passed, and she called her husband to her, and wept and said: "If I die, then bury me beneath the juniper tree."

Then she was quite comforted and happy until the next month was over, and then she had a child as white as snow and as red as blood, and when she beheld it she was so delighted that she died.

Then her husband buried her beneath the juniper tree, and he began to weep sore; after some time he was more at ease, and though he still wept he could bear it, and after some time longer he took another wife.

By the second wife he had a daughter, but the first wife's child was a little son, and he was as red as blood and as white as snow. When the woman looked at her daughter she loved her very much, but then she looked at the little boy and it seemed to cut her to the heart, for the thought came into her mind that he would always stand in her way, and she was for ever thinking how she could get all the fortune for her daughter, and the Evil One filled her mind with this till she was quite wroth with the little boy and she pushed him from one corner to the other and slapped him here and cuffed him there, until the poor child was in continual terror, for when he came out of school he had no peace in any place.

One day the woman had gone upstairs to her room, and her little daughter went up too, and said: "Mother, give me an apple."

"Yes, my child," said the woman, and gave her a fine apple out of the chest, but the chest had a great heavy lid with a great sharp iron lock.

"Mother," said the little daughter, "is brother not to have one, too?"

This made the woman angry, but she said: "Yes, when he comes out of school."

And when she saw from the window that he was coming, it was just as if the Devil entered into her, and she snatched at the apple and took it away again from her daughter, and said: "You shall not have one before your brother."

Then she threw the apple into the chest, and shut it. Then the little boy came in at the door, and the Devil made her say to him kindly: "My son, will you have an apple?" and she looked wickedly at him.

"Mother," said the little boy, "how dreadful you look! Yes, give me an apple."

Then it seemed to her as if she were forced to say to him: "Come with me," and she opened the lid of the chest, and said: "Take out an apple for yourself," and while the little boy was stooping inside, the Devil prompted her, and crash! she shut the lid down, and his head flew off and fell among the red apples.

Then she was overwhelmed with terror, and thought: "If I could but make them think that it was not done by me!" So she went upstairs to her room to her chest of drawers, and took a white handkerchief out of the top drawer, and set the head on the neck again, and folded the handkerchief so that nothing could be seen, and she set him on a chair in front of the door, and put the apple in his hand.

After this Marlinchen came into the kitchen to her mother, who was standing by the fire with a pan of hot water before her which she was constantly stirring round.

"Mother," said Marlinchen, "brother is sitting at the door, and he looks quite white, and has an apple in his hand. I asked him to give me the apple, but he did not answer me, and I was quite frightened."

"Go back to him," said her mother, "and if he will not answer you, give him a box on the ear."

So Marlinchen went to him and said: "Brother, give me the apple." But he was silent, and she gave him a box on the ear, whereupon his head fell off. Marlinchen was terrified, and began crying and screaming, and ran to her mother, and said: "Alas, mother, I have knocked my brother's head off!" and she wept and wept and could not be comforted. "Marlinchen," said the mother, "what have you done? But be quiet and let no one know it; it cannot be helped now, we will make him into black–puddings." Then the mother took the little boy and chopped him in pieces, put him into the pan and made him into black–puddings; but Marlinchen stood by weeping and weeping, and all her tears fell into the pan and there was no need of any salt.

Then the father came home, and sat down to dinner and said: "But where is my son?" And the mother served up a great dish of black–puddings, and Marlinchen wept and could not leave off. Then the father again said: "But where is my son?"

"Ah," said the mother, "he has gone across the country to his mother's great–uncle; he will stay there awhile."

"And what is he going to do there? He did not even say good–bye to me."

"Oh, he wanted to go, and asked me if he might stay six weeks, he is well taken care of there."

"Ah," said the man, "I feel so unhappy lest all should not be right. He ought to have said good–bye to me."

With that he began to eat and said: "Marlinchen, why are you crying? Your brother will certainly come back."

Then he said: "Ah, wife, how delicious this food is, give me some more." And the more he ate the more he wanted to have, and he said: "Give me some more, you shall have none of it. It seems to me as if it were all mine."

And he ate and ate and threw all the bones under the table, until he had finished the whole. But Marlinchen went away to the chest of drawers, and took her best silk handkerchief out of the bottom drawer, and got all the bones from beneath the table, and tied them up in her silk handkerchief, and carried them outside the door, weeping tears of blood. Then she lay down under the juniper tree on the green grass, and after she had lain down there, she suddenly felt light–hearted and did not cry any more. Then the juniper tree began to stir itself, and the branches parted asunder, and moved together again, just as if someone were rejoicing and clapping his hands. At the same time a mist seemed to arise from the tree, and in the centre of this mist it burned like a fire, and a beautiful bird flew out of the fire singing magnificently, and he flew high up in the air, and when he was gone, the juniper tree was just as it had been before, and the handkerchief with the bones was no longer there. Marlinchen, however, was as gay and happy as if her brother were still alive. And she went merrily into the house, and sat down to dinner and ate.

But the bird flew away and lighted on a goldsmith's house, and began to sing:

> "My mother she killed me,
> My father he ate me,
> My sister, little Marlinchen,
> Gathered together all my bones,
> Tied them in a silken handkerchief,
> Laid them beneath the juniper tree,
> Kywitt, kywitt, what a beautiful bird am I!"

The goldsmith was sitting in his workshop making a golden chain, when he heard the bird which was sitting singing on his roof, and very beautiful the song seemed to him. He stood up, but as he crossed the threshold he lost one of his slippers. But he went away right up the middle of the street with one shoe on and one sock; he had his apron on, and in one hand he had the golden chain and in the other the pincers, and the sun was shining brightly on the street. Then he went right on and stood still, and said to the bird: "Bird," said he then, "how beautifully you can sing! Sing me that piece again."

"No," said the bird, "I'll not sing it twice for nothing! Give me the golden chain, and then I will sing it again for you."

"There," said the goldsmith, "there is the golden chain for you, now sing me that song again." Then the bird came and took the golden chain in his right claw, and went and sat in front of the goldsmith, and sang:

> "My mother she killed me,
> My father he ate me,
> My sister, little Marlinchen,
> Gathered together all my bones,
> Tied them in a silken handkerchief,
> Laid them beneath the juniper tree,
> Kywitt, kywitt, what a beautiful bird am I!"

Then the bird flew away to a shoemaker, and lighted on his roof and sang:

> "My mother she killed me,
> My father he ate me,
> My sister, little Marlinchen,
> Gathered together all my bones,
> Tied them in a silken handkerchief,
> Laid them beneath the juniper tree,
> Kywitt, kywitt, what a beautiful bird am I!"

The shoemaker heard that and ran out of doors in his shirt–sleeves, and looked up at his roof, and was forced to hold his hand before his eyes lest the sun should blind him. "Bird," said he, "how beautifully you can sing!"

Then he called in at his door: "Wife, just come outside, there is a bird, look at that bird, he certainly can sing." Then he called his daughter and children, and apprentices, boys and girls, and they all came up the street and looked at the bird and saw how beautiful he was, and what fine red and green feathers he had, and how like real gold his neck was, and how the eyes in his head shone like stars. "Bird," said the shoemaker, "now sing me that song again."

"Nay," said the bird, "I do not sing twice for nothing; you must give me something."

"Wife," said the man, "go to the garret, upon the top shelf there stands a pair of red shoes, bring them down." Then the wife went and brought the shoes.

"There, bird," said the man, "now sing me that piece again." Then the bird came and took the shoes in his left claw, and flew back on the roof, and sang:

> "My mother she killed me,
> My father he ate me,
> My sister, little Marlinchen,
> Gathered together all my bones,
> Tied them in a silken handkerchief,
> Laid them beneath the juniper tree,
> Kywitt, kywitt, what a beautiful bird am I!"

And when he had finished his song he flew away. In his right claw he had the chain and in his left the shoes, and he flew far away to a mill, and the mill went "klipp klapp, klipp klapp, klipp klapp," and in the mill sat twenty miller's men hewing a stone, and cutting, hick hack, hick hack, hick hack, and the mill went "klipp klapp, klipp klapp, klipp klapp." Then the bird went and sat on a lime–tree which stood in front of the mill, and sang:

"My mother she killed me ..."

Then one of them stopped working.

"My father he ate me ..."

Then two more stopped working and listened to that.

"My sister, little Marlinchen ..."

Then four more stopped.

"Gathered together all my bones,
Tied them in a silken handkerchief ..."

Now eight only were hewing.

"Laid them beneath ..."

Now only five ...

"The juniper tree ..."

And now only one ...

"Kywitt, kywitt, what a beautiful bird am I!"

Then the last stopped also, and heard the last words. "Bird," said he, "how beautifully you sing! Let me, too, hear that. Sing that once more for me."

"Nay," said the bird, "I will not sing twice for nothing. Give me the millstone, and then I will sing it again."

"Yes," said he, "if it belonged to me only, you should have it."

"Yes," said the others, "if he sings again, he shall have it." Then the bird came down, and the twenty millers all set to work with a beam and raised the stone up. And the bird stuck his neck through the hole, and put the stone on as if it were a collar, and flew on to the tree again, and sang:

"My mother she killed me,
My father he ate me,
My sister, little Marlinchen,
Gathered together all my bones,
Tied them in a silken handkerchief,
Laid them beneath the juniper tree,
Kywitt, kywitt, what a beautiful bird am I!"

And when he had done singing, he spread his wings, and in his right claw he had the chain, and in his left the shoes, and round his neck the millstone, and he flew far away to his father's house.

In the room sat the father, the mother, and Marlinchen at dinner, and the father said: "How light–hearted I feel, how happy I am!"

"Nay," said the mother, "I feel so uneasy, just as if a heavy storm were coming." Marlinchen, however, sat weeping and weeping, and then came the bird flying, and as it seated itself on the roof the father said: "Ah, I feel so truly happy, and the sun is shining so beautifully outside, I feel just as if I were about to see some old friend again."

"Nay," said the woman, "I feel so anxious, my teeth chatter, and I seem to have fire in my veins." And she tore her stays open, but Marlinchen sat in a corner crying, and held her plate before her eyes and cried till it was quite wet. Then the bird sat on the juniper tree, and sang:

"My mother she killed me ..."

Then the mother stopped her ears, and shut her eyes, and would not see or hear, but there was a roaring in her ears like the most violent storm, and her eyes burnt and flashed like lightning:

"My father he ate me ..."

"Ah, mother," says the man, "that is a beautiful bird! He sings so splendidly, and the sun shines so warm, and there is a smell just like cinnamon."

"My sister, little Marlinchen ..."

Then Marlinchen laid her head on her knees and wept without ceasing, but the man said: "I am going out, I must see the bird quite close."

"Oh, don't go," said the woman, "I feel as if the whole house were shaking and on fire." But the man went out and looked at the bird.

"Gathered together all my bones,
Tied them in a silken handkerchief,
Laid them beneath the juniper tree,
Kywitt, kywitt, what a beautiful bird am I!"

On this the bird let the golden chain fall, and it fell exactly round the man's neck, and so exactly round it that it fitted beautifully. Then he went in and said: "Just look what a fine bird that is, and what a handsome golden chain he has given me, and how pretty he is!" But the woman was terrified, and fell down on the floor in the room, and her cap fell off her head. Then sang the bird once more:

"My mother she killed me ..."

"Would that I were a thousand feet beneath the earth so as not to hear that!"

"My father he ate me ..."

Then the woman fell down again as if dead.

"My sister, little Marlinchen ..."

"Ah," said Marlinchen, "I too will go out and see if the bird will give me anything," and she went out.

"Gathered together all my bones,
Tied them in a silken handkerchief,"

Then he threw down the shoes to her.

"Laid them beneath the juniper tree,
Kywitt, kywitt, what a beautiful bird am I!"

Then she was light–hearted and joyous, and she put on the new red shoes, and danced and leaped into the house. "Ah," said she, "I was so sad when I went out and now I am so light–hearted; that is a splendid bird, he has given me a pair of red shoes!"

"Well," said the woman, and sprang to her feet and her hair stood up like flames of fire. "I feel as if the world were coming to an end! I, too, will go out and see if my heart feels lighter." And as she went out at the door, crash! the bird threw down the millstone on her head, and she was entirely crushed by it. The father and Marlinchen heard what had happened and went out, and smoke, flames and fire were rising from the place, and when that was over, there stood the little brother, and he took his father and Marlinchen by the hand, and all three were right glad, and they went into the house to dinner, and ate.

The Donkey

Brothers Grimm

Once upon a time there lived a King and a Queen, who were rich, and had everything they wanted, but no children. The Queen lamented over this day and night, and said: "I am like a field on which nothing grows." At last God gave her her wish, but when the child came into the world, it did not look like a human child, but was a little donkey. When the mother saw that, her lamentations and outcries began in real earnest; she said she would far rather have had no child at all than have a donkey, and that they were to throw it into the water that the fishes might devour it. But the King said: "No, since God has sent him he shall be my son and heir, and after my death sit on the royal throne, and wear the kingly crown."

The donkey, therefore, was brought up and grew bigger, and his ears grew up high and straight. And he was of a merry disposition, jumped about, played and took especial pleasure in music, so that he went to a celebrated musician and said: "Teach me your art, that I may play the lute as well as you do."

"Ah, dear little master," answered the musician, "that would come very hard to you, your fingers are not quite suited to it, and are far too big. I am afraid the strings would not last."

But no excuses were of any use — the donkey was determined to play the lute. And since he was persevering and industrious, he at last learnt to do it as well as the master himself. The young lordling once went out walking full of thought and came to a well; he looked into it and in the mirror–clear water saw his donkey's form. He was so distressed about it, that he went out into the wide world and only took with him one faithful companion.

They travelled up and down, and at last they came into a kingdom where an old King reigned who had a single but wonderfully beautiful daughter. The donkey said: "Here we will stay," knocked at the gate, and cried: "A guest is without — open, that he may enter."

When the gate was not opened, he sat down, took his lute and played it in the most delightful manner with his two fore–feet. Then the door-keeper opened his eyes, and gaped, and ran to the King and said:

"Outside by the gate sits a young donkey which plays the lute as well as an experienced master!"

"Then let the musician come to me," said the King. But when a donkey came in, everyone began to laugh at the lute–player. And when the donkey was asked to sit down and eat with the servants, he was unwilling, and said: "I am no common stable–ass, I am a noble one."

Then they said: "If that is what you are, seat yourself with the soldiers."

"No," said he, "I will sit by the King." The King smiled, and said good–humouredly: "Yes, it shall be as you will, little ass, come here to me." Then he asked: "Little ass, how does my daughter please you?"

The donkey turned his head towards her, looked at her, nodded and said: "I like her above measure, I have never yet seen anyone so beautiful as she is."

"Well, then, you shall sit next her, too," said the King.

"That is exactly what I wish," said the donkey, and he placed himself by her side, ate and drank, and knew how to behave himself daintily and cleanly. When the noble beast had stayed a long time at the King's court, he thought: "What good does all this do me, I shall still have to go home again," let his head hang sadly, and went to the King and asked for his dismissal.

But the King had grown fond of him, and said: "Little ass, what ails you? You look as sour as a jug of vinegar, I will give you what you want. Do you want gold?"

"No," said the donkey, and shook his head. "Do you want jewels and rich dress?"

"No."

"Do you wish for half my kingdom?"

"Indeed, no." Then said the King: "If I did but know what would make you content. Will you have my pretty daughter to wife?"

"Ah, yes," said the ass, "I should indeed like her," and all at once he became quite merry and full of happiness, for that was exactly what he was wishing for. So a great and splendid wedding was held. In the evening, when the bride and bridegroom were led into their bedroom, the King wanted to know if the ass would behave well, and ordered a servant to hide himself there. When they were both within, the bridegroom bolted the door, looked around, and as he believed that they were quite alone, he suddenly threw off his ass's skin, and stood there in the form of a handsome royal youth.

"Now," said he, "you see who I am, and see also that I am not unworthy of you."

Then the bride was glad, and kissed him, and loved him dearly. When morning came, he jumped up, put his animal's skin on again, and no one could have guessed what kind of a form was hidden beneath it.

Soon came the old King. "Ah," cried he, "so the little ass is already up! But surely you are sad," said he to his daughter, "that you have not got a proper man for your husband?"

"Oh, no, dear father, I love him as well as if he were the handsomest in the world, and I will keep him as long as I live."

The King was surprised, but the servant who had concealed himself came and revealed everything to him. The King said: "That cannot be true."

"Then watch yourself the next night, and you will see it with your own eyes; and hark you, lord King, if you were to take his skin away and throw it in the fire, he would be forced to show himself in his true shape."

"Your advice is good," said the King, and at night when they were asleep, he stole in, and when he got to the bed he saw by the light of the moon a noble looking youth lying there, and the skin lay stretched on the ground. So he took it away, and had a great fire lighted outside, and threw the skin into it, and remained by it himself until it was all burnt to ashes. But since he was anxious to know how the robbed man would behave himself, he stayed awake the whole night and watched. When the youth had slept his fill, he got up by the first light of morning, and wanted to put on the ass's skin, but it was not to be found. At this he was alarmed, and, full of grief and anxiety, said: "Now I shall have to contrive to escape."

But when he went out, there stood the King, who said: "My son, where are you away to in such haste? What have you in mind? Stay here, you are such a handsome man, you shall not go away from me. I will now give you half my kingdom, and after my death you shall have the whole of it."

"Then I hope that what begins so well may end well, and I will stay with you," said the youth. And the old man give him half the kingdom, and in a year's time, when he died, the youth had the whole, and after the death of his father he had another kingdom as well, and lived in all magnificence.

The Children of Queen Dora

A Spanish story

There was once a king who went walking through the streets of his kingdom and came past a house where there lived, with her two sisters, a good and holy girl called Dora. All three girls were standing at the door of their house to watch the king go past.

The eldest sister said to him that if he would take her to be his wife she would make him a cloak without a seam. The middle sister said that if he would marry her she would make him a shirt without a stitch. But the king went on without taking any notice of them. Only to Dora did he listen when she said that if he would accept her as his wife she would give him two children each with a golden star on their foreheads. The king thought to himself that it would be very good to have two children with golden stars on their foreheads and so he went and asked for her hand.

They were married with great pomp and ceremony and, after the wedding, all three sisters went to live in the king's palace. Soon afterwards, the king had to go off to the wars.

As Dora had promised, she gave birth to a boy and a girl, both with a golden star on their foreheads. But because the sisters envied Dora they took the children, tied a bandage round their foreheads to hide the stars, shut them up in a chest and threw it into the river. Then they wrote to the king saying that their sister must be a bad witch because she had given birth to two black cats.

When the king received this letter, he wanted to have his wife put to death straightaway, but he thought that beheading would be too light a punishment. So he had the queen walled up alive and doomed to die of hunger. But because she was so good and holy, her guardian angel brought her bread and water and Dora did not die in her terrible prison.

Now the chest containing the children floated down the river till it came into a mill-race and blocked it so that the mill-wheel stopped turning. The miller came out to see what was wrong, and when he saw the chest he thought it must be full of gold, so he ran and pulled it out. He called his wife to help him open the chest and there they found the two children. They stood looking at them in some perplexity for, as the miller and his wife were poor and already had one son, they did not know what they would do with two more. But in the end they decided to keep them, though they found to their puzzlement that there was simply no way of removing the bandages from their foreheads.

However, the miller had not been completely wrong when he thought that the chest was full of gold. From the very day that he took the children into his house, his business went better and better and he was soon on the way to becoming a rich man.

The children grew and grew and soon showed they were both very clever. The miller sent them to school along with his own son, but they were such quick learners that after a short time the teacher could not teach them any more. The miller's son, however, was as dull as a donkey and did not learn anything, and so he grew angry with them, insulted them and called them "foundlings." One day the children asked the miller why their brother called them foundlings for they had thought that they were all of the same family. Then the miller was obliged to tell them their story.

When they found out that the miller was not their real father, the two children demanded to go out into the world and find their true fortunes. Although the miller resisted as much as he could, they begged so hard that he had no choice but to let them depart. But before they left the house he gave them food for their journey and seven gold coins.

As the two children travelled along the road, they came to a village where they saw a man lying dead on the roadside. When they asked why he was not to be buried, they were told that it was because he had left nothing when he died and no one would pay the seven gold coins needed for his burial. Because that was the exact amount that they carried with them, the children paid for the burial and went on their way.

In time, they came to the king's palace where they sought work as gardeners. Setting to work, they planted a garden that was glorious to behold, with so many wonderful flowers and plants that everyone was amazed. All the people came to look at the garden because of the marvellous hedges and borders that had been created and everybody asked where these two children had come from with the bandages on their foreheads.

The children's aunts also heard of this with some alarm and went to see the new gardeners. When they saw the two children, of course they immediately recognized their nephew and niece and it was as if they were seeing ghosts, for they still believed that the children had been drowned.

The aunts returned to the palace and began to think what the king would do if he came to hear the truth. So they went into the city one dark night and asked a witch for advice how to get rid of the children. She answered that if the aunts paid her well, she would solve the problem for them. The aunts agreed and gave her a bag of gold.

The witch started to go to the garden every day. She praised the lovely flowers and hedges but kept telling the children that something was missing.

"Now I know what is missing to make your garden perfect," she said one day.

"What is that?" the children asked.

"The most beautiful music in the world."

"Where is that to be found?" they asked.

"In the Castle of Never Return."

The two children then decided they must have this music for their garden, and they agreed that the boy would go and look for it. As a sign he left his sister a glass of water that would turn into blood if any danger should befall him.

The boy set off to seek the castle, and as he was going along the road, there appeared to him the figure of the man whom they had had buried, who said: "I am the one whom you buried, and for that I owe you my eternal thanks. Listen, you have been sent to your death but if you do as I say, all will be well. In the Castle of Never Return you will find three harps: one that plays very well, another that plays middlingly well, and a third that plays only such sad music that no one can listen to it. Take the harp that plays the sad music, for if you take the one that plays best, the castle doors will close upon you and you will never get out."

The boy travelled on to the castle, saw the three harps and did as the man had bidden him, taking the one that played the sad music. When he came back to the palace with it, all the people were full of wonder at how beautifully it played.

The witch went wild with rage when she saw that the boy had not been kept prisoner in the castle, but in the end she made herself appear pleasant and came and said to him: "You can hear how beautiful the music is, but there is still something lacking in your garden."

"And what is that?" asked the boy.

"The clearest fountain in the world."

"Where is that to be found?"

"In the Castle of Never Return."

"Then I shall go and fetch it," said the boy bravely.

On the way he again met the man who said to him: "Three fountains you will find in the castle: one with very clear water, another that is a little dirtier, and a third that gives very dirty water. Choose the fountain with the dirtiest water otherwise the castle doors will close upon you and you will be kept prisoner."

Again the boy did as the man had advised and he chose the dirtiest fountain. But when he had brought it to the palace garden, it became as clear as the clearest crystal, so that everyone was filled with wonder who came to look at it.

When the witch heard that the boy had returned safely a second time, she was beside herself with fury. But again she put on a pleasant appearance and came and said to him: "Listen, there is still something missing to make your garden perfect."

"What is that?" asked the boy.

"The bird that can sing in every tongue."

"And where is that?"

"In the Castle of Never Return."

Again the boy set off to the castle and again he met the man as before who said to him: "In the Castle of Never Return you will find three birds: one that sings a lot, another that sings a little, and a third that looks sickly and keeps his beak under his wing. Take the sad bird, because if you take any of the others the doors of the castle will shut and you must stay inside for ever.

But when he got to the castle, the boy did not follow the man's advice for he was afraid that the sick bird would die on him on the way home, so he chose the bird that could sing the most. But hardly had he touched the bird when he fell down as dead and the doors of the castle shut fast.

His sister, however, had been watching the glass of water every day and now saw it turn into blood. So she knew that something evil had happened to her brother. She set off at once to help him. On the way she met the man who had spoken to her brother and he said to her: "I told your brother what he should do in the Castle of Never Return but because he did not heed my advice he has remained a prisoner in the castle. You need have no fear, for all will be well if you listen to me. Now when you go into the castle, you will see three birds: one that sings much, one that sings only a bit, and one that hides its beak under its wing. Take this one, but mark well what you must do. You will see in the castle courtyard three men lying as if dead, two at the entrance and one further in. This last one is your brother. Take water from the dirtiest well that you see there, hold fast to the bird and sprinkle some drops into your brother's face and he will come to himself. Then you must escape quickly for the doors of the castle will soon close again."

She did just as the man had told her. Even so they were almost caught for the doors started to swing shut just as they were going out. Indeed the brother's coat was caught in the doors but, quick as a flash, the girl cut off the piece with a scissor which she had brought with her and so they escaped.

The bird which they had brought was the greatest wonder of the world for there was nothing which it could not say in any known language and it had an answer to everything that it was asked.

Everybody talked so much of the marvellous bird and of the beautiful music and crystal–clear fountain in the garden that these wonders came to the ears of the king and he wanted to see them all for himself. He visited the garden and found that everything was as admirable as he had heard. But when he came to the bird it would not sing for him; it would only stick its beak under its wing. So the children asked the bird why it did that and it answered: "Because the king is deceived and is doing his good queen a dreadful injustice."

Then, with the king standing there, the bird told the children everything that had happened since their birth and said that, if he was to make amends, the king must burn what he had always believed in most.

The king wanted to remove the bandages from the children's foreheads straightaway to see if they bore the gold stars. But the bird said that only the queen could do this.

"Alas," said the king, "she will be dead now, and I blame myself for believing her wicked sisters."

"No," said the bird. "The queen is still alive and well and must be set free."

On hearing this, the king was overjoyed and he sent for the queen to be removed from her prison immediately. When Queen Dora arrived before her husband, out of the goodness of her heart she forgave him everything. Then she embraced her children, took the bandages from their foreheads and showed everyone the gold stars which proved them to be the king's own children. The queen was so very forgiving that she desired the king to spare her sisters. But he answered that, as the bird had bidden him to burn what he had most believed in, no more fitting punishment could be found for the evil deceit of the two sisters, and so he had them taken straight out and burnt at the stake.

The Princess and Prince Hare

A Spanish folk tale

There was once a man who went walking through the streets of a city with a basket full of the most beautiful flowers, calling out: "Who will buy sorrow? Who will buy grief?"

Everyone who heard this laughed at him and no one would buy his flowers, lovely though they were. For who, after all, would buy sorrow and grief, of which there is plenty enough in the world already? But that did not upset the man and he went on walking through the streets and offering his wares for sale: "Who will buy sorrow? Who will buy grief?"

In this way the strange vendor came past the king's palace. The princess heard him calling and, full of curiosity, looked out of the window. When she saw the lovely flowers in the basket, she decided she must have them and called down: "Wait a moment, good man, I'll buy your flowers."

She threw him down a piece of gold and sent her maid to fetch the flowers. They were truly beautiful, flowers such as no one in the palace had ever seen before. Even the royal gardener shook his head in wonder as he planted them carefully in the garden. And the princess was so delighted with the flowers that she stayed all day long in the garden admiring them.

The next morning when she came again with her maid into the garden, up sprang a white hare from among the flowers, and he was so enchanting that the princess had to have him and told her maid: "Quick, catch him for me."

But the enchanting little animal came running up to her all by himself. The princess tied a ribbon round his neck so that he could not run away and went walking with the hare all round the palace garden. When at last they were coming back to the palace because the princess was tired after her walk, suddenly the hare broke loose and disappeared with the ribbon. The princess was vexed at losing her fine ribbon, but even more distressed at losing her hare, so much so that she never slept a wink that night for sorrow.

The next morning she again went walking with her maid in the garden in order to see the flowers. And lo and behold, there came the hare leaping again through the flowers. She did not have to catch him for he came up all by himself. The princess tied her silk scarf round his neck so that he could not run away and now she went walking with the hare through the whole garden. But on their way back to the palace, the hare again broke free and vanished with the silk scarf.

The princess was vexed at losing her fine scarf, but even more distressed at losing her hare and she never closed her eyes all night for sorrow. The next morning she went straight with her maid into the garden and once again the hare came leaping out through the flowers. Yet again, he came to the princess all by himself. This time, the princess put her girdle round his neck so that he would not run away, and all day she went walking with her hare. When at last they were returning to the palace because it was getting late, the hare broke loose again and vanished with the girdle.

The princess was vexed at losing her splendid belt but even more distressed at losing her hare, and she never had a moment's sleep all night for sorrow. On the fourth day the princess fell ill on account of the great desire which she had for her hare and was so weak and unhappy she could not rise from her bed. Now she realized what sorrow and grief she had bought with the flowers. The princess remained sick in her bed and all the most famous doctors came and examined her. After long consultation they all agreed that there was nothing physically wrong with the princess, but that her soul was sick with longing. They prescribed walks, pleasure, song and dance so that she would forget her white hare.

From far and near came the musicians, jugglers and story-tellers and very soon the palace was just like a fair. But all that commotion, all the pleasures, all the jokes and stories told could not help the princess. There she lay pale and sad on her pillows and stared yearningly into the distance as if she were looking out for someone.

At that time there were two sisters living in a poor cottage, two old biddies. When they heard of the strange sickness of the princess, one of the sisters said to the other: "What do you think, sister? Shouldn't I go over to the palace and cheer up the princess a bit? Perhaps she'll cheer up if I tell her a fairy-story."

"I bet the princess is just waiting for you and your fairy-tales. Why, they'll all laugh at you," her sister answered.

But that did not put the old biddy out at all, she just thought she had better give it a try. So she tied up a loaf of bread and a bit of baked fish in a bundle and off she went. Now it was a long way to the city and the old woman was not as young as she was, and so every now and again she had to have a rest. She would go and sit in the shade of a tree, and preferably on a milestone by the side of the road. And once when she was sitting on just such a milestone, something strange happened. As she was getting up to travel on her way, all of a sudden the ground in front of her opened up and out came a donkey with two golden panniers on his back. The donkey was led by two hands on his bridle but there was nobody to be seen.

The old woman stood with her mouth open in amazement because such a thing never even happened in all the fairy–tales which she knew, and they were many. Now because she was curious and wanted to know what it was all about, she decided to wait for the donkey to come back; and it was not long before the donkey did come back. The old woman took firm hold of one of the panniers and so went with the donkey down under the ground. At first all was dark about her but then she saw a meadow in bright sunshine, and in the meadow stood a glorious palace, and that is where the donkey took her.

In the first room of the palace there stood a table ready laid, and when the old biddy went and sat at the table, a hand poured soup into her plate, a second hand placed roast meat before her and a third hand poured out wine, but she could not see the people to whom the hands belonged. When she had eaten her fill, she went into the next room and there stood a white bed all prepared and ready. A hand shook up her pillows, a second folded the sheet back, and a third gave her a candle. But except for the hands, not a living person was to be seen. The old woman lay down in the bed and fell fast asleep.

Early next morning she woke up and again she saw something strange: out of the garden came running a white hare which jumped straight into a pail of water standing in the corner of the room. When the creature came out of the pail, it was no longer a hare but a handsome young prince. The prince stepped in front of the mirror, took a comb and began to comb his hair, all the while speaking with a sad voice: "O mirror, could you not let me see who has such great sorrow on my behalf?"

Then he stepped into the pail again and came out as a white hare. The old woman shook her head for a long time in amazement. Then she went back to the first room and had a good breakfast. After that she waited for the donkey to appear and go up out of the ground again. She went and hung on to one of the panniers and in a few moments there she was standing by the milestone on the road that led to the city.

Once in the city she went straight to the palace and told the guards that she wanted to cheer up the princess with her fairy–tales.

"She has never heard such a story as I shall tell," she assured them.

"Well, go and try, then," said the chief guard and let her in to the princess.

Now the thoughts of our dear princess were not at all upon fairy–tales. She lay on her bed with her head turned away and did not even thank the good old woman for her greeting. But the old woman was not at all put out by that and began to tell her tale. She told how she had been walking towards the town, and had been sitting on a milestone when suddenly the ground had opened and she told how she had gone with the donkey right down to an underground palace and that there, would you believe it, she had seen a white hare.

As soon as the old woman mentioned the hare, the princess became joyful, lifted up her head and wanted to know at once what happened next. So the old woman had to go on telling about the hare who had jumped into the pail of water and had turned into a handsome young prince.

"I must see that for myself," exclaimed the princess and jumped quickly out of bed as if nothing had ever been the matter with her.

The next day the old woman led the princess and her maid to the milestone on the road. There they waited till the donkey with the golden panniers appeared, and they travelled down with him under the ground. At first it was dark round them, but then they saw a meadow in bright sunshine and in the meadow stood a palace. In the place innumerable hands were hard at work, opening doors, serving guests, but they could not see to whom the hands belonged. Then the old woman, the princess and the maid walked through the whole palace and nowhere could they find a living soul. When they came into the last room, they all three cried out in fright, for there lay a dead figure, half a hare and half a man.

The princess's heart filled with compassion for the dead figure lying there so abandoned without a single flower, without a candle and with no one praying for the salvation of his soul. She went up to him, laid a flower from her girdle on his breast, lit a candle and knelt down to say a prayer. But hardly had she spoken the first word before the body stirred and came to life. In front of the princess there now lay a handsome young prince who raised his head and looked into her eyes.

With the prince the whole palace now came to life. Everywhere people were running busily back and forth. Prince Hare knelt before the princess and said: "I thank you, beautiful maiden. With the flower, the candle and your prayer you have broken the wicked enchantment that lay over me and my whole land. How can I repay you?"

Then he led her through the whole palace and showed her all his treasures, saying that she could take whatever pleased her. Such wealth the princess had not seen even in her father's palace but she liked none of it so such as she liked the handsome young prince himself. She stared in amazement at the beautiful rooms and halls which were now full of servants and courtiers.

"Why are they all so busy, prince?" she asked.

"They are making everything ready for my wedding," answered the prince sadly.

Then the princess, too, felt a stab of grief because her heart had been touched by this fine young man. And the prince went on: "Sweetest of maidens, it is written in the stars that, after my enchantment is broken, I am to marry the one to whom destiny has betrothed me. But as I look into your eyes, I wish that it were not so."

"Who, then, are you to marry?" the princess asked, feeling her heart yet again torn with sorrow.

"I am to marry the one to whom I was bound three times during my enchantment," replied the prince.

"But you were bound three times to me," exclaimed the princess joyfully. "I bound you to me with a ribbon, a scarf and a girdle."

"Then will you be my wife?" cried the prince happily.

With joy, the princess gave him her hand and her heart. Prince Hare took her hand and, falling to his knees, pledged her all his love.

After three days, the wedding was held and thereafter the young couple lived happily and contentedly in the prince's palace. And so the princess did not have to suffer any more sorrow and grief for having bought the basket of flowers. And the old woman stayed with them and they loved her for she had brought them their fortune.

But in the end the old woman wanted to go back to the land of her birth, back to her poor cottage and her sister. The prince and the princess tried to persuade her to stay with them, but when they saw how homesick the old woman was, they sent her home in a golden coach laden with gifts.

The Three Hares

A Hindu legend

There were once three hares who lived in three caves side by side. They used to pray to God every day for their heart's desire to be fulfilled, namely that they would one day be taken up into heaven.

The first hare had a brown pelt, the second was white in patches, and the third was white all over and was called Snow. The three hares were very fond of each other and whatever one of them did the others did, too. They devoted many hours to prayer but, so that they would not go hungry, they also had to see about getting food.

So for many years they lived their god–fearing lives. Their prayers reached heaven and God decided to reward their piety. Although he knew them well he resolved to put them to the test. So God the Father said to the Moon: "You do not need to start shining until twelve o'clock, so first go into the mountains, seek out the three hares and ask each of them for something to ward off your hunger. When you have been to all three, come back to me and tell me about it."

The Moon obeyed and went first to the brown hare who was just getting his meal ready. When he saw the Moon standing there before him, he asked the Moon kindly to share his food with him.

The Moon thanked him, shared the meal and then went to the second hare. When the hare heard that someone was coming, he called cheerfully, "Welcome friend!"

When the Moon told him that he was hungry, the hare said: "I should gladly give you something to eat, but today I was praying too long so I forgot to look for food. But if you can wait, I shall get something."

When the hare had prepared the meal, he gave it all to the Moon. After that the Moon came finally to the third hare, Snow. He had to knock at the door for a long time, but at last the hare, who had been deep in prayer, appeared and greeted him.

"I am looking for someone who can give me something to eat," said the Moon. "After my long journey over the snow–covered heights, I am very tired and hungry."

"Just rest for a while," said Snow, "and meanwhile I shall go and see if I can find you something."

The Moon sat down near the entrance to the cave while the hare went to look in his larder. But alas, he had not gathered any food for days as he had been so deep in prayer. Snow thought of the verse: "Whosoever gives lodging to a guest and neither stills his hunger nor quenches his thirst has prayed to God in vain."

What was the poor hare to do now? At that difficult moment a solution occurred to him. He went and lit a fire and invited his guest to come and sit in comfort by the warmth, saying: "Sir, I have prayed so much in the last days, that I was not able to go and get food, and now I have nothing in my house that I can set before you."

The Moon said angrily: "Then I shall go on and I won't sit by your fire."

"But please stay," said Snow. "Do you mind what kind of meat I set before you?"

The Moon answered: "Now that I see that you mean it seriously, I shall eat any kind of meat which you set before me."

"Good," said Snow happily. "But as I have nothing else than myself to offer, I shall cast my own body into the fire and then you will have meat."

"No," cried the Moon in horror. "No, don't do that!"

But it was too late. Before the Moon could stop him, the hare had jumped into the flames and not even a cry was heard.

After this, the Moon went back up to heaven. There he saw that in the lap of God a beautiful white hare was lying.

God said: "Moon, look at this hare who sacrificed himself and jumped into the fire for you. How shall I reward his self–sacrifice?"

Then the Moon said: "Lord, will you give me the hare as a friend and companion? I shall keep him with me always wherever I go."

"Your request is granted," answered the Father. "When you shine upon the earth, let the hare shine down with you so that all men may see him and remember his example of selflessness."

And since then, you can always see the hare in the silvery light of the full Moon; but you will see him best when the Easter Moon shines in the sky in springtime.

The Saint and the Mountain Spirit

Maja Muntz–Koundoury

Through the rugged mountains of the Peloponnese, many narrow paths and tracks wind from town to town, from village to village. They are often hemmed in by steep crags on one side while, on the other, the eye of the traveller peers cautiously over deep precipices or along dark ravines where noisy torrents gush over the boulders in the rainy season.

Beside such a track in the bare grey wall of rock at the top of the mountain was a cave. It was in a lonely place feared by travellers. Here only the cry of the eagles circling the summit of the mountain broke the stillness. In this cave there lived a hermit, a man with mild eyes and grey hair. He spent his life praying for his fellow–men and asking God's grace for them. His prayer always ended with the words: "Lord, they know not what they do."

The track in front of his cave ran beside a deep dark chasm and was particularly dangerous, for it often happened that a strong wind came gusting down from the mountain top, and woe betide the traveller who at that moment was passing along the track. These gusts were so violent and unexpected that the poor wayfarer would be swept off his feet and hurled into the ravine. Occasionally the unfortunate victim might be able to cling to a projecting bush and cry desperately for help, but who would hear him in that wilderness and come to his aid? Well, there was someone and that was the hermit who lived in the cave. He knew the mountain and its ways. The great silence had so sharpened his ears that he could hear the high flute–like noise made by the wind before the gust struck. It sounded as if some mighty being were taking a huge indrawn breath to fill his gigantic lungs to bursting point. Then the old man would go to the entrance of his cave and listen, and if he heard a human cry he would run with a rope in his hand. In this way he had saved the lives of many people.

Near his cave he had built a little stone shrine where he placed an icon of St Nicholas, the holy protector of all travellers. Day and night he kept an oil–lamp burning there, and this showed the weary travellers the way to the safety of the cave. For this deed of compassion the hermit was loved and honoured by the inhabitants of the villages who sometimes had to use this dangerous path. Among them, it was said that a wicked spirit had its dwelling on the top of the mountain, and it was this evil spirit who cast people down into the chasm, and who else but a saint could protect one from such a danger? The hermit however did not think that he was doing anything extraordinary, but thanked God for every successful rescue, for so he loved mankind.

One lovely spring evening when all the flowers of Greece seemed to be holding an assembly, the holy man left his dwelling in order to thank God in the open air for all the beauty bestowed on nature. The air was full of fragrance, the mountain slopes were all golden or purple with innumerable blossoming shrubs, the valleys resembled many–coloured Persian carpets, with here and there bright patches of red, orange and yellow. It was growing darker and the hermit saw lanterns moving in the distant villages: it was Good Friday and away down there the people were walking with candles in procession with the picture of the dead Christ. The cool wind carried the slow mournful tolling of the bells. The old man stayed there until the last light had disappeared. Then he went back to his cave, but when he entered he had a fright. It seemed to him that something was moving near the back wall of his dwelling, something that looked like an enormous boulder. The holy man crossed himself. Suddenly the ground beneath his feet shook and in the cave was heard a heavy voice, like the growl from the depths of the earth during an earthquake.

The voice said: "Do not do that ... or I must go away, and I want to talk to you."

"Who are you?" the hermit managed to ask with some difficulty

"I am he who rules over this mountain, and casts the human ants into the abyss," was the grim answer. "I have come to ask you why and by what power you try to prevent me from doing this? Whenever you appear, I am powerless!"

The holy man could not believe his ears. "Are you the spirit of this mountain?" he stammered.

"Yes, I am," said the voice. "I must make myself visible to you in this way, otherwise your human eyes would not see me." He went on vehemently: "I hate you human beings. You unreliable, ungrateful creatures! The great gods of Hellas turned against you, hunted you and tried to destroy you."

The hermit said to him: "Human beings are God's youngest children, and I love my fellow–men in spite of all their weaknesses and errors. The One God, unknown to you, suffered death for love of us humans and

rose again from the dead. All that I do is in his name, for his love is great."

"Love?" asked the mountain spirit. "The people of my time knew about love, too. But the power of your God must be very great, I see that, and so listen. If you can prove to me that his love is greater than any other power, I shall bow before him and leave people in peace."

The hermit looked towards the picture of Christ above his bed and went and sat beneath it.

"May God help me," he sighed. "I shall tell you about his power. Once I knew an old shepherd who lived with his daughter in a little village not far from here. One evening when he had brought back his flocks to the village houses, he noticed to his horror that one of the sheep was missing. He went back into the mountains to look for the lost animal. Hour after hour went by and he did not return. The whole village was already asleep when his young daughter, full of anxiety for him, went after him. She knew the mountains well but still she searched in vain until she came here and found him. You know what happened then!"

"Yes, I blew the shepherd over the edge," growled the spirit. "But he managed to catch hold of a bush."

"That was so." The hermit sighed. "And I did not hear him for I was on the other side of the mountain. God be thanked I came back at that time but even so I was too late. I found the girl hanging over the precipice, one hand clasping a point of rock, and with the other she was holding on to her half–conscious father. She did not have the strength to pull him up. She was already exhausted and she slipped with him into the abyss." The hermit was silent.

The mountain spirit snorted impatiently. "That's nothing new, a child's love. I've seen that before. Did you never hear of King Oedipus and his daughter?"

The hermit nodded. "You are right."

The mountain spirit roared with laughter, so that the grit fell off the wall of rock. "I'll give you another chance," he growled. "Tomorrow at this time you will see me again." And he vanished.

The next evening the old man was sitting beneath the icon when the cave shook as with an earthquake and the spirit appeared. "Have you anything better to tell me than yesterday?" he asked mockingly.

"Listen and judge for yourself," was the calm answer. "Once war was raging in this land, a dreadful war. The suffering was terrible amongst the people and amongst those who were fighting. Not only danger but also much hunger and hardship had to be borne. Two friends were fighting in the front ranks. They were already at their limit with hunger, cold and exhaustion when one of them was badly wounded in an attack. But worse was to come. Their forces had to fall back before the strength of the enemy and, in the confusion, the wounded man was left behind. But he was not forgotten. His friend, who could hardly walk himself, looked for him and found him. This friend lifted his fellow-soldier on his shoulders and, weary and alone, for he could not catch up with the others, carried him through the mountains. He came this way. As soon as he arrived at my cave, he fell down unconscious. With God's help, I was able to save them both." The hermit was silent.

The mountain spirit spoke: "That is truly great love. For here blood does not speak. But I, too, have seen true friendship in the good old days: Achilles and Patroclus, and many others."

The hermit hung his head. "You are right," he admitted.

"I shall come once more tonight," promised the mountain spirit, "but that will be the last time. Think hard!" And he vanished.

It was late that Holy Saturday night. In the villages people were going to church for the midnight service. The old man knelt before the icon. It was too late to go to a village and hear the joyous tidings in the lighted church: *"Christos anesti!"* "Christ is risen!" God would forgive him as he was missing the service for a good purpose. He closed his eyes and prayed. Soon a dark shadow crept into the cave. A rough hand gripped the hermit's neck and he looked up into a wild distorted face.

"Hand it over!" the rough voice commanded. "Where's the money?"

Trembling the old man raised his hands. "What are you saying, brother? What money? I haven't got any."

A fist struck him in the face. "Don't try and fool me. All that money that people give you for saving them, where is it?"

"Nothing, I have nothing," murmured the hermit in a faint voice.

The robber threw him to the ground and kicked him. In a rage he searched the poor dwelling but found nothing. "Did I come to this damned place just for this?" he screamed and struck again and again like a madman at the defenceless old man. Then he went storming out of the cave.

At that very moment, the badly hurt old man heard the familiar sharp note of the wind and knew what would happen. The mountain shook. A violent gust stormed over the path. A cry rang through the air. The hermit struggled to his feet, seized the rope and staggered out. In the distance the church-bells were starting to ring.

With his last strength, the hermit hastened to the precipice and threw the rope to the robber who was clinging to a bush. The holy man was just able to tie the other end of the rope round a point of rock before he fell to the ground dying and his soul left his body.

The robber climbed up panting, looked at the dead man petrified for a moment and then ran screaming away. The soul of the holy man hovered over his body.

The mountain spirit spoke: "Can you see me?"

The soul answered: "Yes, now I can see you as you really are."

The spirit asked: "Why did you do that? He murdered you."

"Love your enemies, my God has taught me," answered the saint.

Silence fell. Then the mountain spirit said: "That is a greater love than anything that I have ever known. I shall keep my promise. Farewell."

"Peace be with you," said the saint.

In the valley far below, the Easter bells were ringing joyfully.

The Barge–Master's Easter

J.W. Ooms

I knew the master of *Gezina II* well. His boat was a sixty ton canal barge with its painted prow and steel frame. It had lovely lines, that inland waters boat. Some years before the war, when I was trying to find out more about the life and sailing of the canal barges, I was able to go on more than one trip with the *Gezina II*.

The master was an incredibly hard worker. He hardly allowed himself time to eat. I still remember once when we were sailing along above Zwolle on the Zwarte Water, the master said to his crewman and me: "Boys, the potatoes are done. I'll pour the water off over the port side and then I'll bring them down into the cabin. You go on down and get grace said."

The crewman and I went down into the tiny cabin and the master poured off the potatoes. But what happened was that the lid slipped off the pot and all the steaming contents fell out. Then he called down: "Just say thanks for the meal, boys, the potatoes have gone overboard!"

Yes, that was just like him, the burly but honest skipper of the *Gezina II*.

It was in 1944, some weeks before Easter, that he received rather unusual orders. It was still wartime and the Occupation Authorities commandeered him through the freight office to ship a cargo to Lobith, where it was to be loaded on to a bigger boat. What was unusual was that it was a cargo of twenty–eight large bells taken from various church towers. But the master of the *Gezina II* did not like the sound of the job.

"Trina," he said to his wife, "I won't have anything to do with that cargo! The number of times we have lain moored on a Sunday at some place or other and listened to the church bells ringing. Then we say to each other, 'That's God's voice calling' and off we go to church. Have I now got to take God's voice out of the country? That I cannot do, Trina. I can't and I won't."

His wife agreed that he was right, and nodded her approval. But what would they say? In the war years you had to dance to the tune of the enemy. If you refused, you could land up in prison. It was choosing or collaborating. And the captain chose.

"Will I carry away the bells? Never, never! They're going to melt the bells down to make guns and bullets. I'll have no part in that."

So the master wrote to the freight office that he had enough cargo and that he could not take on the freight. A fortnight passed and he heard nothing more about it so he thought that he had got shot of the thing. He had indeed more than enough freight. There was sugar–beet and grain to be carried. Freight charges were high enough, too, as it was dangerous to sail with fighter aircraft sometimes shooting up inland water–boats. The dangers of war threatened everywhere, on land as on water.

The master thought he had got rid of the problem. But shortly before Easter he received an angry letter. He was ordered within four days to load on the twenty–eight church bells at the Oude Hoofd in Rotterdam and to ship them to Lobith.

The master of the *Gezina II* took it calmly. He tore the letter into shreds and threw them overboard. "They'll have to order me harder than that," he said.

But four days later — and it was then two days before Easter — the cat was in among the pigeons. The *Gezina II* was lying berthed at the sugar factory in Puttershoek, when two fellows came on board. Actually there were three, but the third stayed on the wharf with his rifle on his shoulder by the gangway.

Now there was no way out of it. If the bargee did not take the bells right away to Lobith, it would be regarded as hostile and punished accordingly. His boat, *Gezina II,* would be confiscated. "So, get on with it!"

The master spent a good half day with his head bent pacing up and down the deck. It had cost him much sweat and trouble to become owner of the *Gezina II*. For nineteen years he had toiled from morning till night to pay off the loan on the boat. Now he had nearly reached the point where he could go to the lawyer Meijer in the Maaskade and say, "Here's the last instalment on my loan."

The skipper thought to himself: "What is a boatman without a boat?" At last he said gloomily to his wife, "I'll have to do it after all, Trina. We can't get out of it."

Deep in her heart the woman was glad that her husband had given in, for she too loved the *Gezina II*. Their whole life was tied up with the graceful canal barge.

That same evening he sailed to Rotterdam and the next day he loaded the bells on at the Oude Hoofd in Rotterdam. It was fearfully hard work even though he had a powerful winch. But church–bells are unwieldy things.

With those twenty–eight church–bells the *Gezina II* was laden right down below her plimsoll line. An old man had been standing silently on the wharf watching the loading. When at last the *Gezina II* cast off and was gathering way the old man called out grimly: "Bell–skipper, bell–skipper, watch what you're doing."

They did not make much progress, because during the day the air was quite clear with hardly any haze over the water, and many British planes were flying about. Every so often, air–raid sirens sounded on land, and that fearsome sound, carried over the waters, reached the ears of the skipper and his wife aboard the *Gezina II*. The skipper pretended to be deaf and dumb. He did not say anything but his weather–beaten face was strained. Something was going on inside him. He was doing something he did not approve of, something against his conscience. He was carrying bells out of his country, eight and twenty church–bells, from which the enemy would make guns and bullets.

The barge had reached the neighbourhood of Culemborg when British airmen caught sight of it. They first circled it quite high up, then they came diving down, like falcons plunging on to a robin.

The skipper was standing at the tiller. He saw them coming and called: "Trina, take cover, we're being attacked!"

Less than two seconds later, the aircraft's guns started firing. The noise was indescribable: bullets started hitting the bells, ringing the loud church bells. The whole boat sounded like a peal of bells. It was a truly remarkable sound, with the bronze voices sounding the same deep, imploring tone which had once rung out from belfries all over the countryside.

Twice they received the full broadside. Amazingly the skipper and his wife escaped unscathed. Once the aircraft had flown off to the West, the skipper stood again by the wheel. But his face was incredibly pale and his eyes seemed glazed. The bells were still echoing with a strangely beautiful and at the same time melancholy sound.

"D'you hear it now?" called the skipper. "D'you hear it, Trina? It is the voice of God, the same voice that used to call from the church spires on Sundays."

It was too much for the skipper. He collapsed like a sandbag by the tiller. Then Trina saw that they were taking in water. She rushed to the tiller, steered straight for the bank and threw the grapple on to the land. Then she lowered a pail on a rope into the water and pulled up a pailful. She poured water on the skipper's cheeks and dashed some on to his forehead.

By good fortune the skipper soon came to. But Trina had got the *Gezina II* stuck on the mudbank of a narrow dyke. That was dire necessity for the water was already gushing in below the waterline.

People came rushing up from all directions, for they had seen the planes attacking and heard the remarkable sound of bullets on bells ringing over the water.

Suddenly Germans appeared out of the air–raid shelter in the neighbourhood of the waterway. They soon cleared the onlookers and then they saw that the boat was making water and would have to be repaired before it could continue on its way. The soldiers were kind to the skipper and his wife.

"Come with us into the shelter," they said. "We shall tell the Kommandant about your rotten luck. Boat–repairers will have to come. But just come on in to the shelter. We're celebrating Easter, come and join us!"

What else could the skipper and Trina do? The Germans were friendly, of course, because the skipper had a cargo for their homeland, a contribution to their war–machine.

There the skipper and Trina sat among the German soldiers in the shelter. There were candles set on a rough wooden table. The candle flames flickered restlessly and just as restlessly a fire was burning in the skipper's heart. He realized he should have said "No!" He should have refused that cargo. He ought never to have given in, never shipped the voice of God out of the country.

But now it had been done, and he could not undo it. His *Gezina II* lay broken against the summer dyke of a waterway and now he would have to do whatever the Germans commanded him to do. If he refused, they would take *Gezina II* away from him. Confiscated, that's what they had called it. But he could not survive without his boat; *Gezina II* had become part of his life. And now here he was sitting in an air–raid shelter right in the midst of the enemy. They offered him schnapps and made it clear to him that he and his wife were to celebrate Easter with them.

There was nothing else to be done. He would have to go along with it because he did not want to risk them taking his boat from him.

A corporal began to read a story. It was an Easter legend.

"I won't listen to it," thought the skipper. "I won't listen to a legend ... and certainly not to a legend read by an enemy."

The skipper had often sailed into Germany before: iron ore from Ruhrort, coal from Mannheim. He and Trina understood German very well.

No, the skipper did not want to listen. All the same he did listen. Even though there was sometimes a babble of voices, the corporal read on steadily. The story was about one of the soldiers who had to keep watch over the grave where Jesus had been buried. The soldier came from Bethlehem. His father had been a carpenter, and at that time he had received the order to make a crib for the stable of the inn "Good Hope."

The soldier remembered that something special had happened with that crib. When his father had finished the piece, it was discovered that in the wood there was a wonderful marking in the shape of a cross. The father was a pious man looking for the redemption promised by the prophets. The soldier remembered his father saying to him: "This cross is the sign of a king. One day in this crib the promised king and Redeemer will lie as a defenceless human child, but the cross will be a sign of his triumph and his power."

And all at once the soldier at the grave was certain that he was keeping watch over the grave of the promised king. That king had been condemned to the death of the cross and had died on the wood of shame, but would rise again in glory. Then the soldier threw away his arms and he deserted, calling to his companions: "He shall rise again, he shall rise again, it is Easter."

The skipper and his wife listened to the corporal reading. When he had finished — most of the soldiers had been giving more attention to their drink than to the Easter story — the skipper said to Trina in a subdued voice: "I did not believe in God's promise that he would make everything all right. I let myself carry his voice out of the country. Trina, I did not put my trust in him, I did not believe in Easter. I put my boat above everything else."

Suddenly he turned to the Germans and said: "Even if you take everything from me, I won't take church bells any further on my ship, Easter bells for you to make into guns. I won't do it, I won't carry the bells a mile further."

The Germans in the shelter did not understand what the skipper was getting at. Had he drunk too much schnapps?

What could the skipper do now? The twenty-eight bells could not be removed and hidden. Not even ten skippers could move a single bell from the hold of the barge without a strong winch. The skipper walked out of the shelter. Trina followed him, tears streaming down her face.

When they were alone together — meantime dusk had fallen over the land — the skipper said: "If I just do nothing, the Germans will bring another boat and the bells will be loaded on to it and taken to Germany."

Trina sighed: "What can we do? We can do nothing."

They walked along the dyke, the skipper and his wife. They walked there back and forth, just as he had used to pace up and down on the deck of his boat. Darkness fell. The two had been walking for hours on the dyke. But when high tide came about midnight, the skipper said: "Trina, I'm hoping to get her moving. We must try to get the *Gezina* off the mudbank at high water. Then I'll pull her over into the middle of the river."

That is what they did, the two of them. They took their most precious belongings from the cabin and put them into the rowing boat. And when the lovely barge lay in the middle of the river, man and wife stepped into the rowing boat. And they had to hurry. They could see how the *Gezina* was already lying deeper and deeper. There was a gurgling sound of water gushing into the hold. Suddenly quite quickly she slipped away, the lovely *Gezina II*. Down she went and soon there was nothing more to be seen of her.

The skipper and Trina rowed slowly away. They did not get far. Even before they had reached the former towpath, where there is a sharp bend in the Lek, Germans in a patrol boat came upon them. They were taken once more to the air–raid shelter.

"You were ordered to take the bells to Germany, weren't you?" the soldiers accused them harshly. "You are guilty of sabotage."

The skipper kept calm. He pointed to the corporal, who was now sitting with a glass in his hand and appeared to be drunk.

"I did have an order, I did," answered the skipper. "That man read us a story. He gave me the order to believe in the Risen King. And the King said: 'Not through might or power, but through my spirit, shall it happen.'"

"What do you mean?"

"I don't know," said the skipper softly. "All I know is that it is Easter and that Christ has overcome. Easter bells must not become guns. That was a beautiful story, the story of the soldier at the grave. He understood what Easter was all about."

The people in the neighbourhood no doubt still remember that a few days after that Easter 1944, by order of the Occupation, a sunken barge had to be raised because it was blocking the channel in the waterway. Hauled up by three winches from a derrick, the heavy barge was finally raised to the surface. But the bells fell out of the hold and sank again to the muddy bottom.

The skipper lost his *Gezina II*. His boat was confiscated, but he still felt at peace with himself. At least he had stopped them taking away the voice of God, the voice of the bells that every year proclaimed Easter over the land with their metal tongues.

The Crystal Ball

Brothers Grimm

There was once an enchantress, who had three sons who loved each other as brothers, but the old woman did not trust them, and thought they wanted to steal her power from her. So she changed the eldest into an eagle, which was forced to dwell in the rocky mountains, and was often seen flying in great circles in the sky. The second, she changed into a whale, which lived in the deep sea, and all that was seen of it was that it sometimes spouted up a great jet of water in the air. Each of them bore his human form for only two hours daily. The third son, who was afraid she might change him into a raging wild beast — a bear perhaps, or a wolf, went secretly away. He had heard that a King's daughter who was bewitched, was imprisoned in the Castle of the Golden Sun, and was waiting to be set free. Those, however, who tried to free her risked their lives; three–and–twenty youths had already died a miserable death, and now only one other might make the attempt, after which no more must come. And as his heart was without fear, he made up his mind to seek out the Castle of the Golden Sun.

He had already travelled about for a long time without being able to find it, when he came by chance into a great forest, and did not know the way out of it. All at once he saw in the distance two giants, who made a sign to him with their hands, and when he came to them they said: "We are quarrelling about a cap, and which of us it is to belong to, and as we are equally strong, neither of us can get the better of the other. The small men are cleverer than we are, so we will leave the decision to you."

"How can you dispute about an old cap?" said the youth.

"You do not know what properties it has! It is a wishing–cap; whosoever puts it on, can wish himself away wherever he likes, and in an instant he will be there."

"Give me the cap," said the youth, "I will go a short distance off, and when I call you, you must run a race, and the cap shall belong to the one who gets first to me."

He put it on and went away, and thought of the King's daughter, forgot the giants, and walked continually onward. At length he sighed from the very bottom of his heart, and cried: "Ah, if I were but at the Castle of the Golden Sun," and hardly had the words passed his lips than he was standing on a high mountain before the gate of the castle.

He entered and went through all the rooms, until in the last he found the King's daughter. But how shocked he was when he saw her. She had an ashen–grey face full of wrinkles, bleary eyes, and red hair.

"Are you the King's daughter, whose beauty the whole world praises?" cried he.

"Ah," she answered, "this is not my form; human eyes can only see me in this state of ugliness, but that you may know what I am like, look in the mirror — it does not let itself be misled — it will show you my image as it is in truth."

She gave him the mirror in his hand, and he saw therein the likeness of the most beautiful maiden on earth, and saw, too, how the tears were rolling down her cheeks with grief.

Then said he: "How can you be set free? I fear no danger."

She said: "He who gets the crystal ball, and holds it before the enchanter, will destroy his power with it, and I shall resume my true shape. Ah," she added, "so many have already gone to meet death for this, and you are so young; I grieve that you should encounter such great danger."

"Nothing can keep me from doing it," said he "but tell me what I must do."

"You shall know everything," said the King's daughter; "when you descend the mountain on which the castle stands, a wild bull will stand below by a spring, and you must fight with it, and if you have the luck to kill it, a fiery bird will spring out of it, which bears in its body a red-hot egg, and in the egg the crystal ball lies as its yolk. The bird, however, will not let the egg fall until forced to do so. and if it falls on the ground, it will flame up and burn everything that is near, and even the egg itself will melt, and with it the crystal ball, and then all your trouble will have been in vain."

The youth went down to the spring, where the bull snorted and bellowed at him. After a long struggle he plunged his sword in the animal's body, and it fell down. Instantly a fiery bird arose from it, and was about to fly away, but the young man's brother, the eagle, who was passing between the clouds, swooped down, hunted it away to the sea, and struck it with his beak until, in its extremity, it let the egg fall. The egg, however, did not fall into the sea, but on a fisherman's hut which stood on the shore and the hut began at once to smoke and was about to break out in flames. Then arose in the sea waves as high as a house, which streamed over the hut, and subdued the fire. The other brother, the whale, had come swimming to them, and had driven the water up on high. When the fire was extinguished, the youth sought for the egg and happily found it; it was not yet melted, but the shell was broken by being so suddenly cooled with the water, and he could take out the crystal ball unhurt.

When the youth went to the enchanter and held it before him, the latter said: "My power is destroyed, and from this time forth you are the King of the Castle of the Golden Sun. With this can you likewise give back to your brothers their human form."

Then the youth hastened to the King's daughter, and when he entered the room, she was standing there in the full splendour of her beauty, and joyfully they exchanged rings with each other.

The Candle

or
How the Good Peasant Overcame the Cruel Overseer

Leo Tolstoy

"Ye have heard how it has been said, an eye for an eye, and a tooth for a tooth; but I say unto you, resist not evil."

This happened in the time before the serfs were freed from their masters. Of masters there were different kinds. There were those who, remembering God and the hour of death, showed mercy to their serfs, and there were others — sheer brutes — who remembered neither. Of these over-lords, the worst were those who had themselves been serfs — men who had risen from the mire to consort with princes. Life under them was the hardest of all.

Such an overseer was appointed to a seignieurial estate, the peasantry on which worked on the forced labour system. The estate was a large and fine one, comprising as it did both meadow and forest land, as well as good water supply. Both its owner and the peasantry were contented, until the former appointed one of his house–serfs from another estate to be overseer.

This overseer assumed office, and began to press the peasants hard. He had a family — a wife and two married daughters — and meant to make money, by fair means or by foul, for he was both ambitious and thoroughly wicked. He began by compelling the peasants to exceed their tale of days and, having started a brick factory, nearly worked the people (women as well as men) to death, that he might sell and make money by the bricks. Some of the peasants went to Moscow to complain to the owner of the estate, but their representations availed nothing. The owner sent his petitioners away empty–handed, and did nothing to check the overseer. Soon the overseer heard that the peasants had been to complain, and started to take vengeance upon them, so that their daily lot became worse than ever. Moreover, some of them were untruthful men, and began telling tales of one another to the overseer and intriguing among them-selves, with the result that the whole district was set by the ears, and the overseer only grew the more cruel.

Things grew steadily worse, until at last the overseer was as much feared by the peasantry as though he had been a raging wild beast. Whenever he rode through the village, every man shrank away from him as from a wolf, and endeavoured at all costs to avoid his eye. The over-seer saw this, and raged all the more because they feared him so. He flogged and over-worked the peasants, and many a one suffered sore ill at his hands.

In time, however, it came to pass that the peasants became desperate at these villainies, and began to talk among themselves. They would gather together in some secluded spot, and one of the more daring of them would say, "How much longer are we going to put up with this brute who is over us? Let us end it, once and for all. It would be no sin to kill such a man."

Once the peasants had been told off to clear the undergrowth in the forest. It was just before the beginning of Holy Week, and when they gathered together for the mid-day meal they began to talk once more.

"How can we go on like this?" they said. "That man is driving us to desperation. He has so overworked us of late that neither we nor our women have had a moment's rest by day or night. Besides, if anything is not done exactly to his liking, he flies into a passion and beats us. Simon died from his flogging, and Anisim has just undergone torture in the stocks. What are we to look for next? That brute will be coming here this evening, and we shall feel the rough side of his tongue. Well, all we need do is to pull him from his horse, bash him over the head with an axe, and thus end the whole thing. Yes, let us take the body somewhere, cut it up, and throw the limbs into the water. The only thing is — we must all be agreed, we must all stand together. There must be no treachery."

Vassili Minaeff was especially insistent in the matter, for he had a par-ticular spite against the overseer. Not only did the latter flog him every week, but he had also carried off his wife to be his cook.

So the peasants talked among themselves, and in the evening the over-seer arrived. He had hardly ridden up when he flew into a rage because the chopping had not been done to his liking. Moreover, in one of the piles of faggots he detected a hidden bough.

"I told you not to cut the lindens," he said. "Which of you has done this? Tell me, or I will flog the whole lot of you."

So, on his asking them again in whose tale of trees the linden had been included, the peasants pointed to Sidor; whereupon the overseer lashed him over the face till it was covered with blood, gave Vassili also a cut because his pile of faggots was too small, and rode off home again.

That evening the peasants collected together as usual, and Vassili said: "What fellows you are! You are sparrows rather than men. You keep saying to one another, 'Stand ready, now, stand ready,' and yet, when the moment comes, you are every one of you afraid. That is just how the sparrows got ready to resist the hawk. 'Stand ready, now, stand ready — no betrayal of one another,' they said; and yet, when the hawk stooped, they scurried off into the nettle–bed, and the hawk took the sparrow he wanted, and flew off with it dangling in his talons. Then the sparrows hopped out again. 'Tweet, tweet!' they cried — and then saw that one of their number was missing. 'Which of us is gone?' they said. 'Oh, only little Vania. Well, it was fated thus, and he is paying for the rest of us.' The same with you fellows, with your cry of 'No betrayal, no betrayal.' When that man hit Sidor you should have plucked up heart of grace and finished him. But no; it was, 'Stand ready, stand ready! No betrayal, no betrayal!' — and yet, when the hawk stooped, every man of you was off into the bushes."

The peasants talked more and more frequently on this subject, until they were quite prepared to make an end of the overseer.

Now, on the Eve of Passion Week he sent word to them that they were to hold themselves in readiness to plough the land for oats. This seemed to the peasants a desecration of Passion Week, and they gathered together in Vassili's backyard and debated the matter.

"If he has forgotten God," they said, "and orders us to do such things as that, it is our bounden duty to kill him. Let us do it once for all."

Just then they were joined by Peter Michieff. Peter was a peaceable man, and had hitherto taken no part in these discussions. Now, however, he listened, and then said:

"You are meditating a great sin, my brothers. To take a man's life is a terrible thing to do. It is easy enough to destroy another's life, but what about your own? If this man does evil things, then evil awaits him. You need but be patient, my brothers."

Vassili flew into a passion at these words.

"For you," he said, "there is but one consideration — that it is a sin to kill a man. Yes, of course it is a sin, but not in such a case as the present one. It is a sin to kill a good man, but what about a dog like this? Why, God has commanded us to kill him. One kills a mad dog for the sake of one's fellows. To let this man live would be a greater sin than to kill him. Why should he go on ruining our lives? No matter if we suffer for killing him, we shall have done it for our fellows, and they will thank us for it.

Yours is empty talk, Michieff. Would it be a less sin, then, for us to go and work during Christ's holy festival? Why, you yourself do not intend to go, surely?"

"Why should I not go?" answered Peter. "If I am sent to plough, I shall obey. It will not be for myself that I shall be doing it. God will know to whom to impute the sin, and, for ourselves, we need but bear Him in mind as we plough. These are not my own words, brothers. If God had intended that we should remove evil by evil, He would have given us a law to that effect and have pointed us to it as the way. No. If you remove evil by evil, it will come back to you again. It is folly to kill a man, for blood sticks to the soul. Take a man's soul, and you plunge your own in blood. Even though you may think that the man whom you have killed was evil, and that thus you have removed evil from the world — look you, you yourselves will have done a more wicked deed than any one of his. Submit yourselves rather to misfortune, and misfortune will submit itself to you."

After this, the peasants were divided in opinion, since some of them agreed with Vassili, and some of them respected Peter's advice to be patient and refrain from sin.

On the first day of the festival (the Sunday) the peasants kept holiday, but in the evening the *starosta* arrived from the manor house with his messengers, and said:

"Michael Semenovitch, the overseer, has sent us to warn you that you are to plough tomorrow in readiness for the oat sowing."

So the *starosta* and his men went round the village and told all the peasants to go to plough next day — some of them beyond the river, and some of them starting from the highroad. The peasants were in great distress, yet dared not disobey, and duly went out in the morning with their teams, and started ploughing. The church bells were ringing to early mass, and all the world was observing the festival; but the peasants — they were ploughing.

The overseer awoke late that morning and went to make his round of the homestead as usual. His household tidied themselves up and put on their best clothes, and, the cart having been got ready by a workman, drove off to church. On their return a serving–woman set out the samovar, the overseer returned from the farm, and everyone sat down to tea–drinking. That finished, Michael lighted his pipe and called for the *starosta*.

"You set the peasants to plough?" he asked.

"Yes, Michael Semenovitch."

"They all of them went, did they?"

"Yes, all of them, and I divided up the work myself."

"Well, you may have done that, but are they actually ploughing? That is the question. Go and see whether they are, and tell them that I myself am coming when I have had dinner. Tell them also that each two ploughs must cover a *dessiatin,* and that the ploughing is to be good. If I find anything done wrong I shall act accordingly, festival or no festival."

"Very good, Michael Semenovitch," and the *starosta* was just departing when Michael called him back. He called him back because he wanted to say something more to him, though he hardly knew how to do it. He hemmed and ha'ed, and finally said:

"I want you to listen, too, to what those rascals are saying of me. If you hear anyone abusing me, come and tell me all he said. I know those brigands well. They don't like work — they only like lying on their backs and kicking up their heels. Guzzling and keeping holiday, that is what they love, and they will think nothing of leaving a bit of land un-ploughed, or of not finishing their allotted piece, if I let them. So just you go and listen to what they are saying, and mark those who are saying it, and come and report all to me. Go and inspect things, report to me fully, and keep nothing back — those are your orders."

The *starosta* turned and went out, and, mounting his horse, galloped off to the peasants in the fields.

Now, the overseer's wife had heard what her husband had said to the *starosta,* and came to him to intercede for the peasants. She was a women of gentle nature, and her heart was good. Whenever she got an opportunity she would try to soften her husband and to defend the peasants before him.

So she came now to her husband, and interceded.

"My dearest Michael," she implored, "do not commit this great sin against the Lord's high festival, but let the peasants go, for Christ's sake."

But Michael disregarded what she said, and laughed at her.

"Has the whip become such a stranger to your back," he said, "that you are grown so bold as to meddle with what is not your business?"

"Oh, but, Michael dearest, I have had such an evil dream about you. Do listen to me, and let the peasants go."

"All I have to say to you," he replied, "is that you are evidently getting above yourself, and need a slash of the whip again. Take that!" And in his rage he thrust his glowing pipe–bowl against her lips, and, throwing her out of the room, bid her send him in his dinner.

Jelly, pies, cabbage soup with bacon, roast sucking–pig, and vermicelli pudding — he devoured them all, and washed them down with cherry–

brandy. Then, after dessert, he called the cook to him, set her down to play the piano, and himself took a guitar and accompanied her.

Thus he was sitting in high spirits as he hiccuped, twanged the strings, and laughed with the cook, when the *starosta* returned, and, with a bow to his master, began to report what he had seen in the fields.

"Are they ploughing, each man his proper piece?" asked Michael.

"Yes," replied the *starosta*, "and they have done more than half already."

"No skimping of the work, eh?"

"No, I have seen none. They are ploughing well, for they are afraid to do otherwise."

"And is the up–turn good?"

"Yes, it is quite soft, and scatters like poppy–seed."

The overseer was silent a moment.

"Well, and what do they say of me?" he went on presently. "Are they abusing me?"

The *starosta* hesitated, but Michael bid him tell the truth.

"Tell me everything," he said. "'Tis not your own words that you will be reporting, but theirs. Tell me the truth, and I will reward you; but screen those fellows, and I will show you no mercy — I will flog you soundly. Here, Katiushka! Give him a glass of vodka to encourage him."

The cook went and fetched a glassful and handed it to the *starosta*, whereupon the latter made a reverence to his master, drank the liquor down, wiped his mouth, and went on speaking.

"Anyway," he thought to himself, "it is not my fault that they have nothing to say in praise of him, so I will tell the truth since he bids me do so."

So the *starosta* plucked up courage and went on: "They are grumbling, Michael Semenovitch. They are grumbling terribly."

"But what exactly do they say? Tell me."

"There is one thing they all of them say — namely, that you have no belief in God."

The overseer burst out laughing.

"Which of them say that?" he asked.

"They all do. They say, in fact, that you serve the Devil."

The overseer laughed the more.

"That is excellent," he said. "Now tell me what each of them separately has to say of me. What, for instance, does our friend Vassili say?"

The *starosta* had been reluctant hitherto to inform against his own friends, but between him and Vassili there was an old–standing feud.

"Vassili," he replied, "curses you worse than all the rest."

"Then tell me what he says."

"I am ashamed to repeat it, but he hopes you may come to a miserable end some day."

"Oh, he does, does he, that young man?" exclaimed the overseer. "Well, he won't ever kill me, for he will never get a chance of laying his hands upon me. Very well, friend Vassili, you and I will have a settling together. And what does our Tishka say?"

"Well, no one says any good of you. They all curse you and utter threats."

"What about Peter Michieff? What did he say? I'll be bound the old rascal was another one of those who cursed me."

"No, but he was not, Michael Semenovitch."

"What did he say, then?"

"He was the only one of them who said nothing at all. He knows a great deal for a peasant, and I marvelled when I saw him today."

"Why so?"

"Because of what he was doing. The others marvelled at him too."

"What was he doing?"

"A most strange thing. He was ploughing the grass by the Tourkin ridge, and as I rode up to him I seemed to hear someone singing in a low, beautiful voice, while in the middle of his plough-shaft there was something burning."

"Well?"

"This thing was burning like a little tongue of fire. As I drew nearer I saw that it was a five-kopek wax candle, and that it was fastened to the shaft. A wind was blowing and yet the candle never went out."

"And what did he say?"

"He said nothing, except that when he saw me he gave me the Easter greeting, and then began singing again. He had on a new shirt, and sang Easter hymns as he ploughed. He turned the plough at the end of the furrow, and shook it, yet the candle never went out. Yes, I was close to him when he shook the clods off the plough and lifted the handles round. Yet, all the time that he was guiding the plough round, the candle remained burning as before."

"What did you say to him?"

"I said nothing, but some of the other peasants came up and began laughing at him. 'Get along with you!' they said. 'Michieff will take a century to atone for ploughing in Holy Week.'"

"And what did he say to that?"

"Only 'On earth peace, and goodwill toward men'; after which he bent himself to his plough, touched up his horse, and went on singing to himself in a low voice. And all the time the candle kept burning steadily and never went out."

The overseer ceased to laugh, but laid aside the guitar, bowed his head upon his breast, and remained plunged in thought.

He dismissed the cook and the *starosta*, and still sat on and on. Then he went behind the curtain of the bed–chamber, lay down upon the bed, and fell to sighing and moaning as a cart may groan beneath its weight of sheaves. His wife went to him and pleaded with him again, but for a long time he returned her no answer.

At last, however, he said, "That man has got the better of me. It is all coming home to me now."

Still his wife pleaded with him.

"Go out," she implored him, "and release the peasants. Surely this is nothing. Think of the things you have done and were not afraid. Why, then, should you be afraid of this now?"

But he only replied again, "That man has conquered me. I am broken. Go you away while you are yet whole. This matter is beyond your understanding."

So he remained lying there.

But in the morning he rose and went about his affairs as usual. Yet he was not the same Michael Semenovitch as before. It was plain that his heart had received some shock. He began to have fits of melancholy, and to attend to nothing, but sat moodily at home. His reign did not last much longer. When the Feast of St Peter arrived the owner came to visit his estate. He called on his overseer the first day, but the overseer lay sick. He called on him again the second day, but still the overseer lay sick. Then the owner learnt that Michael had been drinking heavily, and deposed him from his stewardship. The ex–overseer still hung about the homestead, doing no work and growing ever more melancholy. Everything which he possessed he drank away, and descended even to stealing his wife's shawls and taking them to the tavern to exchange for drink. Even the peasants pitied him, and gave him liquor. He survived less than a year, and died at last of vodka.

The Easter Grace

From a story by Werner Bergengruen

In the days of the Holy Roman Empire, it was the custom of the Emperor on Easter Eve to dispense mercy to those who made public confession of crimes in his presence. For this ceremony a great candle, called the Candle of Grace, was lit by the Emperor himself in the Lateran Church of St John the Baptist. For as long as the candle still burned, penitents could come and lay their hand upon the candle to make confession. Only those were allowed to seek the Easter Grace whose misdeeds were not already being tried in a court of law or who had not been summoned, so that in order to obtain the Easter Grace it was necessary to make a voluntary confession. Furthermore it was an offence, punishable by death, to prevent anyone who was seeking the Easter Grace from making the journey to Rome.

Now at that time there lived in Syracuse a knight by the name of Caesarius who was married to a lady called Antonia. While Caesarius had been away from home on his journeys, his wife had been unfaithful to him and had given her favours to other admirers. In due time, Caesarius discovered this and, enraged, brought his wife before a court of law on charges of adultery. Antonia, in fear of her husband's wrath and the harsh sentence of the court, escaped from Caesarius and went back to her parents' house. There her mother advised her to flee to Rome, confess her guilt to the Emperor and seek the Easter Grace, even though she had already been summoned by a judge.

Caesarius found out that his wife was going to Rome to seek the Easter Grace wrongfully, but he could not prevent her from going without breaking the law himself. After much thought, he decided to go to Rome himself and present the Emperor with a letter stating the facts, so that his wife would not escape punishment.

"I believe," he ended his letter, "that it is necessary for Your Imperial Highness to know these things so that you may judge whether it is right to grant Antonia the Easter Grace."

Caesarius then rode off to Rome with this letter of denunciation. When the night came for the Easter vigil, he entered the Lateran Church of St

John the Baptist which is called the mother of all churches. He arrived early and took up a position not far from where the Candle of Grace still stood unlit before the Emperor's throne, for he was afraid that otherwise he might not be able to make his way through the great throng of people. Near at hand a table stood ready for the imperial clerk who would enter the names of the lawbreakers in a book and give out the letters of mercy so that the penitents would be allowed to go home and mend their ways without further prosecution.

The huge church where the crowd slowly gathered was poorly lit, and the gloom increased Caesarius' own sadness and inner turmoil. In the half–dark, he could make out the tall decorated stem of the Easter Candle itself, on the far side of the great altar, waiting for its own central moment in the vigil ceremony.

Now, as the bell tolled the hour, the few lit candles in the church were doused and the church was left in grave–like darkness. The great bronze doors opened, and slowly the singing procession entered with the newly–consecrated light. The Emperor and his highest paladins followed behind. Through the blackness nothing could be seen except the tiny flickering light in the hand of the deacon who led the procession. The ceremony proceeded according to ancient custom. At last the tall decorated Easter Candle was lit. Then sounded forth the message of the Easter annunciation and, as the tidings of the Resurrection spread among the faithful, so the light of the Easter Candle was distributed from candle to candle until the whole church blossomed in brightness. Now only the Candle of Grace remained unlit.

After mass had been sung, the Emperor rose from his throne and in his golden cloak strode towards the Easter Candle. There he lit a spill of fragrant wood, raised it above his head and bore it across to the wick of the Candle of Grace as a sign that he would dispense mercy from the Kingdom of the Risen One.

At that moment the side door was opened and from the dark courtyard outside came the long train of miscreants. They came in pairs: men, women and children, barefoot, many wearing penitential clothing, others clad as pilgrims. There came at the head of the procession a seven–year-old waif who, arriving before the resplendent figure of the Emperor and placing his tiny hand on the shaft of the candle, could only murmur that he had taken half a pound of honey–cake from a baker. The clergy all smiled. The Emperor, too, smiled and ordered the clerk to inscribe the boy's name in his book, noting that he should be cared for and that later he should be given a post in the imperial treasury.

One after the other those seeking mercy laid their right hands on the candle and said their piece, some loud, others in fear and shyness, so that many had to be told to raise their voices. Afterwards they went to the clerk's table and thence they departed from the church by another way. There were those who had broken their oaths, murderers, poisoners, those who had killed their own children, robbers of churches, bandits and forgers. Many thrust themselves forward, pushing others aside in the fear that the candle might burn down and the measure of mercy be exhausted before their turn had come. But the candle was as thick as a branch and as high as the back of a throne. It was blood red and was designed so that the heat of the flame allowed the red to melt down and the white inside could then be seen as a symbol of mercy.

The Candle of Grace had now burnt down some way and the press of those desiring mercy had eased, so that the Emperor was already thinking that he would return to his palace leaving the church dignitaries behind to represent him till the candle should burn right down.

Caesarius was holding the letter of denunciation rolled in his hand while he watched the tide of penitents moving slowly on. His only thought was on this roll of paper which he would hand to the Emperor as Antonia made her confession. But still he had not yet caught sight of her. Then at last she emerged from the darkness of the pillars, coming forward hesitantly as if she had overcome some inner struggle.

Meanwhile in the church the people were growing tired but, as Antonia appeared with her golden hair reflecting the glory of all the thousand candles in the church, every head craned forward for no one could be unaffected by the dignity and beauty of this high-ranking lady. The Emperor, too, and the bishops and priests around him looked in admiration. Antonia stood thus in her dark penitent's gown, with her golden hair glowing, in the rapt gaze of hundreds of eyes.

Raising her eyes to the Emperor, she slowly laid her hand upon the candle-shaft and right through the church nothing could be heard but the breathing of the populace. In this sudden hush, every one of her words could be heard even though she spoke in a low hesitant voice.

Caesarius was standing to one side, so that he could not be seen by Antonia. He trembled and his hands gripped the scroll even more tightly than before.

Antonia started to confess that she had committed adultery with men who had admired and paid court to her during the absence of her husband. This admission caused a loud tumult in the congregation, so much so that her voice quavered and stopped and she gazed at the red candle in confusion. She saw the red outer wax layer dripping down, and she remembered the candle-lit hours in which she had been unfaithful to

Caesarius. The wax of the great candle ran and formed itself into all manner of shapes, and it was now as if she saw Caesarius' figure hanging in torture, humiliated and pierced by the shafts of wit and mockery which she and her suitors had shot at him. All this was now revealed to her in the extravagant forms made by the melting and congealing wax. Slowly her eyes filled and tears welled forth, glistening.

She could not go on. For a moment, she swayed, unsteady on her feet. There was a moment of absolute stillness. Then she cried aloud: "I have sinned in candle–glow, and it is not right for me to beg mercy in candle–glow." And without taking her hand from the candle she bent forward and blew out the flame.

The whole populace stirred with shock and amazement. Antonia took no notice. Pale, with her eyes shut she continued her confession, but now with a loud voice. There was a sudden movement in the church and quick steps, and further cries of astonishment. But Antonia heard none of this.

"I do not deserve Your Highness's mercy. I do not even deserve my husband's mercy for these things," cried Antonia when she had ended her confession. "That is why I blew the candle out, for I know that the Easter Grace can only be given as long as the candle is burning."

But now she was silent and opened her eyes, she saw that the great candle was burning still. On the stone floor, a roll of paper had burnt out leaving a thin smoke. Her husband, Caesarius, stood beside her.

The stern voice of the Emperor was ringing out: "Who are you, knight? And how do you dare to interrupt these imperial proceedings?"

Caesarius answered: "I am Caesarius of Syracuse. I am the husband of this lady, Antonia. I came here in anger to denounce her. But as I listened to her confession and watched her tears falling, I could find in my heart only mercy and forgiveness towards her. And the paper with which I lit again the flame of the candle was my own letter of denunciation."

The Emperor said: "You have done right. And we shall follow your example. For even as God loves us and forgives us eternally, so we must learn to forgive a thousand times and a thousand times again. Go back to your home in peace, and with our mercy."

And so Caesarius and Antonia walked from the mighty church arm in arm as they had done on the day of their first wedding vows.

The Resurrection

From the Gospel of Luke

At daybreak on the first day after the sabbath, they came to the tomb carrying the spices which they had prepared and they found that the stone had been rolled away from the tomb. When they went inside, they did not find the body of the Lord Jesus. They were at a loss about this when, see! two men stood by them, clothed in lightning.

As they were filled with fear and bowed their faces to the earth, the men said to them: "Why are you looking for the one who lives among those who are dead? He is not here, but has been raised. Remember what he told you while he was still in Galilee when he said: The Son of Man must be given up into the hands of sinful men and be crucified to rise again on the third day." And they remembered his words.

Then they returned from the tomb to give the news to the eleven and to all the others. Now it was Mary Magdalene, Joanna, Mary the mother of James and the other women with them who told all this to the apostles. And their words appeared to them to be nonsense so that they did not believe them.

But Peter got up and hurried to the tomb. He stooped down and saw only the linen cloths. So he went home, filled with wonder at what had happened.

Kira Kiralina

A Romanian folk tale

There was once, there never was, an emperor and an empress. Although they had prayed fervently, God had denied them the blessing of children. One day however an Arab trader appeared at the palace, stood before the emperor and said: "Your Majesty, I can remove the weight of your sorrow from your shoulders. See this special herb! It has the power to make your wife a mother. What she must do is to boil the herbs in water and drink the potion."

With great joy the emperor heard these words. Out of gratitude, he gave the trader a magnificent robe embroidered with gold and, when the stranger took his leave, the emperor led him to the stables and presented him with a fine white horse.

Then the emperor called the empress and told her about the properties of this marvellous herb. The empress summoned the cook and gave her the herb with instructions what to do with it. So the cook boiled the herbs, and because she did not know what they were for, she tasted the potion before bringing it to the empress. So it came about that the empress and the cook each gave birth to a little boy as round and beautiful as the bud of a tree. The emperor was overjoyed by the birth of his own son and, as the two boys had come into the world together, he gave them both to be suckled by the same wet-nurse. He called his own son Blade and the cook's son Pikestaff.

When Blade and Pikestaff had grown up the emperor had to go to war. He called Blade to him and said: "My son, here is my key-ring with all the keys of the palace. You may enter all the rooms that can be opened with the great silver keys, but you must not put a foot inside the room that can be opened with the little golden key, for it will do you no good."

The emperor then left with his army and Blade, in his absence, started to explore every room in the palace one after the other. They were adorned with the most beautiful tapestries and precious ornaments, but none of the rooms pleased him. When he came to the door which the little golden key could open, he paused outside for a while thinking of his father's command. But his curiosity grew so strong, he opened the door

107

and entered the room. Inside there was only a table and on it lay a silver telescope. He raised it to his eye and looked out of the window. What should he see afar off but a palace made completely of gold. It sparkled and shone like the sun. And at a window of this palace was sitting Kira Kiralina, Moonshine, Fairy Tsina, Mistress Young Child, Beautiful as Flowers. And as she looked up, she saw a fleeting reflection, as if the image of a handsome prince was framed in the window, and she fell instantly in love. But the image disappeared and she was left full of longing.

As for Blade, he gazed through the silver telescope for a long, long time. Then he laid it back in on the table and left the room sighing, with his eyes full of tears.

When the emperor came back from the war, his son did not go to meet him, and the empress told him that Blade was lying gravely ill on his bed. Straightaway the emperor guessed how the illness had arisen, and he called together everyone in the kingdom who was skilled in medicine. They all told him the same thing, that unless his son could obtain Kira Kiralina as his wife, he would not regain his health. But all efforts would be in vain for it was known that the Blue Emperor, Kira Kiralina's father, did not wish his daughter ever to marry.

Then Pikestaff, the cook's son, said that he would go with his foster-brother, Blade, to try to win Kira Kiralina's hand. He roused Blade from his sickbed, encouraged him, and together they set off on their way. They went on and on till summer was over. Then they came to the mother of the forests and knocked at her little hut. She opened the door a fraction, and a cold wind blew through the crack.

"What do you want?" she asked.

"Shelter for the night, good mother, and we ask you to show us the way to the palace of Kira Kiralina, Moonshine, Fairy Tsina, Mistress Young Child, Beautiful as Flowers."

She raised her wrinkled face to them and said: "I am sorry for you, poor lads. But I cannot take you in, for when my son the Autumn Wind comes home, he would turn you into lumps of ice in a single breath. It is better for you to go on further and ask at my younger sister's. She is the mother of the Snowstorm."

Blade and Pikestaff thanked her and went on deeper into the forest until they came again to a tiny hut. They knocked at the door, and the mother of the Snowstorm opened the door a little. She did not take the young men in either, but said: "Go on further to the house of my younger sister, the mother of the Spring Breeze. She can take you in and perhaps she can tell you how to find the way that you seek."

Blade and Pikestaff thanked her and went on until they came to the mother of the Spring Breeze. They knocked at the door, and a beautiful tall woman opened the door. As soon as she saw Blade she exclaimed: "Come in, prince, and I shall give you lodging for the night. I know what you are seeking. You have set off to find Kira Kiralina. Only my son knows how to enter her kingdom and I promise I will ask him for you. But you must hide well because if my son notices that beings from the other shore are here he will eat you up."

Then she clapped her hands and down from the stove there flew a golden bird with a diamond beak and emerald eyes. He took Blade and Pikestaff under his wings and flew back up on to the stove.

It was not long before the two of them felt a mild breath of air with the scent of violets and rosemary, and when they peeped out from under the feathers, they could see the door opening. A boy came in. He had eyes like the skies without a cloud, and hair as shining and soft as the grass in spring. He folded his silvery wings and against the table he placed his staff of hundreds of different blossoms and herbs. Then he sniffed around and said to his mother: "Doesn't it smell of beings from the other shore?"

"It may seem so to you, my son, but what would beings from the other shore be seeking with us?"

That was what his mother said as she placed his food before him. When he had drunk a bowl of sweet goat's milk and had drunk water of lilies of the valley he began to talk, and when his mother saw that he was in a good mood, she spoke to him.

"Tell me, my son, where is the kingdom of Kira Kiralina, Moonshine, Fairy Tsina, Mistress Young Child, Beautiful as Flowers? And what must a human being do to win her?"

"It is a hard thing, Mother. The kingdom of the Blue Emperor with his daughter's golden palace lies ten years away from here. But a man can go all that way as quick as you pass your hand across your eyes if he travels towards the iron forest which belongs to the elves. The iron forest stands beside the black stream, and the black stream runs with tar and pitch, spits out fire and throws stones up to the sky. A man can only cross it on the elves' log, and the elves' log is hidden in the iron forest. But whoever hears what I am telling you and tells it to another will be turned to stone from his feet up to his knees."

After a while the Spring Breeze spoke again: "When a human being reaches the other side, he must beat the elves' log three times to possess the golden stag which sings like all the birds of the world together. He must hide inside the golden stag and stay in the room of Kira Kiralina for three nights, then he can carry her off and take her to his home. But whoever hears what I am telling you and tells another will be turned to stone up to his belt."

After another pause the Spring Breeze went on: "When a human has carried off Kira Kiralina, the mother of the Whirlwind will become jealous. She will send a pedlar to her, a pedlar with shirts which are finer than the spinning of a spider's web. Kira Kiralina will buy two shirts and will put one on, but will fall down deathly sick upon her bed. If no one then comes and sprinkles tears from the turtle-dove on her in the middle of the night, she will die. Whoever hears what I say, and tells it to another will turn to stone from his toes to the crown of his head."

While the Spring Breeze was speaking, Blade, the emperor's son, had fallen asleep under the golden feathers, but the cook's son had remained awake and alert and heard everything.

Early next morning when he awoke, Blade asked the mother of the Spring Breeze whether her son had told her the way which they were seeking. She however feared being turned into a stone, and said that she knew nothing. So leaving the house, the young men went travelling on.

> They found the road with the longest name
> where never a human footstep came,
> where summer day is as long as you will,
> where time is magic and stands quite still;
> Through enchanted time they made their way
> where the sun never sets on the summer day;
> They followed the road with the longest name
> until to the forest of iron they came.

Blade stopped at the edge of the forest of iron and did not wish to go further, but Pikestaff encouraged him again and said: "Don't be afraid. Just follow me and do as I say."

Now they heard a terrible roaring, rushing and hissing. Pikestaff led them on straight towards it till they came to the black river spitting fire and stones up to the sky. Pikestaff looked for the log of the elves and found it. They rode upon the log of the elves, crossed the stream and reached the land of the Blue Emperor and soon arrived at the golden palace.

Kira Kiralina was at the window looking out and, as soon as she saw the emperor's son coming towards her, she recognized him and fell fainting to the ground. After a time, she opened her eyes but she would not stand up or leave her room. Her father, the Blue Emperor, did everything he could to cure her. He sought advice from everyone he could, but all to no avail. Then Pikestaff came into the palace, stood before the emperor and said: "Your Majesty, famous and fortunate, may you live all the days that God grant you. If you would bring your daughter back to life, you must bring her the golden stag that sings like all the birds of the world together, and you must leave the stag in her room for three nights. Then you shall see how quickly she will recover."

So the emperor sent out his heralds to find the stag. And Pikestaff said he would go and hunt for it, too. Then Pikestaff went back into the forest and beat thrice upon the elves' log and what happened? The log changed into the golden stag that sings like all the birds of the world together. Pikestaff hid his foster–brother Blade in the stag's belly and went with the stag to the palace. The emperor saw him at once and came down to meet him, delighted that the stag had been found.

Now the Blue Emperor himself led the stag into his daughter's room and left it there. When the stag saw that it was alone with Kira Kiralina it began to sing, and what it sang was a song of longing that would have melted wood and stone. Listening to it, Kira Kiralina fell asleep. In the darkness of the night, Blade came out and kissed her on the forehead, and then he went back into the stag.

Next morning Kira Kiralina said to her maids: "When the golden stag sang to me, I dreamed a beautiful dream. I dreamed that the handsome youth that I saw from my window came and kissed me on the forehead."

"Mistress," said her most trusted maidservant, "if the golden stag sings again tonight, only pretend to sleep. Then take hold of the youth when he kisses you."

That night the stag sang the song of longing even more beautifully than before and the princess only pretended to go to sleep. When Blade came out and kissed her on her forehead, she took him in her arms and called out: "Now you shall not escape me, for I have so long wished to find you!"

When the three days were past, the Blue Emperor came and saw with joy that his daughter was now cured. Then Pikestaff arrived and said he wished to take away the golden stag. But Kira Kiralina wept and did not want to part with her stag for anything in the world. Pikestaff whispered in her ear: "Ask your father to let you go out with the stag as far as the edge of the town. There stands a coach with twelve horses ready to carry you off with your loved one."

The princess asked her father permission and it was granted to her. When they reached the edge of the town, Pikestaff struck the golden stag three times and it turned into a coach with twelve winged horses. Then Pikestaff took Princess Kira Kiralina by one hand and his foster–brother by the other and leapt into the coach with them. The horses flew off as if they had eaten fire, vanished into the blue of the sky and flew through enchanted time until the brothers reached their own country.

Heralds proclaimed the return of the emperor's son with Kira Kiralina, Moonshine, Fairy Tsina, Mistress Young Child, Beautiful as Flowers, and the emperor held a wedding feast that lasted for three days and three nights.

Soon afterwards Kira Kiralina was sitting at the window when a pedlar came, selling shirts finer than the spinning of a spider. The princess called him up and bought two shirts from him. She put one of the shirts on but instantly, as if the hour of her death had sounded, she sank down on her bed.

When Pikestaff heard that she was ill, he remembered the warning given by the Spring Breeze. In the middle of the night, he came into the princess' room and sprinkled her with the tears of the turtle–dove. The princess immediately stirred and grew better. But as Pikestaff crept away, the guards seized him. They took him before the emperor and his son, saying: "This man clearly crept into the princess's room to steal a kiss from her."

Blade asked his foster–brother to explain but Pikestaff would not speak. And then the emperor's son grew angry and, in his wrath, he handed over his foster–brother to the executioner.

As he was being led away, Pikestaff cried out: "Before I die, I ask only for one thing. May the emperor's son call the great council together. Then before them, before the emperor's son and before Kira Kiralina I shall tell you the whole truth."

Blade granted the boon and called together the imperial council. When he and Kira Kiralina had taken their places, Pikestaff began: "There was once an emperor's son who fell in love with a princess from the other shore, and because he could no longer live without her he set off to find her or to perish in the attempt. He took his foster–brother, the cook's son, with him. When they had gone right across the world and further, they came to the house of the mother of the Spring Breeze and asked her the way. She promised to ask her son, and she kept her promise. But only the cook's son stayed awake and heard how the Spring Breeze said these words to his mother: 'The kingdom of Kira Kiralina lies ten years away from here. But the way can be travelled as quickly as you pass your hand over your eyes if you go through the iron forest that belongs to the elves. Then you will come to the black stream that spits fire and casts up stones to the sky. It can only be crossed on the elves' log. And he who repeats this to another will be turned to stone from his feet to his knees.' "

When Pikestaff reached this far in his story, he was turned to stone from his feet to his knees. The court all saw this and the entire imperial council went rigid with fright. They begged Pikestaff not to tell any more, but he went on: "The Spring Breeze then told how after crossing the river, 'You must beat the elves' log three times to have the golden stag that sings like all the birds in the world together, and hidden in the golden stag you must stay three nights in the princess's room. Then you may carry her off and bring her home. But he who repeats this to anyone will be turned to stone up to his belt.'"

When Pikestaff reached this point in his story, he became stone right up to his belt. Then Blade burst into tears and begged his foster–brother not to tell any more. But Pikestaff continued: "'When a man has made the princess his wife,' went on the Spring Breeze, 'the mother of the Whirlwind will be angry and will send a pedlar with shirts finer than the spinning of the spider. The princess will put one on and she will sink down as if the hand of death were upon her. Then if no one comes in the middle of the night and sprinkles her with the tears of the turtle–dove she must die. And if anyone repeats these words to another, he will turn to stone from his toes to the crown of his head.'"

Hardly had Pikestaff finished speaking than he turned to stone from his toes to the crown of his head. Too late Blade saw how unjust he had been. In vain he begged his foster–brother a hundred and a hundred times for forgiveness.

The emperor's son and Kira Kiralina wept for Pikestaff for three days and three nights. Then they had the stone placed in their room so that they would always have the statue of their benefactor before their eyes.

After a time they had a child, and they cared for him like the light of their eyes. One morning however Blade woke up and said to Kira Kiralina: "I have just had a dream. A lady clad in a white robe stood before me and said: 'If you wish your brother to live again, you must sacrifice your precious child and sprinkle the statue with three drops of his blood.'"

"This lady in the white robe also appeared to me," said Kira Kiralina, "and said the same."

Then the mother and father realized that, cruel though it seemed, they must do as was bidden them and sacrifice their child. And the very moment that a drop of the child's blood dripped on to the statue, the stone began to move. When three drops of the child's blood had fallen on the stone, the statue walked and began to speak.

"Mother of God!" exclaimed Pikestaff, "What a long sleep I have had!"

"Yes, brother," answered Blade, "and you would have slept on and on had we not restored you with the blood of our child."

When Pikestaff heard what they had done for him, he cut his hand and let three drops of his own blood fall on to the dead child, and the child came to life at once. Now they praised heaven and gave thanks. And then they arranged such a feast of celebration that it was even merrier and longer than their own wedding.

Koshchey the Deathless

Alexander Afanasiev

Once there was a king who had an only son. When the prince was small, his nurses and governesses sang lullabies to him. "Prince Ivan, when you grow up, you will find your bride," they would sing. "Beyond thrice nine lands, in the thrice tenth kingdom, Vasilisa Kirbitievna sits in a tower, and her marrow flows from bone to bone."

When the prince had passed his fifteenth year, he began to ask the king's leave to set out in search of his bride. "Whither will you go?" the father asked. "You are still too young."

"No, father, when I was little, my nurses and governesses sang lullabies to me and told me where my bride lives; and now I wish to go and find her." The father gave the prince his blessing and sent word to all the kingdoms that his son, Prince Ivan, was setting out to find his bride.

One day the prince came to a certain town, put up his horse to be cared for, and went to walk in the streets. He came to the square and saw that a man was being flogged with a whip. "Why do you whip him?" he asked.

"Because he borrowed ten thousand roubles from a prominent merchant," they told him, "and did not pay them back at the agreed time. As for the man who redeems him, his wife will be carried off by Koshchey the Deathless."

The prince thought and thought and went away. He walked through the town, then came to the square again, and saw that the man was still being flogged; Prince Ivan took pity on him and decided to redeem him. Since I have no wife, he thought, no one can be taken from me. He paid the ten thousand roubles and went home. Suddenly the man whom he had redeemed ran after him, crying: "Thank you, Prince Ivan! If you had not redeemed me, you would never have won your bride. But now I will help you. Buy me a horse and a saddle at once."

The prince bought him a horse and saddle and asked: "What is your name?"

"My name is Bulat the Brave," the man said.

They mounted their horses and set out. As soon as they arrived in the thrice tenth kingdom, Bulat said: "Well, Prince Ivan, order chickens, ducks, and geese to be bought and roasted, so that there will be plenty of everything. And I will get your bride. But mind you: every time I come to you, cut off the right wing of a fowl and serve it to me on a plate."

Bulat the Brave went straight to the lofty tower where Vasilisa Kirbitievna was sitting, gently threw a stone, and broke the gilded top of the tower. He ran to Prince Ivan and said: "Why are you sleeping? Give me a chicken."

The prince cut off the right wing of a chicken and handed it to him on a plate. Bulat took the plate ran to the tower, and cried: "Good day, Vasilisa Kirbitievna. Prince Ivan sends you his greetings and has asked me to give you this chicken."

The maiden was frightened and sat in silence. But he answered himself in her stead: "Good day, Bulat the Brave! Is Prince Ivan well? Thank God, he is well. And why do you stand like that, Bulat the Brave? Take the key, open the cupboard, drink a glass of vodka, and God speed you."

Then Bulat ran to Prince Ivan. "Why are you sitting?" he said. "Give me a duck."

The prince cut off the right wing of a duck and handed it to him on a plate. Bulat took the plate and carried it to the tower. "Good day, Vasilisa Kirbitievna! Prince Ivan sends you his greetings and has asked me to give you this duck."

She sat in silence, and he answered himself in her stead: "Good day, Bulat the Brave! Is the prince well? Thank God, he is well. And why do you stand like that, Bulat the Brave? Take the key, open the cupboard, drink a glass of vodka, and God speed you."

Then Bulat ran home and again said to Prince Ivan: "Why are you sitting? Give me a goose."

The prince cut off the right wing of a goose and handed it to him on a plate. Bulat the Brave took it to the tower. "Good day, Vasilisa Kirbitievna! Prince Ivan sends his greetings and has asked me to give you this goose."

Vasilisa Kirbitievna straightway took a key, opened a cupboard, and gave him a glass of vodka. Bulat did not take the glass, but seized the maiden by her right hand, drew her out of the tower, and seated her on Prince Ivan's horse, and the good youths galloped away at a headlong pace, taking the lovely maiden with them.

Next morning King Kirbit woke up and arose, saw that the top of the tower was broken and his daughter stolen, grew terribly angry, and ordered pursuers to set out after her in all directions. Our knights–errant rode a long time or a short time, then Bulat the Brave removed the ring from his hand, hid it, and said: "Ride on, Prince Ivan; but I will turn back and look for my ring."

Vasilisa Kirbitievna began to beseech him: "Do not leave us, Bulat the Brave! If you wish, I will give you my ring."

He answered: "That is impossible, Vasilisa Kirbitievna. My ring is priceless; my own mother gave it to me, and when she gave it she said: "Wear it, lose it not, forget not your mother.""

Bulat the Brave rode back and met the pursuers on the road; he straightway slew them all, leaving only one man to bring the news to the king, and hastened to catch up with Prince Ivan. They rode for a long time or a short time, then Bulat the Brave hid his handkerchief and said: "Ah, Prince Ivan, I have lost my handkerchief; ride on, and I will catch up with you soon."

He turned back, rode several versts, and met twice as many pursuers; he slew them all and returned to Prince Ivan. The prince asked: "Have you found your handkerchief?"

"I have," said Bulat.

Dark night overtook them. They pitched a tent; Bulat the Brave lay down to sleep, set Prince Ivan to guarding the tent, and said to him: "If anything happens, rouse me."

The prince said and stood, then grew tired; drowsiness overcame him, and he sat down at the door of the tent, and fell asleep. Suddenly Koshchey the Deathless appeared and carried off Vasilisa Kirbitievna. At daybreak Prince Ivan awoke, saw that his bride was gone, and wept bitterly. Bulat the Brave woke up too and told him: "Why are you weeping?"

"How can I help weeping? Someone has stolen Vasilisa Kirbitievna."

"I told you to keep watch. This is the work of Koshchey the Deathless; let us set out to find the old rattlebones."

They rode for a long, long time, and they beheld two shepherds grazing a flock. "Whose flock is this?" they asked.

The shepherds answered: "It belongs to Koshchey the Deathless."

Bulat the Brave and Prince Ivan questioned the herdsmen as to whether Koshchey the Deathless were far from there; how to get to him; when they, the herdsmen, were accustomed to return home with the flock; and where it was shut up for the night. Then they climbed down from their horses, wrung the necks of the herdsmen, dressed themselves in the latter's clothes, and drove the flock home; when they came to the place they stood at the gate.

Prince Ivan had a gold ring on his hand which Vasilisa Kirbitievna had given to him. And Vasilisa Kirbitievna had a goat: mornings and evenings she washed in the milk of that goat. A maid came with a cup, milked the goat, and turned back with the milk. Bulat took the prince's ring and threw it into the cup.

"Oh, my friends," said the maid, "you are playing pranks." She came to Vasilisa Kirbitievna and complained: "The herdsmen are now making mock of us; they threw a ring into the milk."

The maiden answered: "Leave the milk, I will strain it myself."

She strained it, saw the ring, and ordered the herdsmen to be brought before her. The herdsmen came.

"Good day, Vasilisa Kirbitievna," said Bulat the Brave.

"Good day, Bulat the Brave. Good day, prince. How has God brought you here?"

"We have come for you, Vasilisa Kirbitievna. Nowhere shall you hide from us; even in the depths of the sea we shall find you."

She seated them at the table, gave them a variety of viands to eat and wines to drink. Bulat the Brave said to her: "When Koshchey returns from hunting, ask him where his death is. And now it would not be a bad idea for us to hide."

The guests had no sooner hidden than Koshchey the Deathless came flying back from the hunt. "Fie, fie!" he said. "Formerly there was no breath of anything Russian here, nor could a glimpse be caught of it, but now something Russian has come here in person and is offending my nose."

Vasilisa Kirbitievna answered him: "You have been flying through Russia, and yourself have become full of it, and now you fancy it is here."

Koshchey ate his dinner and lay down to rest. Vasilisa came to him, threw herself on his neck, and kissed him and fondled him, saying: "My beloved friend, I could hardly wait for you; I began to think that I would never again see you alive, that wild beasts had devoured you."

Koshchey laughed. "You foolish woman! Your hair is long, but your wit is short. How could wild beasts devour me?"

"But where is your death then?"

"My death is in that broom that stands at the threshold." As soon as Koshchey flew away, Vasilisa Kirbitievna ran to Prince Ivan. Bulat the Brave asked her: "Well, where is Koshchey's death?"

"In that broom that stands on the threshold."

"No, that is a deliberate lie; you must question him more cunningly."

Vasilisa Kirbitievna thought up something: she took the broom, gilded it, decorated it with many ribbons, and put it on the table. When Koshchey the Deathless came home and saw the gilded broom on the table, he asked her why she had arranged it so.

119

"I could not allow your death to stand thus unceremoniously at the threshold," said Vasilisa Kirbitievna. "It is better to have it on the table."

"Ha, ha, ha, you foolish woman! Your hair is long but your wit is short. Do you think my death is here?"

"Where is it then?"

"My death is hidden in the goat."

As soon as Koshchey left for the hunt, Vasilisa Kirbitievna adorned the goat with ribbons and bells and gilded his horns. Koshchey saw it, and he laughed again and said: "Eh, you foolish woman, your hair is long but your wit is short. My death is far away. In the sea there is an island, on that island stands an oak, under the oak a coffer is buried, in the coffer is a hare, in the hare is a duck, in the duck is an egg, and in the egg is my death."

Having said this, he flew off. Vasilisa Kirbitievna repeated all this to Bulat the Brave and to Prince Ivan; they took provisions and set out to find Koshchey's death. After a long time or a short time they had used up all their provisions and began to feel hungry. They happened to come upon a dog with her young. "I will kill her," said Bulat the Brave, "for we have nothing more to eat."

"Do not kill me," begged the dog. "Do not make my children orphans. I will be useful to you."

"Well," they said, "God be with you."

They walked on, and saw an eagle with her eaglets sitting on an oak. Bulat the Brave said: "I will kill the eagle."

The eagle said: "Do not kill me, do not make my children orphans, I will be useful to you."

"So be it," they said, "live in health."

They came to the wide ocean. A lobster crawled on the shore. Bulat the Brave said: "I will kill him."

The lobster answered: "Do not kill me, good youth! There is not much substance in me; even if you eat me, you will not be sated. The time will come when I may be useful to you."

"Well, crawl on with God," said Bulat the Brave. He looked at the sea, saw a fisherman in a boat, and cried: "Come to shore!"

The fisherman brought the boat; Prince Ivan and Bulat the Brave seated themselves in it and sailed for the island. They reached the island and went to the oak. Bulat grasped the oak with his mighty hands and tore it out by the roots. He got the coffer from under the oak and opened it, and from the coffer a hare jumped out and ran away as fast as it could.

"Ah," said Prince Ivan, "if we had a dog here, he would catch the hare."

Lo and behold, the dog was already bringing the hare. Bulat the Brave took it, tore it open, and from the hare a duck flew out and soared high into the sky.

"Ah," said Prince Ivan, "if we had the eagle now, he could catch the duck." Lo and behold, the eagle was bringing the duck. Bulat the Brave tore open the duck, and an egg rolled out from it and fell into the sea.

"Ah," said the prince, "if only the lobster would bring it up!"

And lo and behold, the lobster was crawling toward them with the egg. They took the egg, went to Koshchey the Deathless, struck him on the forehead with the egg, and he instantly fell sprawling to the ground and died. Prince Ivan took Vasilisa Kirbitievna and they set out on their way.

They rode and rode. Dark night overtook them; they pitched a tent, and Vasilisa Kirbitievna lay down to sleep. Bulat the Brave said: "Lie down too, prince, I will keep watch."

At midnight twelve doves came flying, struck wing against wing, and turned into twelve maidens. "Now, Bulat the Brave and Prince Ivan," they said, "you have killed our brother, Koshchey the Deathless, and stolen our sister–in–law, Vasilisa Kirbitievna. But you won't profit by it. When Prince Ivan comes home, he will order his favourite dog to be brought out, and she will break away from the dog keeper and tear the princess into little pieces. And he who hears this and tells it to the prince will become stone to the knees."

Next morning Bulat the Brave roused the prince and Vasilisa Kirbitievna, and they made ready and set out on their way. A second night overtook them; they pitched their tent in the open field. Bulat the Brave said again: "Lie down to sleep, Prince Ivan, and I will keep watch."

At midnight twelve doves came flying, struck wing against wing, and turned into twelve maidens.

"Well, Bulat the Brave and Prince Ivan," they said, "you have killed Koshchey the Deathless, our brother, and stolen Vasilisa Kirbitievna, our sister–in–law, but you won't profit by it. When Prince Ivan comes home, he will order his favourite horse to be brought out, the horse on which he has been wont to ride since childhood; the horse will break away from the groom and kill the prince. And he who hears this and tells it to the prince will become stone to the waist."

Morning came and they rode on again. A third night overtook them; they stopped to spend the night and pitched their tent in the open field. Bulat the Brave said: "Lie down to sleep, Prince Ivan, and I will keep watch."

Again at midnight twelve doves came flying, struck wing against wing, and turned into twelve maidens.

"Well, Bulat the Brave and Prince Ivan," they said, "you have killed Koshchey the Deathless, our brother, and stolen Vasilisa Kirbitievna, our sister–in–law, but you won't profit by it; when Prince Ivan comes home, he will order his favourite cow to be brought out, the cow whose milk has nourished him since childhood: she will wrench herself free from the cowherd and spear the prince on her horns. And he who sees and hears us and tells this to the prince, will become stone altogether." When they had said this, they turned into doves and flew off.

Next morning Prince Ivan and Vasilisa Kirbitievna awoke and set out on their way. The prince came home, married Vasilisa Kirbitievna, and after a day or two said to her: "Do you want me to show you my favourite dog? When I was little I played with it."

Bulat the Brave took his sabre, whetted it — he made it very sharp — and stood near the porch. The dog was led out; it wrested itself free from the dog keeper and ran straight toward the porch, but Bulat swung his sabre and cut the dog in twain. Prince Ivan was angry at him, but remembering his former services, did not say a word.

The next day Ivan ordered his favourite horse to be brought out; the horse broke his halter, wrested himself free from the groom, and galloped straight at the prince. Bulat the Brave cut off the horse's head. Prince Ivan grew even angrier than before and ordered Bulat to be seized and hanged, but Vasilisa Kirbitievna obtained his pardon. "Had it not been for him," she said, "you would never have won me."

On the third day Prince Ivan ordered his favourite cow to be brought out; she wrested herself free from the cowherd and ran straight toward the prince. Bulat the Brave cut off her head, too.

Now Prince Ivan became so enraged that he refused to listen to anyone; he ordered the hangman to be summoned and commanded that Bulat be put to death at once.

"Ah, Prince Ivan," Bulat said, "now that you have ordered your hangman to put me to death, I would rather die by my own hand. Only let me speak three speeches."

Bulat told him about the first night, how twelve doves came flying, and what they had said to him — and straightway he became stone to the knees. Then he told about the second night, and became stone to the waist. Prince Ivan besought him not to speak to the end. Bulat the Brave answered: "Now it is all the same; I am half stone, it is not worthwhile living longer."

He told about the third night and became stone altogether. Prince Ivan put him in a separate chamber and went there every day with Vasilisa Kirbitievna and lamented bitterly.

Many years went by. One day Prince Ivan was lamenting there Bulat when he heard a voice coming from the stone figure. "Why are you weeping?" the voice said. "I am grieved even without your weeping."

"How can I help weeping? After all, it is I who destroyed you."

"If you wish, you can save me. You have two children, a son and a daughter; slay them, draw their blood."

Prince Ivan told this to Vasilisa Kirbitievna; they grieved and lamented, but decided to slay their children. They slew them, drew their blood, and as soon as they smeared the stone with it Bulat the Brave came to life. He asked the prince and his wife: "Are you heartbroken over your children?"

"We are, Bulat the Brave."

"Well then, let us go to their rooms." They went, and lo and behold, the children were alive. The father and mother were overjoyed and in their joy gave a feast for all.

I was at that feast too, I drank mead and wine there; it ran down my moustache but did not go into my mouth, yet my soul was drunk and sated.

The Water of Life

Alexander Afanasiev

A certain King grew very old and his eyes began to fail. He heard that beyond the ninth land, in the tenth kingdom, there was a garden with the apples of youth, and in it a well with the water of life; if an aged man ate one of those apples, he would grow young, and if a blind man's eyes were bathed with that water, he would see. That king had three sons. So he sent his eldest forth on horseback to find that garden and bring him the apples and the water, for he wanted to be young again and to see. The prince set out for the distant kingdom; he rode and rode and came to a pillar. On this pillar three roads were marked: if he followed the first, the marker said, his horse would be sated and he himself would be hungry; if he followed the second, it said, he would lose his own life; if he followed the third, it said, his horse would be hungry and he himself sated.

He thought and thought and finally took the road that promised food for himself; and he rode and he rode till he saw a very beautiful house in a field. He approached it, looked all around, opened the gates, did not doff his cap nor bow his head, and galloped into the yard. The owner of the house, a widow who was not very old, called to the young man: "Welcome, dear guest!"

She led him in, seated him at the table, prepared all sorts of viands, and brought him large beakers of heady drinks. The young man regaled himself and lay down to sleep on the bench. The woman said to him: "It is not fitting for a knight nor honourable for a gallant man to lie alone! Lie with my daughter, the beautiful Dunia."

He was quite pleased with this proposal. Dunia said to him: "Lie closer to me, so that we will be warmer."

He moved toward her and fell through the bed. In the cellar into which he fell he was compelled to grind raw rye all day long and he could not climb out. In vain the king waited and waited for his eldest son to come back. Finally he gave up waiting.

Then he sent his second son to get the apples and the water. This prince took the same road and suffered the same fate as his elder brother. From long waiting for his sons, the king became very sad.

Now the youngest son began to beg his father's permission to go forth to seek the garden. But his father absolutely refused to let him go and said to him: "A curse is on you, little son! Your older brothers perished on this quest and you, who are still a tender youth, will perish even sooner than they."

But the young prince kept imploring his father and promised him that he would bear himself more bravely for the king's sake than any brave knight. His father thought and thought and finally gave the boy his blessing for the journey.

On his way to the widow's house, the young knight passed the same pillar as his older brothers had. He, too, came to the widow's house, dismounted from his horse, knocked at the gate, and asked whether he could spend the night there. The widow received him kindly just as she had his brothers, and invited him in, saying: "Welcome, unexpected guest!"

She bade him sit down to table and placed all kinds of meat and drink before him, enough to stuff himself. He ate his fill, and asked whether be might lie down on the bench. The woman said to him: "It is not fitting for a knight nor honourable for a gallant man to lie alone! Lie with my beautiful Dunia."

But he answered: "No, little aunt! A visitor must not do that without first making certain preparations. Why don't you heat up a bath for me? And let your daughter lead me to the bathhouse."

So the widow prepared a very, very hot bath and led him to the bathhouse with the beautiful Dunia. Dunia was just as wicked as her mother; she made him go in first, locked the door to the bath, and stood in the hall. But the bold knight pushed open the door and dragged Dunia with him into the bathroom. He had three rods — one of iron, one of lead, and one of cast iron — and with these rods he began to belabour the young girl. She wept and implored him to stop. But he said: "Tell me, wicked Dunia, what you have done with my brothers!"

She said that they were in the cellar grinding raw grain. Then only did he let her go. They came back to the main room, tied one ladder to another, and freed his brothers. He told them to go home; but they were ashamed to appear before their father, because they had lain down with Dunia and had failed in their mission. So they wandered about in the fields and woods.

The knight went on; he rode and rode till he came to a farmhouse. He entered; there sat a pretty young girl weaving towels. He said: "God bless you, pretty maiden!"

And she answered: "Thank you! What are you doing, good knight? Are you running away from an adventure or are you trying to find one?"

"I am trying to carry out a mission, pretty maiden," said the knight. "I am going beyond the ninth land, to the tenth kingdom, to a certain garden, where I hope to find the apples of youth and the water of life for my aged, blind father."

She said to him: "It will be hard, very hard, for you to reach that garden. However, continue on your way; soon you will come to the house of my second sister. Go in to see her; she knows better than I how to find the garden and will tell you what to do."

So he rode and rode till he came to the house of the second sister. He greeted her just as he had the first, and told her who he was and where he was going. She bade him leave his horse with her and ride on her own two–winged horse to the house of her older sister, who would tell him what to do — how to reach the garden and how to get the apples and the water.

So he rode and rode till he came to the house of the third sister. She gave him her four–winged horse and told him: "Be careful. In that garden lives our aunt, a terrible witch. When you come to the garden, do not spare my horse. Spur him strongly, so that he clears the wall in one bound; for if he touches the wall, the strings with bells that are tied to it will sing out, the bells will ring, the witch will awaken, and you won't be able to get away from her! She has a horse with six wings; cut the tendons under his wings so that she cannot overtake you."

He did as she bade him. He flew over the wall on his horse, but his horse lightly touched one string with his tail; all the strings sang and the bells rang, but softly. The witch awoke but did not clearly distinguish the voice of the strings and the bells, so she yawned and fell asleep again. And the bold knight galloped away with the apples of youth and the water of life. He stopped at the houses of the sisters, where he changed horses, and darted off to his own kingdom on his own horse. Early next morning the terrible witch discovered that the apples and the water had been stolen from her garden. At once she mounted her six–winged horse, galloped to the house of her first niece, and asked her: "Has someone passed by here?"

The niece answered: "A bold knight went by here, but that was long ago."

The witch galloped on farther and asked her second and her third niece the same question, and they gave her the same answer. She rode on and almost overtook the bold knight, but he had reached his own land and no longer feared her: there she dared not enter. She only looked at him and in a voice hoarse with spite said: "You are a fine little thief! You have succeeded very well in your mission! You got away from me, but nothing will save you from your own brothers." Having thus foretold his fate, she returned home.

Our bold knight went on his way in his own land, and found his vagabond brothers sleeping in a field. He set his horse loose, did not awaken his brothers, but lay down beside them and fell asleep. The brothers awoke, saw that their brother had returned to his own land, softly took the apples of youth out of his breast pocket, and threw him, still sleeping, over a precipice. He fell for three days, till he reached the dark kingdom where people do everything by firelight. Wherever he went, he found the people sad and weeping. He asked the cause of their sorrow and was told that their king's only daughter, the beautiful princess Paliusha, was to be given the next day to a terrible dragon, who would eat her up. In that kingdom, they explained, a maiden was given to the seven-headed dragon every month; that was the law! And now it was the turn of the king's daughter.

When our bold knight heard this, he went straightway to the king, and said to him: "King, I will save your daughter from the dragon, but later you must do for me whatever I ask of you."

The king was overjoyed, promised to do anything for him, and to give the princess to him in marriage.

The next day came. The beautiful princess Paliusha was led to a three-walled fortress on the edge of the sea and the knight went with her. He took with him an iron rod that weighed about two hundred pounds. He and the princess waited there for the dragon; they waited and waited, and while they waited they conversed. He told her about his adventures and said that he had the water of life with him. Then the bold knight said to the beautiful princess Paliusha: "Pick the lice out of my head, and should I fall asleep before the dragon comes, waken me with my rod — otherwise you will not arouse me!" And he laid his head in her lap. She began to look for lice in his hair; he fell asleep.

The dragon flew inshore and circled above the princess. She tried to waken the knight by shaking him, but did not hit him with his rod as he had asked her to do, for she did not wish to hurt him. She could not waken him and began to weep; a tear dropped on his face, and he woke up and exclaimed: "Oh, you have burned me with something pleasant!"

Meanwhile the dragon had begun to swoop down on them. The knight took up his two-hundred pound rod, swung it, and at one stroke knocked off five of the dragon's heads. He swung back a second time, and knocked off the remaining two. He gathered up all the heads, put them under the wall, and cast the monster's trunk into the sea.

An envious fellow saw all this, stole lightly around the other side of the wall, cut off the knight's head, cast it into the sea, and bade the beautiful princess Paliusha tell her father, the king, that he had saved her. He swore that if she did not say this, he would strangle her. There was nothing to be done; Paliusha wept and wept as they went to her father, the king. The king came out to meet them. She told him that this fellow had saved her. The king was enormously happy and at once set about the preparations for the wedding feast. Guests arrived from foreign lands, kings, tsars, and princes, and all of them drank and amused themselves. The princess alone was sad; she would go into a corner behind the barn and shed burning tears for her bold knight.

It occurred to her to ask her father to send fishermen to catch fish in the sea, and she herself went with them. They cast a net and drew out fish, an enormous quantity! She examined them and said: "No, that is not the fish I want!" They cast another net and dragged out the head and trunk of the bold knight. Paliusha rushed to him, found a phial with the water of life in his breast pocket, placed the head on the body, and wet it with the water from the phial, and he came to life. She told him how she loathed the man who wanted to take her. The knight comforted her and told her to go home; later he would come himself and set things right.

So the knight came to the royal palace and found all the guests drunk, sporting and dancing. He declared that he could sing songs in various modes. The guests were pleased at this idea and asked him to sing. First he sang for them a gay song, full of jests and old saws, and the guests were all charmed and praised him for singing so well; then he sang a song so sad that all the guests burst into tears. The knight asked the king: "Who saved your daughter?"

The king pointed out the envious fellow.

"Well, king," said the knight, "let us go to the fortress with all your guests. If he can find the dragon's heads there, I will believe that he saved Princess Paliusha."

All of them went to the fortress. The fellow pulled and pulled but could not pull out even one head: it was far beyond his strength. But the knight pulled them all out as soon as he tried. Then the princess told the whole truth about who saved her. Everyone realized that the bold knight had saved the king's daughter; and the fellow was tied to the tail of a horse and dragged over a field till he died.

The king wanted to marry the bold knight to his daughter. But the knight said: "No, king, I don't need anything from you. Only take me back to our bright world; I have not yet finished my mission for my father — he is still waiting for me to bring him the water of life, for he is blind."

The king did not know how to take the knight up to the bright world; and his daughter did not want to part from him, she wanted to go up with him. She told her father that there was a spoonbilled bird that could take them there, provided she had enough to feed it on the way.

So Paliusha had a whole ox killed and took it with her as a store of food for the spoonbill. She and the knight said farewell to- the under-ground king, seated themselves on the bird's back, and set out for God's bright world. When they gave more food to the bird, it flew upward faster; thus they used up the whole ox to feed it. Now they were perplexed and afraid lest the bird should drop them down again. So Paliusha cut off a piece of her thigh and gave it to the spoonbill; the bird straightway brought them up to this world and said: "Throughout our journey you fed me well, but never in my life did I taste anything sweeter than that last morsel."

Paliusha showed the bird her thigh, and the bird moaned and spat out the piece; it was still whole. The knight put it on Paliusha's thigh, wet it with the water of life, and healed the princess.

Then they went home. The father, the king of the land in our own world, met them and was overjoyed to see them. The knight saw that his father had grown younger from having the apples, but that he was still blind. The knight at once anointed his father's eyes with the water of life. The king began to see; he embraced his son, the bold knight, and the princess from the dark kingdom. The knight told how his brothers had takes his apples and thrown him into the nether world. The brothers were so frightened that they jumped into the river. And the knight married the princess Paliusha and gave a most wonderful feast.

I dined and drank mead with them, and their cabbage was toothsome. Even now I could eat some!

The Two Old Men

Leo Tolstoy

The woman saith unto Him: "Sir, I see that Thou art a prophet. Our fathers worshipped in this mountain; and ye say that in Jerusalem is the place where men ought to worship." Jesus saith unto her: "Woman, believe me, the hour cometh when ye shall neither in this mountain nor yet at Jerusalem worship the Father. Ye worship ye know not what; we know what we worship; for salvation is of the Jews. But the hour cometh, and now is, when the true worshippers shall worship the Father in spirit and in truth: for the Father seeketh such to worship Him."

(John 4:19–23)

I

Two old men took it into their heads to go and pray to God in ancient Jerusalem. One of them was a rich peasant named Efim Tarassitch Sheveloff, and the other was a poor man named Elijah Bodroff.

Efim was a sober man. He drank no vodka, smoked no tobacco, took no snuff, had never breathed an oath in his life, and was altogether a strict and conscientious citizen. Twice he had served a term as *starosta,* and left office without a figure wrong in his books. He had a large family (his two sons, as well as a grandson, were married), and they all lived together. In person he was an upright, vigorous muzhik, with a beard only begun to be streaked with grey now that he had attained his seventieth year. Old Elijah, on the other hand, was a man neither rich nor poor who, formerly a travelling carpenter, had now settled down and taken to bee-keeping. One of his sons earned his living at home, and the other one away. He was a good–hearted, cheerful old fellow, and drank vodka, smoked tobacco, took snuff, and loved a good song. None the less, he was of peaceable disposition, and lived on excellent terms both with his household and the neighbours. In himself he was a man of medium height, with a swarthy complexion and curly beard. Moreover, like his holy namesake, the Prophet Elijah, he was bald.

The two old men had long ago agreed to go upon this pilgrimage together, yet Efim had never been able to find time from his business. As soon as he had got one thing out of hand he would find himself hatching a new scheme. Now he would be marrying a granddaughter, now expecting his younger son home from military service, now planning to erect a new hut.

One day the old men met at a festival, and seated themselves together on a bench.

"Well," said Elijah, "when are we going to carry out that long–agreed–upon scheme of ours?"

Efim frowned. "We must wait a little yet," he said. "This last year has been a heavy one for me. When I planned to build that new hut I reckoned it would cost me about a hundred roubles only, but already the estimate is rising up to three times that amount, and it hasn't come in yet. I must certainly wait until the summer. Then, if God pleases, we will go."

"Well," replied Elijah, "it seems to me that we ought not to put it off any longer, but to go now. Spring is the very time for it."

"Time or no time, the work is begun now. How can I go and leave it?"

"But have you no one to leave in charge? Surely your son could see to it?"

"He indeed! Why, that eldest son of mine is perfectly useless. He would spoil it all."

"No, no, my old friend. Even if you and I died tomorrow, the world would still go on without us. Your son only needs a little teaching."

"That may be; yet I want to see the work finished under my own eyes."

"Pooh, my dear sir! One never really gets to the end of things. Why, only the other day our women at home were washing the linen and get–ting ready for the festival — first one thing having to be done, and then another, as if there would never be an end to it all — when at last my eldest daughter–in–law (and she is a clever woman) exclaimed: 'Never mind if the festival is coming on and we shan't be ready. However much we do, we can't do everything.' "

Efim reflected a moment — then said: "I have laid out a lot of money already on this building scheme, and it would hardly do to set forth on a journey with empty hands. A hundred roubles is no light sum to raise, you know."

Elijah smiled.

"Yes, you must be careful," he said. "Why, your income is ten times as much as mine, yet you worry far more about money than I do. Look at me. Merely tell me when to start, and, little though I possess, I shall be there."

Efim smiled in his turn.

"Are you such a rich man, then, after all?" he said. "Where is it all going to come from?"

"Oh, I shall scrape it together somehow — raise it somehow. If there is no other way of doing so, I shall sell a dozen of my range of bee–hives to a neighbour. He has long been after them."

"And then the swarms will turn out well, and you will be sorry for it."

"Sorry for it? No, no. I have never been sorry for anything in my life except for my sins. There is nothing worth troubling about except one's soul."

"That may be; yet it is awkward to have things go wrong at home."

"But it is still more awkward to have things go wrong with one's soul. Come now! You have as good as promised me, so we must really go. It would be only right of us to do so."

II

Thus Elijah won over his comrade. Next morning Efim took counsel with himself, and then went to see Elijah.

"Yes, we will go very soon now," he said. "You were quite right. In life or in death we are in God's hands. We ought to go while we are still alive and well."

A week later the two got themselves ready. Efim always kept his money at home, and of it he took 190 roubles for the journey, and left 200 for the old woman. Elijah likewise made his preparations. He sold the neighbour ten out of his range of bee–hives, together with whatever stock of honey they might produce. That brought him in seventy roubles. Another thirty he swept together from one corner and another. His wife gave up the whole of her funeral savings, and their daughter–in–law did the same.

Efim confided the entire direction of his affairs at home to his eldest son, telling him which crops to pull while he was away, and how much of them, where to spread the manure, and how to build and roof the new hut. He thought of everything, left directions for everything. Elijah, on the other hand, merely told his old wife to be careful to collect such young bees as might leave the hives which he had disposed of, and deliver full tale of them to the neighbour. On other domestic matters he said not a word. Circumstances themselves would show what was to be done, and how it was to be done, as circumstances arose. Housewives, he thought, know their own business best.

So the two old men made them ready for the journey. Home–made cakes were baked, wallets contrived, new leggings cut out, new boots procured, and spare shoes provided. Then they set off. Their respective households escorted them to the parish boundary, and there took leave of them. Thus the old men were fairly launched upon their way.

Elijah walked along in high spirits, and forgot all his domestic concerns immediately he had left the village. His only cares were how to beguile the way for his companion, to avoid uttering a single churlish word, and to arrive at his destination and return thence in perfect peace and goodwill. As he walked along he whispered silent prayers to himself or thought over his past life so far as he could remember it. Whether he fell in with a fellow–traveller, or whether he were begging for a night's lodging, with each and all he endeavoured to associate amicably and with a pious word upon his lips. As he went he rejoiced in heart. One thing, however, he could not do. He had resolved to leave off tobacco, and to that end had left his pipe at home — and he missed it sadly. On the way a man gave him one. Thereafter, lest he should cause his fellow–traveller to stumble, he would fall behind him and smoke quietly.

As for Efim, he walked circumspectly, determined to do nothing amiss and speak no light word, since frivolity was foreign to his soul. Likewise, his domestic cares never left his thoughts. He was forever thinking of how things might be going at home and of the directions he had given to his son, as well as wondering if those directions were being carried out. Whenever he saw peasants setting potatoes or carting manure he at once thought to himself: "Is my son doing as I instructed him?" Sometimes, indeed, he felt like turning back to give fresh directions and see them carried out in person.

III

When the old men had been on the tramp five weeks their home–made bast shoes gave out, and they had to buy new ones. In time they arrived at the country of the Kholkhi where, although by this time they were far from the district where they were known and had for some time past been accustomed to pay for their board and lodging each night, these good people vied with each other in entertaining them. They took them in and fed them, yet would accept no money, but sped them on their way with food in their wallets and sometimes new bast shoes as well. Thus the old men covered 700 versts with ease, until they had crossed another province and arrived in a bare and poverty–stricken land. Here the inhabitants were willing to take them in, and would accept no money for their night's lodging, yet ceased to provide them with food. Nowhere was even bread given to the travellers, and occasionally it could not be bought. Last year, the people said, nothing had grown. Those who had been rich had ploughed up their land and sold out; those who had been only moderately rich were now reduced to nothing; while those who had been poor had either perished outright or emigrated, with the exception of a few, who still eked out a wretched existence somehow. During the past winter, indeed, such people had lived on chaff and weeds.

One evening the old men stayed the night at a hamlet, and, having bought fifteen pounds of bread, went on before dawn, so as to get as far as possible while it was yet cool. They covered ten versts, and then sat down by a brook, ladled some water into a bowl, soaked and ate some bread, and washed their feet. As they sat and rested Elijah pulled out his horn tobacco-box, whereupon Efim shook his head in disapproval.

"Why not throw that rubbish away?" he said.

"Nay, but if a failing has got the better of one, what's one to do?" replied Elijah with a shrug of his shoulders.

Then they got up and went on for another ten versts. The day had now become intensely hot, and after reaching and passing through a large village, Elijah grew weary, and longed to rest again and have a drink. Efim, however, refused to stop, for he was the better walker of the two, and Elijah often found it difficult to keep up with him.

"Oh, for a drink!" said Elijah.

"Well go and have one. I myself can do without."

Elijah stopped. "Do not wait for me," he said. "I will run to that hut there and beg a drink, and be after you again in a twinkling."

"Very well," said Efim, and he went on along the road alone, while Elijah turned aside to the hut.

When he came to it he saw that it was a small, plastered cabin, with its lower part black and the upper part white. The plaster was peeling off in patches, and had evidently not been renewed for many a long day, while in one side of the roof there was a large hole. The way to the hut door lay through a yard, and when Elijah entered the latter he saw a man — thin, clean-shaven, and clad only in a shirt and breeches, after the fashion of the Kholkhi — lying stretched beside a trench. Somehow he looked as though he were lying there for coolness' sake, yet the sun was glaring down upon him. There he lay, but not as though asleep. Elijah hailed him and asked for a drink, but the man returned no answer. "He must be either ill or uncivil," thought Elijah, and went on to the door of the hut, within which he could hear the voices of two children crying. He knocked first with the iron ring of the door-knocker, and called out "Mistress!" No one answered. Again he knocked with his pilgrim's staff and called out, "Good Christians!" Nothing stirred within the hut. "Servants of God!" he cried once more, and once more received no response. He was just on the point of turning to depart when he heard from behind the door a sound as of someone gasping. Had some misfortune come upon these people? He felt that he must find out, and stepped inside.

IV

The door was unlocked, and the handle turned easily. Passing through a little entrance–porch, the inner door of which stood open, Elijah saw on the left a stove, and in front of him the living portion of the room. In one corner stood an icon frame and a table, while behind the table stood a wooden bench. Upon this bench was seated an old woman — bareheaded, and clad in a simple shift. Her head was bowed upon her arms, while beside her stood a little boy — thin, waxen in the face, and pot–bellied — who kept clutching her by the sleeve and crying loudly as he besought her for something. The air in the hut was stifling to the last degree. Elijah stepped forward and caught sight of a second woman stretched on a shelf–bunk behind the stove. She was lying face downwards, with her eyes closed, but moaned at intervals as she threw out one of her legs and drew it back again with a writhing movement. An oppressive odour came from the bunk, and it was clear that she had no one to attend to her. All at once the old woman raised her head and caught sight of the stranger.

"What do you want?" she asked in the Little–Russian dialect. "What do you want? Nay, my good man, we have nothing for you here."

None the less, Elijah understood her dialect, and took a step nearer.

"I am a servant of God," he said, "who crave of you a drink of water."

"Nay, but there is no one to get it for you," she replied. "You must take what you require and go."

"And is there no one well enough to wait upon this poor woman?" went on Elijah, presently.

"No, no one. Her man is dying in the yard yonder, and there are only ourselves besides."

The little boy had been stricken to silence by the entry of a stranger, but now the old woman had no sooner finished speaking than he clutched her again by the sleeve.

"Some bread, some bread, granny!" he cried, and burst out weeping.

Elijah was about to question the old woman further when a peasant staggered into the hut, supporting himself by the wall as he did so, and tried to sit down upon the bench. Missing his footing in the attempt, he rolled backwards upon the floor. He made no attempt to rise, but struggled to say something, speaking a word only at a time, with rests between each one.

"We have sickness here," he gasped, "and famine too. That little one there" — and he nodded towards the boy — "is dying of hunger." He burst into tears.

Elijah unslung his wallet from his shoulders, freed his arms from the strap, and lowered the wallet to the floor. Then he lifted it, placed it on the bench, unfastened it, and, taking out some bread and a knife, cut off a hunch and held it out towards the peasant. Instead of taking it, the man made a movement with his head in the direction of the two children (there was a little girl there also, behind the stove), as much as to say, "Nay, give it to them." Accordingly Elijah handed the piece to the little boy, who no sooner caught sight of it than he darted forward, seized it in his tiny hands, and ran off, with his nose fairly buried in the crumb. At the same moment the little girl came out from behind the stove, and simply glued her eyes upon the bread. To her too Elijah handed a piece, and then cut off another for the old woman, who took it and began to chew it at once.

"I beseech you, get us some water," she said presently. "Our mouths are parched. I tried to draw some water this morning (or this afternoon — I hardly know which), but fell down under its weight. The bucket will be there now if you could only bring it."

Upon Elijah asking where the well was, the old woman told him, and he went off. He found the bucket there as she had described, brought some water, and gave each of them a drink. Now that they had had the water, the children managed to devour a second hunch apiece, and the old woman too, but the peasant would not touch anything. "I do not feel inclined," he said. As for his wife, she lay tossing herself to and fro on the bunk, unconscious of what was passing. Elijah returned to a shop in the village, bought some millet, salt, meal, and butter, and hunted out a hatchet. Then, having cut some firewood, he lighted the stove with the little girl's help, cooked some soup and porridge, and gave these poor people a meal.

V

The peasant ate but little, but the old woman did better, while the two children cleared a bowlful apiece, and then went to sleep in one another's arms. Presently the man and the old woman began telling Elijah how it had all come upon them.

"We used to make a living," they said, "poor though it was; but when the crop failed last year we found we had exhausted our stock by the autumn, and had to eat anything and everything we could get. Then we tried to beg of neighbours and kind–hearted folk. At first they gave, but later they began to refuse us. There were many who would have given, but they had nothing to give. In time, too, it began to hurt us to beg, for we were in debt to everyone — in debt for money, meal, and bread."

"I tried to get work," went on the peasant, "but there was almost none to be got. Everywhere there were starving men struggling for work. A man might get a little job for one day, and then spend the next two in looking for another. The old woman and the little girl walked many a long distance for alms, though what they received was little enough, seeing that many, like ourselves, had not even bread. Still, we managed to feed ourselves somehow, and hoped to win through to the next season. But by the time spring came people had ceased to give at all, and sickness came upon us, and things grew desperate. One day we might find a bite of something to eat, and then nothing at all for two more. At last we took even to eating grass; and whether that was the cause or something else, the wife fell ill as you see. There she lay on the bed, while I myself had come to the end of my strength, and had no means of reviving it."

"Yes, I was the only one who held up," went on the old woman. "Yet hunger was pulling me down as well, and I was getting weaker every day. The little girl was in the same plight as I was, and taking to having nervous fits. One day I wanted to send her to a neighbour's, but she would not go. She just crept behind the stove and refused. The day before yesterday another neighbour came and looked in; but as soon as she saw that we were ill and starving she turned round and went away again. You see, her own husband had just died, and she had nothing to give her little children to eat. So, when you came, we were just lying here — waiting for death to come."

Elijah listened to their tale, and decided that, as it was doubtful whether he could overtake Efim that day, he had better spend the night here. The next morning he rose and did the housework, as if he himself were the master. Then he helped the old woman to make dough, and lighted the stove. After that he accompanied the little girl to some neighbours' huts, to try and borrow what else was needed, but was unsuccessful everywhere. No one had anything at all — everything had been disposed of for food, down to household necessaries and even clothes. Consequently Elijah had to provide what was needed himself — to buy some things and make others. He spent the whole day like this, and then the next, and then a third. The little boy recovered himself, and began to walk along the bench and to frisk about Elijah, while the little girl grew quite merry and helped in everything. She was forever running after Elijah with her "Nuncle, nuncle!" The old woman likewise picked up again, and went out to see a neighbour or two, while as for the husband, he progressed so far as to walk a little with the help of the wall. Only his wife still lay sick. Yet on the third day she too opened her eyes and asked for food.

"Now," thought Elijah to himself, "I must be off. I had not expected to be detained so long."

VI

It chanced, however, that the fourth (the next) day would be the first of the *rozgovieni,* or days of flesh–eating, and Elijah thought to himself: "How would it be if I were to break my fast with these people, buy them some presents for the festival, and then go on my way in the evening?" So he went to the village again, and bought milk, white meal, and lard. Everyone, from the old woman downwards, boiled and baked that day, and next morning Elijah went to Mass, returned to the hut, and broke his fast with his new friends. That day, too, the wife got up from her bed, and walked about a little. As for the husband, he shaved himself, put on a clean shirt (hastily washed for him by the old woman, since he had only one), and went off to the village to beg the forbearance of a rich peasant to whom both corn– and pasture–land had been mortgaged, and to pray that he would surrender them before the harvest. Towards evening the husband returned with a dejected air, and burst into tears. The rich peasant, it seemed, had refused his request, saying, "Bring me the money first."

Elijah took counsel with himself again. "How are these people to live without land?" he thought. "Strangers will come and reap the crops, and leave nothing at all for them, since the crops are mortgaged. However good the rye may turn out to be (and Mother Earth is looking well now), strangers will come and harvest it all, and these people can look to receive nothing, seeing that their one dessiatin of corn–land is in fee to the rich peasant. If I were to go away now, they would come to rack and ruin again."

He was so distressed by these thoughts that he did not leave that evening, but deferred his departure until the next morning. He went to sleep in the yard as usual, and lay down after he had said his prayers. Nevertheless his eyes would not close. "Yes, I ought to go," he thought "for I have spent too much time and money here already. I am sorry for these people, but one cannot benefit everyone. I meant only to give them a drop of water and a slice of bread: yet see what that slice has led to! Still," he went on, "why not redeem their corn– and meadow–land while I am about it? Yes, and buy a cow for the children and a horse for the father's harvesting? Ah, well, you have got your ideas into a fine tangle,

Elijah Kuzmitch! You are dragging your anchors, and can't make head or tail of things."

So he raised himself, took his cloak from under his head, turned it over until he had found his horn tobacco–box, and smoked to see if that would clear his thoughts. He pondered and pondered, yet could come to no decision. He wanted to go, and at the same time felt sorry for these people. Which way was it to be? He really did not know. At last he refolded his cloak under his head and stretched himself out again. He lay like that until the cocks were crowing, and then dozed off to sleep. Suddenly someone seemed to have aroused him, and he found himself fully dressed and girded with wallet and staff — found himself walking out of the entrance–gates of the yard. But those gates were so narrow, somehow, that even a single person could hardly get through them. First his wallet caught on one of the gates, and when he tried to release it, the gate on the other side caught his legging and tore it right open. Turning to release it also, he found that, after all, it was not the gate that was holding it, but the little girl, and that she was crying out, "Nuncle! Nuncle! Give me some bread!" Then he looked at his leg again, and there was the little boy also holding on to the legging, while their father and the old woman were looking from a window. He awoke, and said to himself: "I will buy out their land for them tomorrow — yes, and buy them a horse and cow as well. Of what avail is it to go across the sea to seek Christ if all the time I lose the Christ that is within me here? Yes, I must put these people straight again" — and he fell asleep until morning. He rose betimes, went to the rich peasant, and redeemed both the rye–crop and the hay. Then he went and bought a scythe (for these people's own scythe had been sold, together with everything else), and took it home with him. He set a man to mow the hay, while he himself went hunting among the muzhiks until he found a horse and cart for sale at the inn–keeper's. He duly bargained for and bought it, and then continued his way in search of a cow. As he was walking along the street he overtook two Kholkhi women, who were chatting volubly to each other as they went. He could hear that it was of himself they were speaking, for one of the women said:

"When he first came they could not tell at all what he was, but supposed him to be a pilgrim. He only came to beg a drink of water, yet he has been there ever since. There is nothing he is not ready to buy them. I myself saw him buying a horse and cart today at the innkeeper's. There cannot be many such people in the world. I should like to see this marvellous pilgrim."

When Elijah heard this, and understood that it was himself they were praising, he forbore to go and buy the cow, but returned to the innkeeper and paid over the money for the horse and cart. Then he harnessed the horse, and drove home to the hut. Driving right up to the gates, he stopped and alighted. His hosts were surprised to see the horse, and although it crossed their minds that possibly he might have bought it for themselves, they hesitated to say so. However, the husband remarked as he ran to open the gates: "So you have bought a new horse, then, grandfather?" To this Elijah merely answered: "Yes, but I only bought it because it happened to be going cheap. Cut some fodder, will you, and lay it in the manger for its food tonight?" So the peasant unharnessed the horse, cut some swathes of grass, and filled the manger. Then everyone lay down to rest. But Elijah lay out upon the roadway, whither he had taken his wallet beforehand; and when all the people were asleep he arose, girded on his wallet, put on his boots and cloak, and went on his way to overtake Efim.

VII

When Elijah had gone about five versts, the day began to break. He sat down under a tree, opened his wallet, and began to make calculations. According to his reckoning, he had seventeen roubles and twenty kopeks left. "Well," he thought, "I can't get across the sea on that, and to raise the rest in Christ's name would be a sin indeed. Friend Efim must finish the journey alone, and offer my candle for me. Yes, my vow must remain unfulfilled now until I die; but, thanks be to God, the Master is merciful and long–suffering."

So he rose, slung his wallet across his shoulders, and went back. Yet he made a circuit of the village — of that village — so that the people should not see him. Soon he was near home again. When he had been travelling away from home, walking had been an effort, and he had hardly been able to keep up with Efim; but now that he was travelling towards home it seemed as if God helped his steps and never let him know weariness. As he went along he jested, swung his staff about, and covered seventy versts a day.

So he came home. A crowd gathered from the fields, far and near, and his entire household ran to greet their old head. Then they began to ply him with questions — as to how, when, and where everything had happened, why he had left his comrade behind, why he had returned home without completing the journey, and so on. Elijah did not make a long story of it.

"God did not see fit to bring me to my goal," he said. "I lost some money on the road, and got separated from my companion. So I went no

further. Pardon me, for Christ's sake," — and he handed what was left of
the money to his old goodwife. Then he asked her about his domestic
affairs. All was well with them, everything had been done, there had been
no neglect of household management, and the family had lived in peace
and amity.

Efim's people heard the same day that Elijah had returned, and went
to him to ask about their own old man. Elijah merely told them the same
story. "Your old man," he said, "was quite well when he parted from me.
That was three days before the Feast of Saint Peter. I meant to catch him
up later, but various matters intervened where I was. I lost my money,
and had not enough to continue upon, so I came back."

Everyone was surprised that a man of such sense could have been so
foolish as to set out and yet never reach his journey's end, but only waste
his money. They were surprised — and then forgot all about it. Elijah did
the same. He resumed his household work — helping his son to get
firewood ready against the winter, giving the women a hand with the
corn–grinding, roofing the stable, and seeing to his bees. Likewise he
sold another ten hives, with their produce, to the neighbour. His old wife
wanted to conceal how many of the hives had been swarmed from, but
Elijah knew without her telling him which of them had swarmed and
which were barren, and handed over seventeen hives to the neighbour
instead of ten. Then he put everything straight, sent off his son to look
for work for himself, and sat down for the winter to plait bast shoes and
carve wooden clogs.

VIII

All that day when Elijah found the sick people in the hut and remained
with them, Efim had waited for his companion. First he went on a little
way and sat down. There he waited and waited, dozed off, woke up
again, and went on sitting — but no Elijah appeared. He looked and
looked about for him, while the sun sank behind a tree — yet still no
Elijah. "Can he have passed me," thought Efim, "or have been given a lift
and so have driven past me, without noticing me where I sat asleep? Yet
he could not have helped seeing me if that had been the case. In this
steppe country one can see a long way. It would be no good my going
back for him, since he might miss me on the road, and we should be
worse off than ever. No, I will go on, and we shall probably meet at the
next halting–place for the night." In time Efim came to a village, and
asked the headman there to see to it that if such and such an old man
(and he described Elijah) arrived later he should be directed to the same
hut as himself. But Elijah never arrived to spend the night, so Efim went

on again the next morning, asking everyone whom he saw if they had come across a bald–headed old man. No one had done so, however. Efim was surprised, but still pushed on alone. "We shall meet somewhere in Odessa," he thought, "or on board the ship," and forthwith dismissed the matter from his mind.

On the road he fell in with a travelling monk who, dressed in skull–cap and cassock, had been to Athos, and was now on his way to Jerusalem for the second time. They happened to lodge at the same place one night, and agreed henceforth to go together.

They arrived at Odessa without mishap, but were forced to wait three days for a ship. There were many other pilgrims waiting there, come from all parts of Russia, and among them Efim made further inquiries about Elijah, but no one had seen him.

The monk told Efim how he could get a free passage if he wished, but Efim would not hear of it. "I would much rather pay," he said. "I have made provision for that." So he paid down forty roubles for a passage out and home, as well as laid in a stock of bread and herrings to eat on the way. In time the vessel was loaded and the pilgrims taken on board, Efim and the monk keeping close to one another. Then the anchor was weighed, sail set, and they put out to sea. All that first day they had smooth sailing, but towards evening the wind arose, the rain came down, and the vessel began to roll heavily and ship water. The passengers were flung from side to side, the women began wailing, and those of the men whose stomachs were weaker than those of their fellows went below in search of berths. Efim too felt qualms, but repressed any outward manifestation of them, and remained sitting the whole of that night and the following day in the same position on deck which he had secured on embarking, and which he shared with some old people from Tambov. They held on to their baggage, and squatted there in silence. On the third day it grew calmer, and on the fifth they put into Constantinople, where some of the pilgrims landed and went to look at the Cathedral of Saint Sophia, now a Muhammadan mosque. Efim did not land, but remained sitting where he was. After a stay of twenty–four hours they put to sea again, and, calling only at Smyrna and Alexandria, arrived without mishap at their port of destination, Jaffa. There all the pilgrims disembarked for the seventy versts' tramp to Jerusalem, the business of landing being a nerve–shaking one for the poor people, since they had to be lowered into small boats, and, the ship's side being high and the boats rocking violently, it always looked as though the passenger would overshoot the boat. As a matter of fact, two men did get a ducking, but eventually everyone came safely to land. Once there, they lost no time in pushing forward, and on the fourth day arrived at Jerusalem. They passed through the city to a Russian hostel, showed their passports, had some food, and were conducted by the monk around the Holy Places. To the actual Holy Sepulchre itself there was no admission that day, but they first of all attended Matins at the Greek Monastery of the Patriarch (where they said their prayers and offered votive candles) and then went to gaze at the outside of the Church of the Resurrection, in which lies the actual Sepulchre of the Lord, but which is so built as to conceal all view of the Sepulchre from outside. That first day also they were afforded a glimpse of the cell where Mary of Egypt took refuge, and duly offered candles there and recited a thanksgiving. They next wished to return to Mass at the Church of the Holy Sepulchre, but found that they were too late, and so went on to the Monastery of Abraham in the Garden of Saveki, where Abraham once wished to sacrifice his son to the Lord. Thence they proceeded to the place where Christ appeared to Mary Magdalene, and thence to the Church of Saint James, the brother of Our Lord. At all these places the monk acted as their guide, telling them everywhere how much to pay and where to offer candles. At length they returned to the hostel, and had just retired to rest when the monk suddenly sprang up, and began rummaging among his clothes. "Someone has stolen my purse and money!" he exclaimed. "The purse had twenty-three roubles in it — two ten-rouble notes and three roubles in coin!" He raged and stormed for some time, but there was no help for it, and eventually they all lay down to sleep.

IX

Efim lay down with the rest, and a temptation fell upon him. "I do not believe," he thought to himself, "that the monk was robbed, for he had nothing which thieves could take. He never gave anything anywhere. He told me to give, but never gave anything himself, and even borrowed a rouble of me."

But almost instantly he began to reproach himself for thinking so. "Who am I," he said, "to judge another? It is sinful of me, and I will refrain from these thoughts." It was not long, however, before he found himself remembering again how watchful of money the monk had been, and how unlikely it was that his tale of being robbed could be true. "He had nothing to be robbed of," thought Efim once more. "It was a mere excuse."

In the morning they rose and went to early mass at the great Church of the Resurrection — at the Holy Sepulchre itself. The monk never left Efim, but walked by his side all the way. When they entered the church they found a great crowd there, both of monks and pilgrims — Russian, Greek, Armenian, Turkish and Syrian, as well as of obscurer nationalities. Efim approached the Holy Gates with the others, passed the Turkish guards, and reached the spot where the Saviour was taken down from the Cross, and where now stood nine candlesticks with lighted tapers. There he offered a candle, and was then conducted by the monk up the steps on the right to Golgotha, to the spot where the Cross had stood. There Efim knelt down and prayed. Then he was shown the cleft where the earth was rent, the spot where Christ's hands and feet were nailed to the Cross, and the Tomb of Adam, where Christ's blood had trickled down upon Adam's bones. Next they came to the stone on which Christ sat while the Crown of Thorns was being placed upon His head, and then to the pillar to which He was bound for the scourging. Finally Efim saw the stone with the two holes for the feet of Christ. They would have shown him something more had not the crowd hurried forward, for all were eager to reach the actual catacomb of the Lord's Sepulchre. There a foreign Mass had just ended, and the Orthodox was beginning. Efim entered the Sepulchre with the rest.

He wanted to get rid of the monk, for he found himself continually sinning in his thoughts against him; but the monk still kept by his side, and entered with him into the Holy Sepulchre to hear Mass. They tried to get nearer to the front, but found it impossible, since the people were so closely packed that any movement either backward or forward was out of the question. As Efim stood gazing to the front and trying to pray, he found himself continually feeling for his purse. Two thoughts kept passing through his mind. The first was — "Is the monk cheating me all the time?" and the second was — "If he has not been cheating me, and really had his purse stolen, why did they not do the same to me as well?"

X

As Efim stood thus, praying and gazing towards the chapel in which the actual Sepulchre stood, with thirty–six lamps always burning above it — suddenly, as he stood peering through the heads in front of him, he saw a strange thing. Immediately beneath the lamps, and ahead of all the congregation, he perceived an old man, dressed in a rough serge kaftan, and with a shining bald head like Elijah Bodroff's. "How exactly like Elijah he is!" thought Efim to himself. "Yet it cannot possibly be he, for it would have been impossible for him to get here before myself. The last ship before our own sailed a whole week before we did, so he could never have caught it. And he certainly was not on our own, for I looked at every pilgrim on board."

Just as these thoughts had passed through Efim's mind, the old man in front began to pray, with three bows as he did so: one forwards, to God, and one on either side of him, to the whole Orthodox world. And lo! as the old man turned his head to bow towards his right, Efim recognized him beyond all possibility of doubt. It was Elijah Bodroff! Yes, that was Elijah's curly black beard — those were his eyebrows, his eyes, his nose — those were his features altogether! Yes, it was he, and nobody else — Elijah Bodroff!

Efim was overjoyed at having found his comrade, though also not a little surprised that Elijah could have arrived before him.

"He must have slipped past me somewhere, and then gone on ahead with someone who helped him on the way," thought Efim. "However, I will catch him as we pass out, and get rid of this monk in the skull–cap. After that Elijah and I will keep together again. He might have got me to the front now if he had been with me."

So he kept his eyes fixed upon Elijah, determined not to lose sight of him. At last the Mass came to an end, and the people began to move. Indeed, there was such a crush as everyone pressed forward to kiss the Cross that Efim got jammed into a corner. Once more the thought that his purse might be stolen from him made him nervous, so he squeezed it tightly in his hand and set himself to force his way clear of the throng. Succeeding at last, he ran hither and thither, seeking Elijah, but eventually had to leave the church without having come across him. Next he visited the various hostels, to make inquiries about him, but, although he traversed the whole city, he could not find him anywhere. That evening, too, the monk did not return. He had departed without repaying the rouble, and Efim was left alone.

Next day, Efim went to the Holy Sepulchre again, accompanied by one of the old men from Tambov who had been with him on the ship. Once more he tried to get to the front, and once more he got thrust aside, so that he had to stand by a pillar to say his prayers. He peered through the heads in front of him again, and, behold! ahead of all the congregation, and under the very lamps of the Lord's Sepulchre, stood Elijah as before! He had his arms spread out like those of a priest at the altar, and his bald head was shining all over.

"Now," thought Efim, "I do not mean to lose him this time." So he started to worm his way forward, and eventually succeeded — but Elijah had vanished. He must have left the church.

The third day also Efim went to Mass, and once more looked for Elijah. And once more there stood Elijah, in the same position as before, and having the same appearance. His arms were spread out and he was gazing upwards, as though beholding something above him, while his bald head again shone brightly.

"Well," thought Efim, "come what may, I am not going to lose him this time. I will go straight away and post myself at the entrance, where we cannot possibly miss each other."

So he did so, and stood waiting and waiting as the people passed out; but Elijah did not come with them.

Efim remained six weeks in Jerusalem. He visited all the holy spots — Bethlehem, Bethany, the Jordan, and the rest — as well as had a new shirt stamped with a seal at the Holy Sepulchre (to be buried in one day), took away water from the Jordan in a phial, took away also earth and candles from the Holy Place, and spent all his money except just what was sufficient to bring him home again. Then he started to return, reached Jaffa, embarked, made the passage to Odessa, and set out upon his long overland tramp.

XI

Efim travelled alone, and by the same route as on the outward journey. Gradually as he drew nearer home there came back to him his old anxiety to know how things had been faring in his absence. "So much water passes down a river in a year!" he thought. "A home may take a lifetime to build up, and an hour to destroy." So he kept constantly wondering how his son had managed affairs since his departure, what sort of a spring it had been, how the cattle had stood the winter, and whether the new hut was finished.

When in time he arrived where he had parted from Elijah he found it hard to recognize the people of the locality. Where last year they had been destitute, today they were living comfortably, for the crops had been good everywhere. The inhabitants had recovered themselves, and quite forgotten their former tribulations. So it came about that one evening Efim was drawing near to the identical village where Elijah had left him a year ago. He had almost reached it, when a little girl in a white frock came dancing out of a hut near by, calling out as she did so, "Grandfather! Dear grandfather! Come in and see us." Efim was for going on, but she would not let him, and, catching him by the skirt of his coat, pulled him laughingly towards the hut. Thereupon a woman and a little boy came out onto the steps, and the former beckoned to Efim, saying: "Yes, pray come in, grandfather, and sup and spend the night." So Efim approached the hut, thinking to himself, "I might get news of Elijah here, for surely this is the very hut to which he turned aside to get a drink." He went in, and the woman relieved him of his wallet, gave him water to wash in, and made him sit down at the table; after which she produced milk, and dumplings, and porridge, and set them before him.

Efim thanked her kindly, and commended her readiness to welcome a pilgrim. The woman shook her head in deprecation of this. "We could do no otherwise," she answered, "for it was from a pilgrim that we learnt the true way of life. We had been living in forgetfulness of God, and He so punished us that we came very near to death's door. It was last year, in the summer, and things had gone so hard with us that we were, one and all, lying ill and starving. Of a surety we should have died, had not God sent to us just such another old man as yourself. He came in at midday, to beg a drink of water, and was seized with compassion when he saw us, and remained here. He gave us food and drink and set us on our feet, redeemed our land for us, bought us a horse and cart — and then disappeared."

The old woman entered the hut at this moment, and the younger one broke off.

"Yes," went on the old woman, "to this day we do not know whether that man may not have been an angel of God. He loved us, pitied us, and yet went away without saying who he was, so that we know not for whom to pray. Even now it all passes before my eyes. I was lying there, waiting for death, when I chanced to look up and saw that an old man — an ordinary–looking old man, except for his baldness — had entered to beg some water. I (may God forgive me for my sinfulness!) thought to myself: 'Who is this vagabond?' Yet listen now to what he did. No sooner had he seen us than he took off his wallet, and, laying it down here — yes, here, on this very spot — unfastened it and —"

"No, no, granny," broke in the little girl, eagerly. "First of all he laid the wallet in the middle of the hut, and then set it on the bench" — and they fell to vying with one another in recalling Elijah's every word and deed — where he had sat, where he had slept, and all that he had said and done to everybody.

At nightfall the master of the house came riding up to the hut on horseback, and soon took up the tale of Elijah's life with them. "Had he not come to us then," he said, "we should all of us have died in sin; for, as we lay there dying and despairing, we were murmuring both against God and man. But this holy pilgrim set us on our feet once more, and taught us to trust in God and to believe in the goodness of our fellow men. Christ be with him! Before, we had lived only as beasts: 'twas he that made us human."

So these good people entertained Efim with food and drink, showed him to a bed, and themselves lay down to sleep. But Efim could not sleep, for the memory of Elijah — of Elijah as he had three times seen him at the head of the congregation in Jerusalem — would not leave him.

"Somewhere on the road he must have passed me," he thought. "Yet, however that may be, and no matter whether my pilgrimage be accepted or not, God has accepted him."

In the morning his hosts parted with Efim, loaded him with pasties for the journey, and went off to their work, while Efim pursued his way.

XII

Just a year had passed when Efim arrived home — arrived home in the spring. The time was evening, and his son was not in the hut, but at a tavern. At length he came home in drink, and Efim questioned him. There was abundant evidence that his son had been living a dissolute life in his absence. He had wasted all the money committed to his care, and neglected everything. His father broke out into reproaches, to which the son replied with insolence.

"You went gaily off on your travels," he said, "and took most of the money with you. Yet now you require it of me!" The old man lost his temper and struck him.

Next morning, as he was going to the *starosta* to give up his passport, he passed Elijah's yard. On the lodge–step stood Elijah's old wife, who greeted Efim warmly.

"How are you, my good sir?" she said. "So you have returned safe and well?"

Efim stopped. "Yes, I have returned, glory be to God," he replied. "But I lost sight of your good husband, although I hear that he is back now."

The old woman responded readily, for she loved chatting.

"Yes, he is back, good sir," she said. "He returned some while ago — it was just after the Feast of the Assumption — and glad we were that God had brought him safely! We had been sadly dull without him. He can work but little now, for his best years lie behind him, but he remains always our head, and we are happier when he is here. How delighted our boy was! 'Life without daddy,' said he, 'is like having no light to see by.' Yes, we found it dull indeed without Elijah. We love him too well not to have missed him sorely."

"Then perhaps he is at home at this moment?"

"Yes, he is at home, and busy at his hive–bench, taking a swarm. He says that the swarms have been magnificent this year — that God has given the bees such health and vigour as he has never known before. Truly, he says, God does not reward us after our sins. But come in, my dear sir. He will be delighted to see you."

So Efim stepped through the lodge, crossed the courtyard, and went to find Elijah in the bee-garden. As he entered it he caught sight of him — unprotected by netting or gloves, and clad only in a grey kaftan — standing under a young birch tree. His arms were spread out and his face turned upwards, with the crown of his bald head shining all over, as when he had stood those three times by the Lord's Sepulchre in Jerusalem; while above him — as also in Jerusalem — the sun was playing through the birch branches like a great burning lamp, and around his head the golden bees were dancing in and out and weaving themselves into a diadem, without stinging him. Efim stood still where he was.

Then Elijah's wife called out: "Husband! A friend has come to see you." Elijah looked round, his face broke out into smiles, and he ran to meet his comrade, gently brushing some bees from his beard as he did so.

"Good day to you, good day to you, my dear old friend!" he cried. "Then did you get there safely?"

"Yes, of a surety. My feet carried me safely, and I have brought you home some Jordan water. Come and see me some time and get it. Yet I know not if my task has been accepted of God, or —"

"Surely, surely it has. Glory be to Him and to Our Lord Jesus Christ!"

Efim was silent a moment; then continued: "Yes, my feet carried me thither; but whether I was there also in spirit, or whether it were another who —"

"Nay, nay. That is God's affair, my old comrade — God's affair."

"Well, on my way back," added Efim, "I stopped at the hut where you parted from me."

Elijah seemed frightened, and hastened to interrupt him. "That also is God's affair, my friend — God's affair," he said. "But come into the hut, and I will get you some honey" — and he hurried to change the conversation by talking of household matters.

Efim sighed, and forbore to tell Elijah of the people in the hut or of his having seen him in Jerusalem. But this clearly did he understand: that in this world God has commanded everyone, until death, to work off his debt of duty by means of love and good works.

The Devil and the Ploughman

Ernst Wiechert

This story happened before I was born, and I remember well the day when it was told to me by my father. We were digging over a few square yards of heath to make a child's garden; and when I could not succeed in pulling out a root of heather with my little hands I called out loud, "The Devil take it," for children love to imitate a grown–up's anger. Thereupon my father took the spade out of my hand without saying a word, and went on digging over the ground. He refused to answer my clamorous questions and only looked very serious, so that I felt confused and rejected and had to stand around in the gloomy knowledge that I had been naughty and foolish; and so time dragged until it was evening.

When at last twilight came, my father took me across the heath to the ruined Swedish redoubt where we often used to sit in that poor and lonely country. He said nothing by way of introduction. He only lifted a bit of earth up and crushed it between his fingers. Then he told this story.

Many years ago in this district there lived a farmer called Michael. He worked a poor farm, for the land here is hard, and here he sowed and reaped and in his hard work he had peace. He did no wrong, did not go to the inn, nor did he steal wood. The only stain on his name was his flaring temper, which burst out from time to time. Then he would strike his beasts and his farm–servants, even his own flesh and blood. But always afterwards he would go off in sombre sadness and lose himself in the heath or in the forest. He would only come back after many hours, sometimes even in the night, and carry on as before: a tired and kind man going on with his work, so that no one could reproach him and everyone pitied this terrible weakness in the blood.

Now it happened once that he had cleared a bit of heath hard by a boggy and neglected wood, and now he was driving his plough for the first time through the fresh unworked soil. By evening his arms were aching. When the ploughshare for the thousandth time was thrust from the crooked furrow by a stone or root his temper rose so that he struck the exhausted horses and kicked the plough wishing aloud that Satan might take it, and without turning round he left the piece of ground, went home, tossed down a few glasses of brandy, threw himself on his bed and fell into a dark and angry sleep.

It was already dark when he woke up with a bitter taste in his heart, and after he had quietly taken himself to task, he went into the stables to have a look at the animals and the men before the end of the day. He never said a word when he did not find the horses by their food trough, but put some oats in his pocket and went off secretly to bring the horses in from the field.

Late that night he came home. Neither horse nor plough was there. He asked the farm servant, the shepherd, he asked the child in the cradle. No one had been to the cleared field. He and his men lit lanterns and went out. Heavy rain was falling. What they found was the furrow that suddenly came to an end, and the stone deeply scored by the ploughshare. Nothing else. We are told that they searched for two weeks day and night, and that the farmer's hair turned grey. Nor did he tell anyone that on the first evening when he was crossing the empty field he had heard a voice calling from the moors: "Micha–el!" it had called, but he did not know whether it was a human or an animal's voice, nor even if it was only the sound of his own blood flowing heavily to his heart.

Then Michael left the farm to his wife and went away silently without saying farewell, with a stick in his hand and a grey linen bag over his bent shoulder. He did not search any more. He went away from all his kith and kin right to the edge of our province, where every year they gather stones from the field before ploughing. And there he soon became known to everyone. "For the sake of Christ," he said standing up at the edge of the field from which he had been carrying stones to a hill, "let me plough a little." And after the wonder and suspicion of the first time there was now joy without mockery when the "Christ–farmer" came along and took on the heaviest work quietly and without payment. In this way the farmers were disappointed when he missed them out or when he did not come back to them. No one found out who he was or why he suffered.

On one day in the year he begged, not for Christ's sake but for his own poor salvation, to be allowed to pull the plough himself for one hour in the evening, with harness round his shoulders and a maiden holding the handle of the plough. He had to suffer much before this strange request was granted. Only in the third year of his wanderings he met at last people who showed a grudging pity, but even so he had to promise to work on the farm without payment for three weeks of the following year before they would help him with his curious penance.

In this way he travelled about for ten years round the country, trying to make amends. Then it happened one year that on the day of the special penance he could find no one who was prepared to lend daughter and plough for the cleansing ritual. It was already growing dark as he, rejected everywhere, came to a derelict field where a rusty plough stood, and he raised his arms in despair.

Then there came a man over the fields in the dusk, bare–headed and barefoot, not at all clothed after the fashion of those parts. The man nodded silently to the farmer, took the handle of the plough and went with him through the heavy fulfilment of his vow, just as one takes pity in silence on the trouble of a child or sick person. But when they had finished, the stranger remained standing by the plough, clearing the earth away from the share which was now shining, and said that he could now go home, they had found what had been lost. And then he walked off.

So the farmer returned home, walking barefoot and bareheaded like his helper, and having no doubt that a miracle had touched him. And he returned to his life as if he had only been away for one circle of the sun, without telling anyone where he had been, without excusing himself. On arriving, he learned that just a few days before, they had found the plough and the remains of the two horses in a peat–moss in the forest. He did not ask the day, but buried the plough, the harness and the bones.

From that time on, Michael did all the heavy and menial work of the homestead by himself and cleared the heath round his farm with his own hands, using the help of neither man nor beast. He was also a quiet and highly esteemed evening guest with the minister of his parish, and to–gether they arranged that he should be buried where the furrow ended at the stone, and that on his tombstone should be written: *Glory to God on high, and to the poorest field below.*

And so it was done, according to his wish.

Sister Amelia

Gerhard Klein

Some time ago, now, someone phoned me from a long way off. I did not catch the name but the voice sounded familiar. The person calling asked if he could visit me soon. He would bring the last greetings from Aunt Amelia. Then it suddenly came to me who the caller was. It was Edward, a childhood playmate of days long past; Amelia had taken him under her wing particularly because he had been orphaned as a very young child. We agreed on a time for his visit. I was too affected to ask for more details on the telephone. I should soon enough hear all about it.

So she was no longer with us, Sister Amelia, who for us children had always been "Aunt" Amelia. The images which had so impressed themselves upon my mind as a boy came flooding back: the great park with the wall lined with chestnut trees which was our annual holiday paradise, the bridge over the pond, the winding path leading through the rose-hedges to the green wood on the hill, the rambling mansion built in the English style. There she stood, the object of the boy's shy devotion and childlike love. She was dressed all in white, according to the fashion of the time, in a blouse with a high stiff collar, in a wide skirt of many pleats and a broad brimmed hat; while the great black Newfoundland dog, Wotan, stood close beside her; there she stood looking at the setting sun. Again in my mind I felt her near as she bent over the impatient boy struggling to stick on cardboard a church which he had cut out. Her warm and kindly voice reassured him, and then she showed him how to do it, and the work of art came right at once.

Early in the morning the boy would slip out of bed, quickly wash himself and dress. Then he would wait at the window till he saw the two figures coming, Uncle Richard and Aunt Amelia. She carried her long riding coat over her arm. The boy then jumped out of the window, and raced towards them, to receive a hearty good–morning kiss, and then he was allowed to go with them to the stable, where the coachman, a former groom of the cavalry captain, was holding ready the two horses, Caesar and Cilly. How proud the boy was to be allowed to hold the stirrup, and how he admired the lady elegantly sitting side–saddle as she trotted away with her friend on their morning ride.

Then all at once the beloved aunt wore the uniform of a nursing sister of the Order of St John. The boy was allowed to carry her basket and accompany her to the miners' camp to visit a woman in childbed. There she would put on her apron, clean everything, cook and look after the baby, and the young mother could lie back on her pillow without being embarrassed at her being "a lady of quality" for, as a nurse, Aunt Amelia was one of them. That was still at a time when children had to change for the main evening meal and to greet the lady of the house, Uncle Richard's old mother, by kissing her hand.

The boy felt almost with secret jealousy that there was an understanding between Uncle Richard and Aunt Amelia. Only much later did he learn the facts about their relationship. For many years Uncle Richard had wooed Aunt Amelia. But she was so committed to her work as a nurse that she hesitated. Also she was impoverished as her father had left the huge estate in the East of Germany heavily in debt. When her friend left for the front in 1914, she had said "yes" to him. But he did not wish to marry her until he had returned safe and sound, believing that children should not have to grow up without a father. Sister Amelia also felt that she should serve at the front herself. Indeed, they may have met now and again.

Then another picture flashed before me: Sister Amelia, still in her uniform, staying in our own home. She had come to us for comfort, following the death of Uncle Richard at the front.

She and the young boy, I remember, now heard the Sunday sermon together, and she was happy and sad at the same time. Sad because she had had to give up so much, she who needed much strength to comfort the wounded and to help the dying over the threshold. The boy promised to write down from memory the sermons or his father's wartime Sunday service and to send it to her. This he did over a long period.

Now other pictures sprang to mind. The war had come to an end. Aunt Amelia was now the matron of a large hospital in Berlin. And now her little flat had become the refuge of numerous "nephews" and "nieces." A free and easy sociability developed in her home. She had always something to eat for the poor students.There was a signal for those of us who were regulars: we rang her bell long–short, short–long. And she always found time for us even though it was only sometimes ten minutes after a long wait. She could listen as very few people can. She had a clear matter–of–fact way of reducing a problem to its true dimensions in a few words. Although she was still fairly young she had been tried by suffering, and all her powers of love she gave to the sick, the nurses and her protegés. She had a cheerful saying: "Swallow it dry." She often knew things even before you had said them. And she knew when to keep silent.

Two young people were particularly close to her. One was her god-daughter Amy, and the other was that same Edward whose visit I was expecting. I had lost touch with both. However I had exchanged greetings from time to time with Aunt Amelia but the events of the Second World War then separated us. I knew only that after the death of Amelia's brother, she had managed the estate in Eastern Germany for a time, and then had been able to flee to the West with her old mother and her brother's wife.

Some years earlier than this, her god-daughter Amy, as a student of philology, had had to write a thesis about a medieval saint. The result was that she was converted to Roman Catholicism and entered a convent of very strict rule. This decision was quite foreign to Aunt Amelia and the separation grieved her, but she kept up the connection inwardly as if towards one who has died, for indeed the girl Amy wished to be dead to her former life.

Of Edward I knew only that he had gone to America as an engineer, and had thrown himself into the technical world and into business. Edward's chosen path was certainly also difficult for Aunt Amelia to understand.

Now Edward was sitting in my home. Strange how common experiences of childhood and youth can often create a bond which survives such a long separation. It is not necessary at all to exchange memories first. I gazed silently across at him. Those clear-etched features, deep-set eyes that could often look at you sadly, were his already when young.

He began to speak with hesitation: "I would not have come to you but Aunt Amelia specially asked me to see you and tell you about her and about myself. And now I am here, I am very glad that she sent me."

He paused for a long time. I now saw in his face the evidence of hard struggles; but still from his eyes shone a certain peace.

"I must tell you a little about myself," he continued, "before I come to Aunt Amelia. Perhaps you know that as a young man I was in the United States for many years. What you cannot know however is that from childhood on I was firmly convinced that Aunt Amelia's god-daughter was destined to be my life-companion and that while I was a student I maintained a close friendship with her. But I never gave the slightest hint that I loved her or that I wished to marry her. I was firmly convinced that she really knew it, but I did not wish to put out feelers prematurely because I wished to make something of myself first.

"For this reason I went to the United States. In my determination to become something there, I did well, and succeeded much better and faster than I had expected. Then I went back to Germany to find her. I visited Amy's parents in order to press my suit with her father, the old lieutenant–colonel. And only then I found out: Amelia was in a convent. She had left the world for good. Aunt Amelia helped me enormously at that time. She told me that Amy believed that only in the sheltered surroundings of the convent could she find the strength to devote herself to spiritual exercises. Amelia said to comfort me that Amy would be praying for the souls of others, perhaps also for my own. She told me not to hold that lightly. She said that perhaps Amelia had to atone for something."

Edward then went on to tell how he wished to see and speak with his young friend Amy. He obtained leave to visit her. They sat opposite each other but it was not just the grille which separated them. With downcast eyes she showed no response to the strong feelings welling up within him as he saw her once again. He told her that he could not understand the path which she had chosen. She told him how she had found peace and her last words as they parted were: "I shall pray for you."

With even greater grimness he plunged into his work. He travelled all over the world involved in planning and supervising major projects. Then the war came. He volunteered. He was a prisoner of war for a long time in Russia, suffering, as he thought, with no one to think of him. What moved him deeply there was the Russian people's great capacity to suffer. In many, especially in the women, he encountered the soul of the people. But his loneliness became harder and harder to bear. He made up his mind to die but when the actual moment came to carry out his resolve he suddenly heard a warm clear voice warning him and calling, "No!" and again "No!" Twice he went to kill himself, twice he was held back by this voice. It was Aunt Amelia's voice. That was it! How could he ever have forgotten it.

"Back home again," he went on, "I wanted to give all strength to rebuilding my shattered country. Soon I was again in an important position, became as they say, an important person. Of Aunt Amelia I only heard that she had survived the flight to the West with her fragile old mother. She was living with her and looking after her until she died.

"Amelia visited me once, and said incidentally: 'I know you were once in great danger.' But I was so taken up with my work that only later did I realize what she had meant.

"Now and then I sent her greetings, and every year through my secretary I sent her a large parcel. Once I went out specially to find her an art print, for she loved such things. But knowing how proud she was, I did not dare offer to support her on a regular basis.

"I myself was living with a divided soul. I longed to go back to Russia to the breadth and stillness of Siberia, to the warm humanity that survives there even under the most terrible pressures. I knew however that I could not belong to those people and to their destiny, for I had a western soul. But I grew to dislike more and more the world in which I was living and working. A verse from my childhood came into my mind: 'What shall it help a man if he should gain the whole world and yet receive damage to his own soul?' Yes, I had received damage to my own soul, great damage. I became more and more aware of that.

"I became ill, and one day my doctor broke the news to me that I only had a short time to live. According to his reckoning, the illness was too far advanced and incurable. I was not upset, it was all right as far as I was concerned. Gradually I released myself from my duties. But a long illness seemed to me to be senseless. I prepared calmly and carefully for my death. I proposed to die on New Year's Eve. Was there anyone to whom I owed anything? I remembered Aunt Amelia. I wished to write a farewell letter to her."

He told me that it took a long time to finish the letter. He made perhaps four attempts. Each one was torn up. In the end only a few lines were left, saying only that he was sure she would understand. Even so he hesitated to carry out the deed that night. It was not that his resolve had weakened, but he kept remembering things which still had to be put in order. He was alone. The servants had been given a holiday. Everyone was involved with the rituals of bringing in the New Year, but for him the New Year would not come. He had lit his candle, and laid his gun ready. He waited for the midnight chime. In all the general fireworks his shot would not be noticed. But suddenly the doorbell rang, not a normal ring but long–short, short–long.

"In me," he went on, "everything rose in rebellion. No, it couldn't be. No, not now. But it was clear to me that I could not leave the old lady out there in the cold. Quickly I opened the drawer in the desk and hid the gun. Perhaps however I left the drawer a bit open. Then I went to the door. There before me, tall and slender, looking very serious, stood Aunt Amelia, in a coat that was far too thin. At first I was disconcerted and stammered out something or other.

"Silently she went past me into my room without taking off her coat. She looked calmly at the candle, looked at me, looked round the room, opened the drawer, took out the gun, unloaded it expertly as in her youth, and put it in her pocket, saying, 'That's better out of the way.' Then she went on, 'and now I'm so hungry after the long journey, I hope you've got something to eat in the house. We'll have a proper New Year's Eve meal together.' She went before me into the kitchen, as if it were the most natural thing in the world for her to be there. Then I noticed that she was wearing her nurse's uniform. Yes, she had come to someone who was seriously ill, ill in body and soul. Suddenly everything fell away from me, the iron band about my breast burst open. I remembered Amelia once telling us children the story of the Frog King and I heard the words, ' Henry, the coach is breaking.' 'No, sire, it is not the coach, but it is the iron band round my heart.'

"We had a quiet meal together. We talked about all our different experiences during the war. Not once did she allude to the situation in which she had found me. She told me of a time when she was completely exhausted in the field hospital and was near to despair. Many of the nurses were absent because of sickness, on all sides sounded the groans and cries of the wounded. The doctors could not cope any more. She herself was bandaging quite mechanically, while the noise of the front was coming nearer. Suddenly she noticed how quiet it was in one corner of the large barn which was being used as a field hospital. She looked across and saw a man whom she did not know, a medical orderly whom she thought she should have recognized. She saw how he went along the rows of the wounded, now stroking someone's brow, now saying some comforting words, now closing the eyes of one who had just died; then again giving a drink to someone in agony. Peace and strength flowed from him. She wanted to go to him but already he was at the other end of the room. She herself felt strengthened by his presence, and found fresh courage. That night the place had to be evacuated. She never saw the stranger again. He had vanished, but because he had been there it helped her in the grave illness which came upon her shortly afterwards. Always after that, she kept the picture of him ever in mind, his comforting speech, his expert touch. She knew who he was. She kept on thinking of the words, 'I shall come again to you.'

"Suddenly I realized how exhausted Sister Amelia must be and I took her to her room. Immediately there was a task for me for now I had to look after her: as a result of her night journey she caught pneumonia and never recovered from it. We had many good talks, and I learned that at the time when I was writing my farewell letter to her, she had felt very uneasy, and had left her place immediately to come to me. All during the journey she had been thinking of me with the greatest intensity of mind, and had tried to sustain me in her thoughts.

"She allowed herself gladly to be looked after by me. Before she felt herself going she told me that she now felt at ease about me, all would turn out well. She asked me earnestly to come to you. Yesterday I accompanied her on her last journey. Today I have come to you. How good it is that in this world there are nurses and aunts who have forces of love that are free and not used up in their own destinies. By her I have been saved, for ever, even if this 'ever' is only for a short while."

There followed days of fruitful conversations between us. It is remarkable to report that Edward's condition did not get worse, as had been expected. He is still alive and well and now devotes all his experience and skills to working for a large charitable organization.

Offerus the Giant

Jakob Streit

There was once a giant so strong that he could pull out a whole fir–tree by the roots. His name was Offerus. He had worked for many farmers, but he never stayed very long at any one farm because before long he had done all the work and then became bored with doing nothing.

So one day he said to himself: "I shall go and seek the mightiest lord on earth, and him alone will I serve, for only the strongest lord can use all my strength."

So Offerus travelled from land to land, from town to town, and every–where he asked for the mightiest lord. At last he came to a king's court where a young lad told him that this king was the mightiest far and wide. Offerus had himself led to the throne and there he offered his services.

Now on that very day the king had summoned all the knights of his country to form an army because a neighbouring king had invaded and burnt down a town. Against this invader the king now wished to send a strong force. So when the king saw the powerful giant he said: "Never did I need you more than I do now. You shall be the mightiest of my soldiers, and with you I shall win every battle."

With all speed the royal armourer set himself to forge a gigantic sword for Offerus, for all the other swords were far too small for him. The very next day the king went off to battle with the giant at the head of his army.

On the third day a messenger raced back to the palace to announce: "Our army has gained the victory. It was terrible to behold how Offerus fought. There was hardly anything left for the others to do. The enemy fled from the sweep of his gigantic sword and scattered in the woods and mountains. The invader has been beaten!"

Victory wreaths were hung from the gates and towers. Bells were rung all over the town. The doors and stairways of the palace were adorned with flowers. On his return, the king commanded the table to be set in the great hall for a great feast of victory.

In the evening the hall was lit with many lights and the feast began. A harper sang to the music of the strings, and sword dances were performed by the best dancers.

Offerus sat beside the king. He noticed that as the harper played and sang a song in which the Devil was mentioned, the king unobtrusively made the sign of the cross over his brow.

"That is very strange," Offerus thought to himself.

The song came to an end and the festive throng lifted their goblets and drank merrily. When the king asked the giant how he had liked the song, the latter replied: "There is just one thing that I am wondering about, Your Majesty. Why did you make that sign on your brow during the song?"

"Oh," replied the king, "I do that whenever I hear the name of the Devil, whose power is great in this world!"

Offerus then asked: "Is the Devil's power greater than yours, then?"

"I rule over one country, but the Devil has power in the whole world!" replied the king.

Offerus had never heard of the Devil before so he thought to himself: "If there is another king who is mightier than this one I shall go and seek him. I want to serve the *very greatest* king."

The next day Offerus took his leave even though the king was unwilling to let him go. The giant wandered through the world. Everywhere he asked where the kingdom of the Devil was but no one would tell him. Indeed many people took fright at the question so that Offerus held the unknown king in even greater respect.

One day when the giant was going through a dark forest, a stranger came up to him from behind. His clothes were greenish, from his chin a pointed beard stuck into the air, and his hat was adorned with a black feather.

Offerus at once asked him: "Wayfarer, can you tell me where I may find the Devil who people say has the greatest power on earth?"

"He is walking beside you, I am he," replied the man in green.

"Is it true that you have power over the whole world?"

"That is so," answered the Devil.

"Then please let me serve you, Your Majesty. Have you work for me?"

"I do have work for you. Come with me!" the Devil beckoned and led the way into the forest ahead. When they had walked some way, the green man stopped by a huge fir tree and commanded: "Pull it out!"

Offerus pulled it out of the ground with one tug. Then he was told to break off the branches. Once more the Devil beckoned him and he followed carrying the huge trunk on his shoulder. Soon they came out of the wood to a place where men had been busy for weeks building a chapel. The rafters and roof–timbers were already in place and bright strips flapped on the little fir–tree set on the gable–end. It was the end of the working day and the workers had left the place intending to cover the roof with tiles the next morning.

"Strike it really hard," cried the Devil pointing to the building. Immediately Offerus struck with the mighty fir–tree trunk at the roof and smashed the walls so that not one stone remained upon another.

"You have done your work well," said the Devil, grinning.

Offerus only wanted to do what his master commanded and so continued to follow him.

When the workmen came to the chapel the next morning, they stared sadly at the ruins of the building.

"That has been done by the Evil One," exclaimed one of them. "Let us set up a cross here on the path before we start building again. That will keep him away."

They did as the man suggested and set up a wooden cross in the middle of the path leading up to the chapel. Then they sang a hymn before they set to work to restore the ruin.

After some time, when the walls and roof had been rebuilt over the holy place, the Devil came back with Offerus. The giant still carried about his huge fir–tree trunk. The Devil walked in front. But when he came near the cross he trembled, sprang aside and made a wide circle round it. Offerus stopped in surprise.

"Tell me, Your Majesty, why do you jump aside and walk round the cross in the path?"

"Do not ask but strike the roof. Look, the tiles are already on it."

"I shall not strike one blow until you tell me the meaning of this wooden cross."

"The cross is the sign of another lord, but I shall be very careful not to speak his name," said the Devil.

"Is his name so powerful and dangerous that the Devil must be careful not to mention it?" asked Offerus. "Is this other lord then mightier than you?"

Then the Devil went up close to him and whispered: "He is one who has power in heaven and on earth. But ask no more. Come, strike hard."

"If there is a lord who has power not only over one country, not only over the world, but also in heaven, then surely he is the greatest king, and only him will I serve," said Offerus, throwing the tree trunk down on to the ground, where it happened to catch the Devil's foot. Then he walked off towards the chapel and left the Devil to limp away, cursing.

Early next morning the workmen arrived. They found the smashed up tree–trunk on the path and the giant asleep within the walls. He was wakened by their voices and, jumping up, gave the men a fright. He took little notice of their fear but immediately pointed to the wooden cross and asked: "Who is the king to whom this sign belongs? And what kind of a king is he?"

The builders answered: "The king's name is Christ. We know how to build his house, but we are not so good at explaining exactly who he is. If you travel east for an hour you will come to a river and above the river you will find a cave in the rock–face where an old man, a hermit lives. He will be able to tell you more."

Offerus set off and found everything just as the men had told him. He climbed up to the rock–face above the river following a narrow path which led to the cave. The hermit looked in astonishment at the giant standing before him.

"What do you want from me?" he asked

"Tell me, old man," said Offerus, "where can I find this king called Christ who has power in all the earth and in heaven?"

"There are two ways," declared the hermit. "One is to find a quiet spot like mine. Then you must eat only a very little and you must read the stories of holy scripture."

"That is not the way for me," replied Offerus. "I cannot read, and I cannot keep still. Look at the strength of my arms. They want to be doing things."

The hermit nodded and went on: "Listen then to the second way. The second way is to serve people with all your strength. Do you see the broad river down there? There is no bridge across it, and yet every day many wayfarers wish to cross to the other side. Go down there, build a hut by the stream and ferry people over on your strong shoulders."

"Then will I meet the king called Christ?" asked the giant.

"One day he will come for you," answered the old man.

"Then I will gladly do as you say!" exclaimed Offerus. He thanked the old man and walked down to the river. There he soon built a hut by the bank, cut himself a strong staff from a young tree, and from that time he ferried the travellers across without ever thinking of asking payment. If anyone gave him bread or fruit, he would thank them.

The first year came to an end. Offerus climbed up to the hermit's cave and said: "Old man, the king has not yet come."

"Carry for another year. He will come."

Once more the faithful giant went down to the river. Every year he climbed up to the hermit to say that his king had not yet come. The old man sent him down for the seventh time, and still Offerus did not grumble.

One wild night when a terrible storm was raging outside, Offerus was sleeping in his hut. Although he was in a deep sleep he suddenly awoke. He thought he could hear a voice calling him from the other side. He rose up, seized his strong staff and stepped into the raging waters. But arriving at the other side he found no one. Only the wind roared in the trees.

"Did I only hear the wind roaring in my sleep?" he thought. He went back and lay down again in his hut. But hardly had he fallen asleep before he woke again with a start. He had quite clearly heard a child calling. Once more Offerus waded through the water. The waves were not so high any more, and the wind had died down. But on the other side there was still no one to be seen. Offerus called out into the night, but there came no answer.

"Strange," he growled into his beard. "I am quite sure I did hear someone calling."

But there was nothing he could do except go back and lie down in his hut.

For the third time he awoke. Outside the waves and the wind were silent. A silver clear voice was calling: "Come over, Offerus."

As he came out of the hut, he could see a light shining on the other side. It seemed to him that a child was standing in the light waiting for him. Offerus waded through the river and could now see the slender figure completely surrounded by the light. Once on the other side, Offerus knelt before the child and lifted him gently on to his shoulders.

"Are you sure you can carry me?" asked the child gently.

Offerus laughed and stepped into the flowing water. But as he waded back through the torrent, the child began to grow heavier and heavier on him. With every step Offerus sank lower and lower. The wind and the water again began to roar, and the waves rose high against his beard and clothing. In the middle of the river Offerus almost stumbled on to his knees, and he felt as if he were carrying the whole burden of the earth upon his shoulders. Just as he thought that he was going under, he turned his head to look up and said in despair: "O child, how heavy you are!"

The child above him answered with a clear voice: "Offerus, you are carrying more than the world, you are carrying him who has created it."

The giant renewed his efforts and struggled on as far as the riverbank, each step becoming harder and harder. At last he set down the child and sank exhausted to the ground.

"Who are you?" he murmured, at the end of his strength.

"I am the king called Christ," answered the child quietly.

Then, as Offerus looked up, he saw a wonderful light surround the child and the child's face shining like the sun, and a wreath of stars round his head.

"You have waited seven years and have served me faithfully. So now I shall baptize you with my name: from now on you shall be called Christ–Offerus. When you go back to your hut, place your staff in the earth. When green leaves shoot from the dead wood, then you will be with me."

The light faded away and the child was gone. Christofferus' shoulders ached still with the burden he had borne but he straightened up, strode to his hut and planted his staff deep into the earth.

The following day, when travellers called to the giant to come and ferry them, no one came out of the hut. They went to the door of the hut and found the giant's staff in the ground, shooting all over with green leaves. The travellers called loudly to the giant but he did not come. Inside the hut, they found his lifeless body lying on the ground.

When this became known many people came from far and near to mourn the good ferryman who had carried them across the river by day and night, in storm and bad weather. A messenger went up to the hermit and told him what had happened.

The old man nodded and said: "I know that Christofferus met his king. One day the king called Christ will come for me, too."

Busy Lizzy of Clausthal

Karl Paetow

A long time ago, in the town of Clausthal in the Harz region of Germany, there lived two poor girls. They had neither father, mother nor relations, and while still young they had to earn a sparse living by their own hands. In those days women's work was limited to housework and distaff and so the girls tried to earn their daily bread by spinning.

Now the two sisters were as unlike each other as straw–stalks and ears, which of course grow out of the same root and yet are so different in their nature. One of the girls was arrogant and stupid; the other was thoughtful and hard working; one was a gossip and lazy; while the other was quiet, got on with her work and tried to increase her means. When the industrious one, Lizzy, put her spinning–wheel away in the corner by the stove at eleven o'clock at night, the lazy one had already been taking her ease for a couple of hours or had gone to sleep.

One Easter Eve, busy Lizzy sat as usual and span her distaff. The even thread ran smoothly from her fingers. But the lazy one had not even started her task. She went out after the lads and ran and jumped with them round the Easter fire. Meanwhile Lizzy went on spinning and thought only of her work. The night–watchman sang out the hours over the rooftops. Then, as she had just spun the last of her flax, the latch of the door rattled and in came a beautiful lady clothed in white. Lizzy knew at once that it was Mother Holle, the fairy godmother of those parts. She had long golden hair, and held in her hand a full distaff as white as silver and shining like silk.

Mother Holle nodded gravely to Lizzy, came nearer, and tested the girl's thread. The lady then said to her in praise:

> Dearest Lizzy
> always busy,
> fine is your thread,
> well earned is your bread.

Then she touched the spinning–wheel with the silver distaff, smiled and went away.

Soon after this apparition, Lizzy went to bed. But she could only go to sleep once her sister had come back from her gallivanting. The beautiful silly girl laughed and threw herself on to her bed, boasting of all the wonderful things that Lizzy had missed that evening.

When the Easter sun shone in through the window, Lizzy was the first to wake up. In astonishment she rubbed her eyes, for her spinning-wheel was glowing gold and the whole room was full of golden light. Quickly she jumped to her feet and rubbed the golden spinning-wheel with her finger and tried to lift the wheel from the ground. But it was too heavy to lift because right from the distaff to the treadle it was pure solid gold. And the thread which she had been spinning on Easter Eve was shining like silk. She wound off skein after skein and hung them up in tens on the shelf with hooks. But the spool remained full and there was no end to the yarn. So she had an endless source of wealth as recompense for all her faithful work.

Now the lazy one, seeing this, greedily hauled out her own spinning-wheel covered in dust. But oh dear, where usually the unspun flax sat on the distaff there was only grey straw. And then, fearing the worst, she looked at her store of flax in the chest and found there, instead of the lovely bales, only chopped straw and chaff.

That is why people in the Harz region still say today: On Easter Saturday the distaff must be empty, or else Mother Holle will come and bring you chopped straw.

Guracasca

A Romanian folk tale

There was once a farmer's boy, the son of poor parents. He was quiet, gentle and hard—working. And he was kind, too; if anyone ever asked him a favour, he never refused. Because he was usually silent, and more often listened wonderingly than had anything to say, the other lads nick—named him "Guracasca" which means "one whose mouth gapes in amazement." In other words, a bit of a simpleton.

But that did not bother Guracasca too much. Why, he had eyes that made the girls love—sick, and curly hair as black and shining as the feathers of a raven, tumbling down to his shoulders. When he led his cows to the fountain, the girls would all send secret glances his way and more often than not one or other of them would be bold enough to turn and see if he would speak to them.

So Guracasca went happily about his work without any cares at all. He was content above all that his master, the farmer, thought well of him. And the farmer was pleased, extremely pleased. How was it that the cows which Guracasca tended were more beautiful and gave better milk than those tended by the other farmhands? Guracasca always seemed to know where to find the richest pastures and wherever his feet trod, the grass rejoiced and grew twice as quickly. Why was this? Because Guracasca had been born in a good hour. The Ursitori, the fairy fates who know what lies in store for us, had stood at his cradle and prophesied that he would go far in life. But Guracasca had no inkling of what they had in store for him.

One afternoon Guracasca came to a meadow strewn with flowers and saw a large bushy tree in the middle of it. He went up to the tree and because he was tired he lay down in its shade. He had chosen a good spot. The tree was so tall that it seemed to reach the clouds and in its branches lived hundreds of birds, twittering and building their nests. Hardly had he begun to listen to their singing than he fell asleep. But a dream brought him suddenly to his feet. A fairy more beautiful than all the fairies of heaven and earth appeared to him and said: "Stand up and go to the emperor's court." Then the fairy disappeared.

"Hoots, toots, what on earth does that mean?" Guracasca cried out, and all day he puzzled over it in vain. Next afternoon he came to the same meadow and lay down again under the same tree among the many flowers; and again he dreamed the same dream.

"Well, blow me down, who's making a fool of me now?" he cried out jumping up.

Once more he racked his brains but he could not figure out what he should do. On the third day the fairy appeared to him again and threatened him with sickness and the most miserable torments if he did not obey. So in the evening, once he had cared for the animals Guracasca went to his master and said: "Master, the thought has come to me that I should go away and try my luck in the wide world. Be so kind as to pay me my wages."

"But Guracasca, what are you going to do in the wide world? Don't you know how wicked the world is? Are you not contented with your wages, or don't you get enough to eat?"

"I have enough to eat, and it is not because of the wages, but I have a mind to go out into the world."

"Don't let the bees buzz in your bonnet, Guracasca. Listen, I'll have a look round for a girl for you whose mother and father will give her some household things as a dowry, and I myself will add some extras. Then you can set up house and not go wandering about in the world."

"My mind is not bent on setting up house, master. All I want is to go off."

Then the farmer saw that Guracasca would not change his mind and so he paid him his wages. Then the lad went off on his travels. In due time he came to the emperor's court and asked if they needed a manservant. It so happened that the gardener needed a spruce–looking lad as the princesses were always scolding him for taking into his service the roughest and most uncouth fellows to be found anywhere.

Now Guracasca was certainly a fine figure of a lad all right but, as far as clothes went, all he had was the coarse tunic of a herdsman. So the gardener had him all spruced up with a smart outfit and then every day he had to tie up twelve bunches of flowers and take them to the emperor's twelve daughters when they came out to go walking in the garden.

On these twelve young ladies the Ursitori had laid a spell at their birth. They had given them an irresistible desire to dance, and had ordained that they would not marry until a man freed them of this desire to dance and put love into the heart of one of them.

Every night the princesses danced through twelve pairs of white silk slippers, and no one understood how it happened. To try to bring an end to it, the emperor shut his daughters up in their room every night. This room had nine iron doors and at each door there were nine iron padlocks. But the emperor did not know that the Ursitori had ordained that the girls should dance all their lives if no one came to break the spell.

The emperor was extremely worried. Every suitor who came to the palace was rejected by the princesses. How long could he keep up this dreadful expense for so many silk slippers? And were his daughters' hearts made of ice so that no suitor ever pleased them?

In the end he made a proclamation that the man who could solve the mystery and tell him where his children danced in the night would receive one of the princesses as his wife.

Now from all sides new suitors came: emperors' sons, princes' sons, sons of the great nobles and sons of the lesser nobles. One after another, they kept watch at night in front of the doors of the twelve sisters. And one after the other, eleven of them simply disappeared. Each time the emperor came impatiently in the morning to receive their news, he was told that they were not to be found.

Then the remaining suitors lost all desire to keep watch and began to slip away. So the emperor just had to go on buying twelve new pairs of white silk slippers every day, and the worry that his daughters might grow to be old maids with grey hairs never having worn the bridal crown weighed more and more heavily upon him.

Guracasca did his duty excellently. The gardener praised him, and the princesses were happy with his bunches of flowers. When he handed over the bunches to them, he lowered his eyes, and in front of the smallest princess whose hand was as white as milk, he turned as red as a peony. He would have liked to ask the emperor if he could keep watch before the princesses' room but he was afraid that he would be sent away in disgrace and with curses for such presumption. He told himself that his nose was not made for the scent of such a fine flower but nonetheless his heart nearly broke for longing for the littlest princess.

Then one night he had a dream again. The very same fairy of the blossoming meadow appeared to him again and said: "Go into the corner of the garden that lies to the east of the palace. There you will find two shoots of laurel, one the colour of cherry, the other rose–coloured, and beside them a golden hoe, a golden watering–can and a silk towel. Dig out the two shoots, and put them into new pots. Hoe them every day with the golden hoe, water them with the golden watering–can and dry them with the silk towel and care for them like the light of your eyes. When they have reached the height of a man, you may ask them for what you will and they will not fail you."

Before Guracasca could thank her, the fairy had vanished. Still half asleep he went into the garden and was quite dumbfounded to find everything just as the fairy had described to him.

He dug the shoots out and put them in new pots. He hoed them every day with the golden hoe, watered them with the golden watering–can, dried them with the silk towel and looked after them like the light of his eyes. They grew as if by magic and in a very short time they had reached the height of a man. Then he stood before the cherry–red little tree and said:

> Daphne, Daphne, laurel tree,
> with the golden hoe I hoed you,
> with the golden watering–can I watered you,
> with the silken towel I dried you.
> Give me the power to be invisible
> whenever I wish.

Then the tree sent forth a bud. The bud grew bigger and rounder till it burst and opened. Out came a flower such as Guracasca had never seen before. He plucked it and kept it hidden, tucked away in his shirt.

That evening he took the flower in his hand, wished to make himself invisible, and slipped in secretly with the princesses when they went to their bedroom. Then he saw that they did not lie down to sleep. They combed their hair, put on ribbons and wore their most beautiful gowns. Then, when they were all dressed up, the eldest called: "Are you ready, girls?" and the others replied: "Ready." Whereupon the eldest stamped lightly on the floor and the floor opened. They went down a hidden passage into the depths, and Guracasca followed behind. Soon they came to a garden surrounded by a copper wall. In the wall was an iron gate in front of which the eldest stamped her foot again. The gate opened but as they were going out through the gate the gardener's boy trod on the littlest princess's dress. She turned round and called: "Sisters, there is someone behind me who has trodden on my dress."

"Don't be so nervous," the others reproached her. "There is nobody there. You must have caught your dress on a thorn."

They went through a wood with silver leaves; they went through a wood with golden leaves; they went through a wood where diamonds and precious stones hung on the branches and sparkled so brightly that Guracasca's eyes began to hurt. Behind the wood lay a shining lake with a little island where there stood a palace of astonishing beauty. The palace sent out rays of light like the sun and it was so amazingly built that every room was inside another room and still every one had windows on all four sides looking out at the wonderful gardens and waters of the lake.

On the shore lay twelve little boats and in each one waited an oarsman splendidly dressed. The princesses embarked, and Guracasca took his place unseen beside the littlest one. Then the boats rowed away one after the other but the last one lagged a little behind. The oarsman could not understand why his boat was so heavy that night, but using all his strength he managed to reach the island.

Here music was playing, so irresistible that you would have to dance at once whether you wanted to or not: the notes lifted you up and turned you round. As quick as lightning the girls were inside the palace and there were the eleven enchanted suitors waiting for them in a hall that was so long and so wide that you could not see where it began or ended. Guracasca also went in and truly his mouth gaped in astonishment and his eyes nearly popped out with all that there was to see. But was he able to stand quietly gazing at the milk–white walls with their rubies and sapphires, the golden pillars and cornices and the burning torches in their silver stands? Not at all! Here where even the tables and benches and the candlesticks danced, he too danced, hopped and leaped without ceasing. And the princesses, as well, danced and danced with all the steps that there are. They danced the Hora and the Sürba, the Girdle Dance and the Gypsy dance, they played the Pepper Game, One–and–One and In–Front–of–the–Tent until their slippers were worn to bits and dawn came. Suddenly the music stopped, and servants clothed in silk brought in tables laden with the finest foods. The gardener's boy stood there with his mouth watering.

When the table was cleared the princesses started back home and Guracasca followed them. When they came to the silver wood, he thought he would just break off a twig. As soon as he did so, it seemed as if there was a raging storm in the tops of the trees, but not a breath stirred and not a leaf moved. The girls were startled and called out in fright: "What could that be?"

"Well, what could it be?" said the eldest calmly. "I'm sure it was the wonder–bird that nests in our father's palace, flying through the trees, because only the wonder–bird could find its way here."

Then the princesses returned to their bedroom through the same passage in the floor.

When next morning the gardener's boy tied up the bunches, he hid the silver twig in the bunch for the littlest one, and the little princess was puzzled when she found it.

Next night the same happened again only this time the lad broke off a golden twig. When the littlest one found it in her bunch of flowers the next day, it was as if a burning shaft went through her heart. In the afternoon she found an excuse to go for a walk and she met the gardener's boy. She said to him: "Where did you get the twig that you hid in my bunch of flowers?"

"From a place that you know only too well, Your Highness."

"Does that mean that you have followed us and you know where we spend the night?"

"That is right, Your Highness."

"How did you follow us, and how did you reach the place?"

"In secret."

"Take this purse of money and do not betray us with a single word."

"I do not sell my silence, Your Highness."

"If you say a word about us, I will see to it that you lose your head."

These severe words were in her mouth, but in her heart she felt that the gardener's boy was becoming more and more handsome every day.

Next night Guracasca broke a diamond twig from the tree, and at the noise that arose the eldest again calmed her sisters. But when next morning the littlest one found the diamond twig in her bunch, she thought: "The gardener's boy has a bidding look in his eye, and in his figure he is a match for any emperor's son."

In the evening she told her sisters that the gardener's boy knew where they went at night. They crowded together and whispered how they could steal away his senses as they had done with the other eleven. Guracasca, however, heard everything for a hedgehog had come up to him in the garden and murmured "Watch out!" and so he had made himself invisible to listen to the princesses.

When he found out what they were planning, he went to the rose-coloured laurel tree and said:

> Daphne, Daphne, laurel tree,
> with the golden hoe I hoed you,
> with the golden watering–can I watered you,
> with the silken towel I dried you.
> Give me the shape and the sharpness
> of an emperor's son.

The tree sent out a shoot which grew round, burst and opened. A wonderful flower came forth and Guracasca plucked it and hid it tucked away in his shirt. Then his weather–beaten skin fell away from him, his skin became fine and his mind as sharp as a razor, and when he looked down at himself he saw that he was wearing the clothes of an emperor's son.

So he went and presented himself to the emperor as a suitor and said that he wished to spend the night watching his daughters. The emperor of course did not recognize him and said that he would gladly have spared such a handsome prince from his doom, but he introduced him to the princesses. Only the littlest one recognized the gardener's boy.

That night he was taken down the passage in the floor with the girls, and led to the palace. There he danced with the girls and the enchanted suitors, but he took care never to step inside a circle. At the sight of all the delicious food, he curbed his appetite. When they came to the table, the princesses gave him the drink that would cast a spell on him. He lifted the goblet and raised it to the littlest one, saying: "Do you wish me to drink?"

She answered: "Do not drink! I would rather be a gardener's wife with you than an empress without you."

Guracasca threw the drink behind him and cried: "Have no fear, Your Highness. By my heart, you will never be a gardener's wife!"

Everyone heard the words exchanged between the two and as soon as they were spoken, the hall dissolved like mist in the sun. Suddenly it was bright daylight and the twelve maidens found themselves back with the twelve young men in the emperor's palace.

The emperor was so surprised that he took hold of his beard in both hands. Guracasca stood before him and told him the whole story of the slippers and the enchanted palace. Then he asked for the hand of the youngest princess and was gladly given it.

Now the other sisters came before the emperor and each one led a suitor by the hand. Their father granted them their wishes, too, and the general rejoicing was so great that not even a hundred mouths, let alone the one single mouth that God has given me, would be enough to describe it.

The day after the littlest daughter was married, she asked her husband what power he had used to break the spell and he told her. And so that he would never have that power over her again and they could stand as equals, she asked him to go with her and cut down the two laurel trees and burn them. And they did.

The Three Poppies

A Spanish folk tale

There was once a peasant farmer who had only one child, a daughter, and he loved her very much. But it was a great sadness to him that the girl could not speak.

One day when he was travelling past three tall stones far off in the countryside, the farmer saw three very beautiful poppies. Without thinking, he picked them and brought them home for his daughter.

The girl took the poppies with a happy smile and went into the house. But all of a sudden she remembered the country saying that it was bad luck to pick a poppy and take it indoors. So when she reached the kitchen, she decided she would destroy them. With that she threw the first of the poppies into the fire where it burned up. Then instantly a handsome youth appeared to her and asked her: "What is it with you?"

And when she did not answer he said: "You won't speak to me? Well, by the three tall stones you will find me." And he disappeared.

Then she took the second poppy and threw it in the fire. At once there appeared another fine–looking youth who said to her: "What is it with you?"

And when she did not answer he said: "You won't speak to me? Well, by the three tall stones you will find me." And he, too, vanished.

Maria, for that was the maiden's name, took the last poppy and threw it in the fire; then again a youth appeared before her and he was the most handsome of the three, and he asked her: "What is it with you?"

And when she did not answer he said: "You won't speak to me? Well, by the three tall stones you will find me." And he went away.

Then Maria grew very sad for she had fallen in love with the last youth who was the most handsome of the three, and after a few days she decided to leave her home and go and seek the three tall stones.

She set off all alone and travelled on and on until she came to the place where the three tall stones stood and, as the poor girl was very tired, she sat down on the ground and began to weep. In the midst of her tears, she saw that one of the three stones opened and out of it came the youth with whom she had fallen in love and he said to her: "What is the matter? Why are you weeping?"

When he saw that she just went on weeping and did not answer, he said to her: "Do not grieve. Up there on the nearby hill you can see a farmhouse. Take this letter to the mistress of the house and she will take you on as a maid."

The girl got up and when she came to the hill she saw a very lovely farmhouse. Now you must know that the mistress of this house had had three sons who were enchanted when out hunting and they had never returned so that their mother did not know where they were.

As Maria had been told, she went and found the mistress of the house and gave her the letter. And when the mistress saw how young and beautiful Maria was but that the girl could not speak, she felt sorry for her and agreed that she could stay there as her girl. Soon, because she was very industrious and willing, Maria became a favourite of the mistress, so much so that the other maids became jealous and began to hate her. Between them, they decided that they would turn their mistress against her. So one day they went to their mistress and said: "Do you know what Maria has said?"

"How, when the girl cannot speak?"

"She told us with signs that she does not understand why you have so many servants for she says that she could wash all the dirty washing in one day herself."

"Come here, Maria," said the mistress. "Did you say that you could wash all the dirty washing in one day all by yourself?"

Maria just shook her head in silence.

"The maids all say however that you did, so now you will have to do it or leave the house."

Then she commanded some of the servants to take all the washing down to the river. Poor Maria went to the three tall stones and began to weep. At once one of the stones opened and the handsome youth appeared and asked her: "What is the matter? Why are you weeping?"

She did not answer but went on weeping. Then he said: "Go back to the washing that my mother has given you to wash, and do not worry. Go to the river and mouth the words: 'Birds of the whole world come and help me to wash.'"

Then Maria went to the river and hardly had she mouthed the words when she saw coming from all directions a whole flock of birds of different kinds, and they all set to and did the washing. In minutes all was finished, and when the servants came in the afternoon everything was already dry.

The mistress was so happy then that she grew even fonder of her new girl. But that only made the other maids more angry and they set about finding more ways to make Maria lose favour with her mistress.

Now the poor woman had mourned her three sons so much that her eyes had become weak from weeping. The maids went to her and said: "Do you know what Maria has said?"

"How, when she cannot speak?"

"She told us with signs that she knew where the healing water for eyes can be found."

"Indeed," said the mistress. "Come here, Maria. So you know where the water can be found that will make my eyes well again, and you did not tell me?"

Maria shook her head in silence.

"Well, as they have said it, they must have learned it from you, because they would not lie. Either you bring me the water, or you shall never come back into this house."

Poor Maria departed and, as she did not know where the water was, she went to the three tall stones and sat down under them weeping. But the youth who heard her tears appeared again and said to her: "What is the matter? Why are you weeping?"

She did not answer and he went on: "Take this glass, go to the bank of the river and mouth the words: 'Birds of the whole world come and weep with me.' When they have all let a teardrop fall into the glass, the last one will let fall a small feather. Dip this feather in the glass and wipe your mistress's eyes with it and they will be healed."

So Maria did all that: she went to the river with the glass and mouthed the words: "Birds of the whole world, come and weep with me."

As before, flocks of birds came from all sides, and every one let a teardrop fall into the glass until it was full. When the last one flapped its wings, a bright feather fell to the ground. Maria took the glass and the feather and went back to the house to find her mistress. She dipped the feather into the glass, wiped her mistress's eyes with it and, after a few moments, the eyes were better.

The mistress was so delighted with her girl that there was nothing she would not do for her. But the other maids became maddened as if they were possessed of the Devil and could not wait to get Maria put out of the house. One day they went to their mistress and said to her:

"Do you know what Maria has said?"

"How, when she cannot speak?"

"She told us with signs that she knows where to find your sons."

"She cannot possibly know that."

"Yes, mistress, that is what she said."

The mistress called Maria to her and asked her if she had said that she knew where to find her three sons. Maria only shook her head in silence.

"But the maids all say that you did, and so you must find them just as you have done the other two things."

Poor Maria went out to the three tall stones and began to weep. The youth appeared and said: "What is the matter? Why are you weeping?"

She went on weeping without answering and he continued: "I know what it is. My mother has commanded you to find us. But do not worry. Go to her with this note. It tells her that she must gather all the women of the neighbourhood together and they must come in a procession with lighted candles and go three times round the stones. Then we shall be freed. But on no account must any candle blow out."

Then Maria went back to her mistress and told her what to do. The mistress called all the women together and gave each one a lighted candle, and to Maria she also gave one. Then they all went in a procession to the three tall stones and walked three times round them. But as they walked round for the third time, a sudden puff of wind came and blew Maria's candle out. Remembering what the youth had told her, she gave a dreadful cry and said: "Oh alas, my candle has gone out."

Instantly the stones opened and the three brothers appeared, and the youngest declared to Maria: "Thanks be to God that you spoke."

The three youths then recounted how a magician had enchanted them when he had found them in this magic place, and had changed them into poppies, saying that they could only be released when a person who took the three poppies indoors should come and speak by the stones.

The mother and her three sons were overjoyed to be reunited. The youngest son asked Maria to marry him and now, full of happiness at being able to speak, she could hardly stop saying "Yes." The young couple were married and for the rest of their days they were happy and contented. Now Maria was mistress of the maids, and they put nothing more in her way but begged her forgiveness, and she forgave them all.

The Legend of the Hidden Icon

Anne–Monika Glasow

Ever since he had fled from his former master's heavy blows, young Pro–
chor had stayed with Father Makary in the forest hermitage. Prochor was
a poor orphan who had always been in the wrong whatever he did or
said. Father Makary had found him half–dead with fear and hunger on his
doorstep, and had cared for him until he was restored to health in soul
and body. When Father Makary found out that Prochor did not belong to
anyone, he kept him in his small cabin deep amongst the trees. Now
Prochor had been there for a very long time — he did not know how to
count time by years — and he had grown into a strong but quiet lad,
happy in his isolation with Father Makary.

Now he was alone in the cabin for the first time. Father Makary had
gone to the nearest monastery two days' journey away, to take part in the
festival of Christ's Ascension, the festival of the outpouring of the Holy
Spirit and the festival of the Holy Trinity.

Father Makary said to Prochor as he left: "You must stay here, Pro–
chor, and feed the birds and the animals when they come at their accus–
tomed times. Animals are the creatures of God. We should not forget
them on holy days."

Prochor gladly stayed behind. He did not like the monastery. The strict
rules and the narrow cells oppressed him though he was deeply affected
by the burning candles and the resplendent gold of the church. Here in
the simple hermitage in the depths of the quiet forest he was able to pray
more reverently and he felt himself nearer to the saints.

As he had been bidden, he looked after the animals and gave them
crumbs of the dry bread that was often his own and Father Makary's only
food.

He went round the little hut and made sure that all was clean and in
order. The room seemed to him bigger than usual, big in the stillness and
loneliness. But he was not afraid. In the corner over the perpetual lamp
there was a Christ–icon which Father Makary had painted. Prochor knew
that Father Makary never made any decision without seeking advice

before the icon in prayer. The old man would never part with it however much he was offered by the rich merchants and high-ranking officers who came to seek his wisdom. They had offered him great sums of money and generous gifts, saying: "Give us the icon, little father, to save us and strengthen us poor sinners against the Evil One."

But he would give them other icons of saints which he had painted and told them to take their gifts to the monastery. For himself, for Prochor and for the birds and animals he kept only the essentials.

"I wonder why it is only this icon that he never gives away," Prochor wondered to himself and asked Father Makary about it.

"If our Redeemer bestows his grace on us through his image being present in our simple hut, and so gives us healing and blessing, and keeps us from Evil, then we cannot betray him like Judas for money even though it should be thirty times thirty pieces of silver."

Father Makary had painted many icons, but only "when God called upon him to do so" and let him "see" what he should paint. For this work he had received permission from the Oldest Monks in the monastery. Whenever Father Makary knelt before the icon of Christ all night in deepest prayer, then Prochor knew that soon the old man would begin to paint. He would rise from his prayer and go out at sunrise to a nearby hill, and when he came back he was so remote and strange that Prochor did not dare to speak to him. The old man would open the door to the little room and close it behind him. Prochor only went to him when called. That might not be for many days. Then Prochor would help him to prepare new colours. Everything that was needed Father Makary would gather himself and mix every colour with his own hands.

"If grace is given to us to make visible to men what is holy, then we shall be given the colours for it, for ordinary colours with which we paint earthly things are not fit for it."

Only at those times when he was allowed to help the old man did Prochor enter that room. Then he could see how the picture was developing and how a living spirit-filled icon came into being.

Now Prochor opened the door of the room. There were the colours which Father Makary had used for the last icon. On the simple easel stood a wooden board divided into three parts and prepared for painting. Prochor stared at it for a while with great longing.

"I wonder if I shall ever paint as Father Makary does," he thought. "To be sure I have never yet seen an angel or a saint, and Father Makary says that we may not paint what comes out of ourselves but only what is given to our sight."

Furthermore, he knew that one was allowed to begin this holy work of painting only with the permission of the Oldest Monks in the monastery. He sighed deeply, left the room and carefully closed the door.

It was still three days before the festival of the Ascension. As Father Makary had taught him, Prochor fasted and prayed by day and by night. On the last night of the three days he was kneeling as usual before the Christ-icon. No words could he find but his heart was full of devotion, reverent love and dedication. Shortly before sunrise he left the hut. It was almost as if he was taken by the hand and led up to the open hill. There he knelt down to await the sunrise.

The stars had paled and the sky was bathed in a green and yellow light. Now the first gold-red rays of the sun appeared shimmering through the silver birch woods. Prochor spread his arms out: "Lord, I am ready." He spoke without knowing it. And then he saw before him a heavenly form, more radiant than the sun and purer than snow. Human words could not describe what he saw. From this vision rays of light emanated, spreading out in all directions. More and more brightly the vision shone, losing its original form and becoming like a cloud. The rays reached up into the heavens and down deep into the earth, and those rays that spread across the horizon bent down as if they would encompass the whole earth. Prochor sank with outspread arms to the ground as if he too would embrace the earth. Then he heard a voice from the depths of the earth and from the heights of heaven, saying: "Lo, I am with you always even until the end of the world."

All was still, Nature held her breath. Then a rustling began in the branches of the trees; a little uncertain twitter of birds began, growing stronger and surer until at last the whole rejoicing choir of birds sounded in the air. Two roe-deer came trustingly through the forest, and hares began to play at the edge of the meadow.

As in a dream, Prochor went back down the hill to the hut. He walked across the first room and opened the door to the second. There the wooden board stood as if it were waiting. Still as in a dreamlike state, he picked up the brush, prepared the colours and began to paint. He painted what he had seen. He knew that he had seen Christ's Ascension.

For days he painted as long as daylight lasted. At night he knelt before the Christ-icon. He neither ate nor drank. He felt no difficulty, no hesitation while he painted. How could it be otherwise; grace was upon him. Then at last a voice said to him; "Lay down your paintbrush now." He obeyed. "Look at the picture," said the voice. He looked at the picture and found in it everything that he had seen. And the picture had holy life in it: it was an icon. He sank back on to the floor and remained lying there before the finished picture.

That is how Father Makary found him. He saw the youth lying with closed eyes in a kind of radiant peace. Then Father Makary saw the picture and he knew everything that had happened.

That night he fought for the life of the youth, just as he had once fought for the life of the little child found upon his doorstep. Towards morning he heard the faint voice of the young man, saying: "Father, are you angry with me?"

"It is good that this question is your first one, but your question should be: 'Is my Redeemer angry with me?' That you were allowed to behold him was a grace and the beginning of a path of grace. But only the beginning. That you went on, following your own wishes was not right. Who gave you permission to paint what appeared to you in a blessed moment? Only the Fathers whom God has chosen can decide that, and their decision is reached only after fervent prayer."

Prochor wanted to speak but he mastered himself and kept silent in obedience.

Father Makary now pondered for a long time what should be done. He prayed for guidance before the Christ–icon. Should he report the youth's wilful action to the Oldest Monks? The rules of the monastery were very strict. Should he destroy the picture? But God was in it and it bore holy life. Should he say it was his own in order to protect the youth? How could he sully a holy thing with a lie? But to give the picture to the faithful for their worship he could not do either, for it had been created in disobedience. Could it bring healing and blessing to those who prayed?

In prayer Father Makary found what to do. He took the picture and covered it with a transparent varnish which would protect it from destruction by the elements. Then he called Prochor.

"Say farewell to the picture."

Prochor reached out his arms to the picture; with fearful eyes he looked at the stern old man, but he said not a word. Father Makary's tone became more gentle: "The picture will not be destroyed, for it is an icon in spite of everything. It will lie hidden until God himself bestows upon mankind the revelation that it bears within it."

He commanded the youth to stay behind while he took the icon and left the hut. Through the deep and trackless forest he carried the picture until he reached a spring where silver bright waters gushed from a cliff to flow down through meadows filled with flowers, bushes and trees on either hand. The old man diverted the flow of the stream with a large stone; then he made a shallow pit in the empty bed of the stream and crossing himself reverently he laid the picture in it. He anchored the edge of the picture with some heavy stones; then he removed the dam. The water, now freed, flowed back into its former bed and covered over the Ascension–icon lying in the bed of the stream.

As Father Makary left, the bushes closed behind him around the hiding place. All grew still. The water from the spring murmured mysteriously. Sunbeams fell obliquely through the branches of the tall birch–trees and when the sunbeams met the waters of the spring they sparkled in them like heavenly light. In the evening the animals came to their accustomed watering place. They bent down over the water. Their bright eyes looked intently at into the crystal–clear water. Then the animals left without drinking, and from that time on they drank lower down the stream.

Father Makary went back to the hermitage through the trackless forest. He spent the night in prayer. In the morning he called the youth.

"There are many ways of serving God," he said. "You cannot remain here with me any longer. You must leave and go into the monastery. Submit to everyone in absolute obedience and, with everything you do, bear constantly in your heart the prayer of Christ: "Jesus Christ have mercy on me and be gracious unto me." Then he will always be with you. When the Oldest Monk tells you that your time has come, return to men and serve the poor and destitute, and proclaim to them what you have seen."

Prochor obeyed and lived for many years in silent obedience. He did what Father Makary had commanded him and in due time he returned into the world to serve and help the poor. He became known as a holy man who travelled through the land seeking out the poor and wretched, the dying and the abandoned, and comforted them with the words that Christ was with them and never would leave them. He reminded the people of the words of the Redeemer: "I am with you always even until the end of the world."

People remembered afterwards that the holy man had spoken of a wonderful Ascension–icon, through which the great love of the Redeemer would be revealed; but he had said that the icon would remain hidden until the time came for it to be revealed. Asked when that should be, he smiled and said: "I do not know. We must be patient. The day will come."

Pentecost

From the Acts of the Apostles

While the day of Pentecost was running its course they were all together in one place, when suddenly there came from the sky a noise like that of a strong driving wind, which filled the whole house where they were sitting. And there appeared to them tongues like flames of fire, dispersed among them and resting on each one. And they were all filled with the Holy Spirit and began to talk in other tongues, as the Spirit gave them power of utterance.

Now there were living in Jerusalem devout Jews drawn from every nation under heaven; and at this sound the crowd gathered, all bewildered because each one heard his own language spoken. They were amazed and in their astonishment exclaimed, "Why, they are all Galileans, are they not, these men who are speaking? And how is it then that we hear them, each of us in his own native language? Parthians, Medes, Elamites; inhabitants of Mesopotamia, of Judea and Cappadocia, of Pontus and Asia, of Phrygia and Pamphylia, of Egypt and the districts of Libya around Cyrene; visitors from Rome, both Jews and proselytes, Cretans and Arabs, we hear them telling in our own tongues the great things God has done." And all were amazed and perplexed, saying to one another, "What can this mean?" Others said contemptuously, "They have been drinking!"

But Peter stood up with the Eleven, raised his voice, and addressed them: "Fellow Jews, and all you who live in Jerusalem, mark this and give me a hearing. These men are not drunk, as you imagine; for it is only nine in the morning. No, this is what the prophet spoke of: 'God says, "This will happen in the last days: I will pour out upon everyone a portion of my spirit; and your sons and your daughters shall prophesy; your young men shall see visions, and your old men shall dream dreams. Yes, I will endue even my slaves, both men and women, with a portion of my spirit, and they shall prophesy. And I will show portents in the sky above, and signs on the earth below — blood and fire, and drifting smoke. The sun shall be turned to darkness, and the moon to blood, before that great, resplendent day, the day of the Lord, shall come. And then, everyone who invokes the name of the Lord shall be saved." ' "

The Six Swans

Brothers Grimm

Once upon a time, a certain King was hunting in a great forest, and he
chased a wild beast so eagerly that none of his attendants could follow
him. When evening drew near he stopped and looked around him, and
then he saw that he had lost his way. He sought a way out, but could find
none. Then he perceived an aged woman with a head which nodded
perpetually, who came towards him, but she was a witch. "Good woman,"
said he to her, "can you not show me the way through the forest?"

"Oh, yes, Lord King," she answered, "that I certainly can, but on one
condition, and if you do not fulfil that, you will never get out of the
forest, and will die of hunger in it."

"What kind of condition is it?" asked the King.

"I have a daughter," said the old woman, "who is as beautiful as anyone in the world, and well deserves to be your consort, and if you will
make her your Queen, I will show you the way out of the forest."

In the anguish of his heart the King consented, and the old woman led
him to her little hut, where her daughter was sitting by the fire. She
received the King as if she had been expecting him, and he saw that she
was very beautiful, but still she did not please him, and he could not look
at her without secret horror. After he had taken the maiden up on his
horse, the old woman showed him the way, and the King reached his
royal palace again, where the wedding was celebrated.

The King had already been married once, and had by his first wife,
seven children, six boys and a girl, whom he loved better than anything
else in the world. As he now feared that the stepmother might not treat
them well, and even do them some injury, he took them to a lonely castle
which stood in the midst of a forest. It lay so concealed, and the way was
so difficult to find, that he himself would not have found it, if a wise
woman had not given him a ball of yarn with wonderful properties. When
he threw it down before him, it unrolled itself and showed him his path.

The King, however, went so frequently away to his dear children that
the Queen observed his absence; she was curious and wanted to know
what he did when he was quite alone in the forest. She gave a great deal
of money to his servants, and they betrayed the secret to her, and told her

likewise of the ball which alone could point out the way. And now she knew no rest until she had learnt where the King kept the ball of yarn, and then she made little shirts of white silk, and as she had learnt the art of witchcraft from her mother, she sewed a charm inside them. And once when the King had ridden forth to hunt, she took the little shirts and went into the forest, and the ball showed her the way.

The children, who saw from a distance that someone was approaching, thought that their dear father was coming to them, and full of joy, ran to meet him. Then she threw one of the little shirts over each of them, and no sooner had the shirts touched their bodies than they were changed into swans, and flew away over the forest.

The Queen went home quite delighted, and thought she had got rid of her stepchildren, but the girl had not run out with her brothers, and the Queen knew nothing about her. Next day the King went to visit his children, but he found no one but the little girl.

"Where are your brothers?" asked the King.

"Alas, dear father," she answered, "they have gone away and left me alone!" and she told him that she had seen from her little window how her brothers had flown away over the forest in the shape of swans, and she showed him the feathers, which they had let fall in the courtyard, and which she had picked up.

The King mourned, but he did not think that the Queen had done this wicked deed, and as he feared that the girl would also be stolen away from him, he wanted to take her away with him. But she was afraid of her stepmother, and entreated the King to let her stay just this one night more in the forest castle.

The poor girl thought: "I can no longer stay here. I will go and seek my brothers." And when night came, she ran away, and went straight into the forest. She walked the whole night long, and next day also without stopping, until she could go no farther for weariness. Then she saw a forest–hut, and went into it, and found a room with six little beds, but she did not venture to get into one of them, but crept under one, and lay down on the hard ground, intending to pass the night there.

Just before sunset, however, she heard a rustling, and saw six swans come flying in at the window. They alighted on the ground and blew at each other, and blew all the feathers off, and their swans' skins stripped off like a shirt. Then the maiden looked at them and recognized her brothers, was glad and crept forth from beneath the bed. The brothers were not less delighted to see their little sister, but their joy was of short duration. "Here you cannot abide," they said to her. "This is a shelter for robbers, if they come home and find you, they will kill you."

"But can you not protect me?" asked the little sister. "No," they replied, "only for one quarter of an hour each evening can we lay aside our swans' skins and have during that time our human form, after that, we are once more turned into swans."

The little sister wept and said: "Can you not be set free?"

"Alas, no," they answered, "the conditions are too hard! For six years you may neither speak nor laugh, and in that time you must sew together six little shirts of starwort for us. And if one single word falls from your lips, all your work will be lost."

And when the brothers had said this, the quarter of an hour was over, and they flew out of the window again as swans.

The maiden, however, firmly resolved to deliver her brothers, even if it should cost her her life. She left the hut, went into the midst of the forest, seated herself on a tree, and there passed the night. Next morning she went out and gathered starwort and began to sew. She could not speak to anyone, and she had no inclination to laugh; she sat there and looked at nothing but her work. When she had already spent a long time there it came to pass that the King of the country was hunting in the forest, and his huntsmen came to the tree on which the maiden was sitting.

They called to her and said: "Who are you?" But she made no answer. "Come down to us," said they. "We will not do you any harm."

She only shook her head. As they pressed her further with questions she threw her golden necklace down to them, and thought to content them thus. They, however, did not cease, and then she threw her girdle down to them, and as this also was to no purpose, her garters, and by degrees everything that she had on that she could do without until she had nothing left but her shift. The huntsmen, however, did not let themselves be turned aside by that, but climbed the tree and fetched the maiden down and led her before the King.

The King asked: "Who are you? What are doing on the tree?"

But she did not answer. He put the question in every language that he knew, but she remained as mute as a fish. As she was so beautiful, the King's heart was touched, and he was smitten with a great love for her. He put his mantle on her, took her before him on his horse, and carried her to his castle. Then he caused her to be dressed in rich garments, and she shone in her beauty like bright daylight, but no word could be drawn from her.

He placed her by his side at table, and her modest bearing and courtesy pleased him so much that he said: "She is the one whom I wish to marry, and no other woman in the world." And after some days he united himself to her.

The King, however, had a wicked mother who was dissatisfied with this marriage and spoke ill of the young Queen. "Who knows," said she, "from whence the creature who can't speak, comes? She is not worthy of a king!"

After a year had passed, when the Queen brought her first child into the world, the old woman took it away from her, and smeared her mouth with blood as she slept. Then she went to the King and accused the Queen of being a man-eater. The King would not believe it, and would not suffer anyone to do her any injury. She, however, sat continually sewing at the shirts, and cared for nothing else.

The next time, when she again bore a beautiful boy, the false mother-in-law used the same treachery, but the King could not bring himself to give credit to her words.

He said: "She is too pious and good to do anything of that kind; if she were not dumb, and could defend herself, her innocence would come to light."

But when the old woman stole away the newly-born child for the third time, and accused the Queen, who did not utter one word of defence, the King could do no otherwise than deliver her over to justice, and she was sentenced to suffer death by fire.

When the day came for the sentence to be carried out, it was the last day of the six years during which she was not to speak or laugh, and she had delivered her dear brothers from the power of the enchantment. The six shirts were ready, only the left sleeve of the sixth was wanting. When, therefore, she was led to the stake, she laid the shirts on her arm, and when she stood on high and the fire was just going to be lighted, she looked around and six swans came flying through the air towards her.

Then she saw that her deliverance was near, and her heart leapt with joy. The swans swept towards her and sank down so that she could throw the shirts over them, and as they were touched by them, their swans' skins fell off, and her brothers stood in their own bodily form before her, and were vigorous and handsome. The youngest only lacked his left arm, and had in the place of it a swan's wing on his shoulder. They embraced and kissed each other, and the Queen went to the King, who was greatly moved, and she began to speak and said: "Dearest husband, now I may speak and declare to you that I am innocent, and falsely accused."

And she told him of the treachery of the old woman who had taken away her three children and hidden them. Then to the great joy of the King they were brought thither, and as a punishment, the wicked mother-in-law was bound to the stake, and burnt to ashes. But the King and the Queen with her six brothers lived many years in happiness and peace.

The Gnome

A Swiss folk tale

In Switzerland, high up where the mountain tops almost touch the sky, a fine farmhouse stood on a little plateau. There was an old pine–tree in front of the door. It was said that a gnome lived under its roots. Anton, the hard–working young farmer, had often heard his grandmother speak of the gnome but no one living now had ever seen him, neither Anton himself, nor the old milkmaid nor the farmhand who was not so young either.

On a mild evening in May, Anton was sitting on the bench under the pine–tree, deep in thought. His pipe and tobacco lay beside him untouched. With his head in his hands and his elbows on his knees, he sat there troubled in his mind.

"What can be so bad that you have left your pipe lying there?" asked a little voice suddenly.

Anton looked up in amazement. Before him stood a shrivelled, shaggy, grey little man, staring at him with a friendly smile. Could it be the gnome his grandmother had spoken about so often?

"Won't you answer me, Anton?"

"Forgive me, I was a bit taken aback. But what is the use of my telling you? You won't be able to help me."

"You never know. Just tell me what's wrong."

"Well, you see, since mother died everything in the house goes wrong. Catherine is now too old and she can't manage everything any more by herself."

The mannikin thought deeply for a while, then he said: "Shall I look after the house? I don't ask for any more wages than just a little saucer of warm milk and a piece of white bread to dip into it."

"Is that all?" asked Anton smiling. "I'll certainly give it a try."

"Agreed. But never forget to put the milk and bread out here on the bench."

"I shall see to that," Anton assured him. "You will never be short, I promise you."

From that moment on, everything was kept in perfect order in the house. When the farmer and his man came in at noon from the field, the meal stood steaming on the table and everything had been tidied up and was clean and polished. But the little man was never to be seen.

Anton had no reason to complain about the house any more, but still he was not happy. One evening when the rambler–rose by the front door was just beginning to bloom, he sat gloomily under the pine–tree staring out in front of him. Suddenly the gnome stood again in front of him and clapped him gently on the knee.

"What's the matter this time, Anton?" he asked. "Have I perhaps not done my work well?"

"Oh no, it's not that, little man, everything is done perfectly," answered Anton. "And I am really grateful to you. But I'll tell you what it is, I often feel so lonely. Catherine is old and mopes a lot, and Sepp doesn't say a word all day."

"You should take a wife, Anton."

"You may well say that, but where on earth can I get a good wife? I don't want an old hen and nice young girls don't have a fancy to come and live up here in my lonely farm."

"I know just the one for you," said the gnome.

Then Anton had to laugh, and he asked jokingly: "A little gnome–wife?"

"No, a fresh young human child. But you will need much courage to win her."

"And where is this wonder–girl to be found?" asked Anton, who was now beginning to get curious.

"I will tell you. You know the little lake up on the Nonnenalp, don't you? You must go there on the night after St John's Day. At the edge of the lake lies a large stone that looks like a coffin. There the true bride is hidden."

"Pale and dead?"

"No, alive and with rosy cheeks. Look once in the mirror before you go to bed tonight."

At these words, the little man vanished as if the earth had swallowed him up. Or had Anton only dreamed it all? He stood up and went back into the house. At bedtime, when he was in his room, the words of the gnome came back to him. He took a candle and stood in front of the mirror. To his amazement he did not see his own reflection but that of a girl, more beautiful than he had ever seen. She wore clothes as were worn in olden times and it looked as if she was sleeping on a stone bench. Two thick blond plaits fell over a black velvet bodice with silver buttons. Her lovely face had the colour of honey and roses. Her breast heaved gently with every breath she took.

A puff of wind stirred the curtains and blew the candle out.

When Anton had relit the candle, the picture in the mirror had vanished and the glass just showed him his own reflection as usual. He fell on to his bed but he could not get to sleep.

"Tomorrow is St John's Day. When it is dark, I shall go to the Nonnenalp and wake the girl in the stone," he promised himself. Then he closed his eyes and fell asleep.

Anton did what he had planned and the following night he stood on the Nonnenalp at the edge of the dark lake. There lay the gigantic stone looking like a coffin. He heaved with all his strength but it would not budge. Disheartened, he looked about him. Above the crest of the mountain the moon appeared large and round. Its rays lit up the rock that was like a lid upon the stone and Anton thought he could make out a roughly hewn figure that resembled a hangman. Wonderingly he traced the outline with his fingers. Then suddenly he felt the stone begin to move under his hand. The lid slid gently off. Beneath there was not the beautiful maiden lying there but a shrivelled old woman who opened her eyes in amazement.

"Now the little man has played an ugly trick on me," grumbled Anton to himself. "Does he really think that I'm going to marry this old gnome-wife?"

"Since you have come to me after all," said the old woman in a pinched squeaky voice to the surprised Anton, "help me out of here."

Anton reached down his hand and the old woman sat up with difficulty and climbed out over the edge of the stone chest.

"Will you just give me a kiss, Anton?" she asked crumpling her head-scarf just like a shy young girl.

Anton drew back, disconcerted.

"I knew it. You don't want to. I was afraid of that. Now I shall have to go back under the stone," sighed the old woman. Two big tears rolled down her shrivelled cheeks and as she turned away she dried her eyes with a corner of her apron. Anton suddenly thought of his old mother. She had always turned away and seized her apron when tears came after he had been rough or unkind to her. Suddenly he felt pity for the old woman. He took the old face between his hands.

"Don't cry, little mother," he said, and kissed her wet cheeks.

To a mighty clap of thunder, the mountains roared and echoed, and with a sudden crash, the rock shattered into fragments. A squall screamed over the heights and the lake seethed and stormed like the sea. Thick clouds covered the moon and, in the midst of all that tumult, Anton stood trembling in deep darkness.

Just as quickly as the storm had come, it died away. The moon came out again between the shreds of clouds. It shone upon the woman beside Anton. But she was no longer an old woman. She was the beautiful girl of the mirror. She looked up affectionately at Anton with her dark eyes,

"You have released me," she said. "How can I repay your good deed?"

Anton looked at her in amazement. "What has happened?" he asked. "I do not understand."

"Let us sit down," said the girl, "and I will tell you my story. Listen then. Down in the valley my father once had a fine farm."

"The old farmstead in ruins?" asked Anton.

"Yes, that will be it. But let me go on: up here on the Nonnenalp lived our herdsman, Käse–Hans. He was as big and strong as a giant. My father thought a lot of him, but I was afraid of him. Every Saturday I had to bring him a basket full of food which was to last him a week, and you can imagine that I did not like doing it, but I could not disobey my father. Every time I took longer and longer on the way, and so I kept Käse–Hans waiting longer and longer. One time in addition to that it was bad weather so I did not go at all, but only climbed up the Nonnenalp the next morning when everyone had gone to church. Hans was sitting in front of the shepherd's hut waiting and his eyes were blazing with anger when he saw me coming.

" 'You really want to let me die of hunger up here,' he roared.

" 'One day of fasting won't do you any harm,' I answered spitefully. ' Do you think that I was going to get my feet wet in this foul weather just for you?'

"That was not nice of me, but did I really deserve such a punishment as the vicious herdsman wished upon me? He said:

> ' Keep your feet dry in the stone
> where my curse shall ban you.
> Your epitaph and key shall be
> your own hangman.'

"That same moment I found myself lying in the stone coffin. I could no longer move and a sleep as heavy as lead came over me. Once a year, on St John's Day, when the moonbeam touched the hangman on the chest, my prison would open and I could come out, but only as an old, old woman. Only if someone kissed me could I be released from the curse. Over the years, some young men came who had heard of the story of the girl in the coffin but not one felt compassion enough to kiss me when they saw how old and ugly I was. Your good heart, Anton, has now finally brought me release."

Anton put his arms round the girl's shoulders.

"Now you shall come with me," said he, "and before the corn is ripe, we shall celebrate our wedding."

Fortunately the girl had nothing against that and so the wedding was celebrated with joy and merriment.

"It is really the gnome whom we have to thank for our good fortune," said Anton some time later to his young wife. "I should really like to do something for him."

"He goes about in such a poor old smock," answered his wife. "Don't you think he would be happy if I made him a nice jacket, a little red cap and soft velvet shoes?"

She made the nicest little clothes and laid them all on the bench under the old pine–tree. When the sun had set, the gnome came out, saw the lovely clothes and clapped his hands with joy. He took off his old clothes and put on the new suit, smoothed it down admiringly, turned round on the tips of his toes and sang happily:

> Only an idle gentleman
> has clothes as fine as these.
> So no more household jobs for me,
> but a life that's full of ease.

After that the gnome disappeared and was never seen again. The dish with milk and white bread remained untouched on the bench and the work in the house and farmyard was no longer done by him. But the young couple did not mind. They were so proud of their home and so fond of each other, they did all the jobs between them; and they did them as well as the gnome, you can be sure.

The Goose–Girl

Brothers Grimm

There was once upon a time an old Queen whose husband had been dead for many years, and she had a beautiful daughter. When the princess grew up she was betrothed to a prince who lived at a great distance. When the time came for her to be married, and she had to journey forth into the distant kingdom, the aged Queen packed up for her many costly vessels of silver and gold, and trinkets also of gold and silver; and cups and jewels, in short, everything which appertained to a royal dowry, for she loved her child with all her heart. She likewise sent her maid–in–waiting, who was to ride with her, and hand her over to the bridegroom, and each had a horse for the journey, but the horse of the King's daughter was called Falada, and could speak. So when the hour of parting had come, the aged mother went into her bedroom, took a small knife and cut her finger with it until it bled. Then she held a white handkerchief to it into which she let three drops of blood fall, gave it to her daughter and said: "Dear child, preserve this carefully, it will be of service to you on your way."

So they took a sorrowful leave of each other; the princess put the piece of cloth in her bosom, mounted her horse, and then went away to her bridegroom. After she had ridden for a while she felt a burning thirst, and said to her waiting–maid: "Dismount, and take my cup which you have brought with you for me, and get me some water from the stream, for I should like to drink."

"If you are thirsty," said the waiting–maid, "get off your horse yourself, and lie down and drink out of the water, I don't choose to be your servant." So in her great thirst the princess alighted, bent down over the water in the stream and drank, and was not allowed to drink out of the golden cup. Then she said: "Ah, Heaven!" and the three drops of blood answered:

> "If this your mother knew,
> her heart would break in two."

But the King's daughter was humble, said nothing, and mounted her horse again. She rode some miles further, but the day was warm, the sun scorched her, and she was thirsty once more, and when they came to a stream of water, she again cried to her waiting–maid: "Dismount, and give me some water in my golden cup," for she had long ago forgotten the girl's ill words. But the waiting–maid said still more haughtily: "If you wish to drink, get it yourself, I don't choose to be your maid." Then in her great thirst the King's daughter alighted, bent over the flowing stream, wept and said: "Ah, Heaven!" and the drops of blood again replied:

"If this your mother knew,
her heart would break in two."

And as she was thus drinking and leaning right over the stream, the handkerchief with the three drops of blood fell out of her bosom, and floated away with the water without her observing it, so great was her trouble. The waiting–maid, however, had seen it, and she rejoiced to think that she had now power over the bride, for since the princess had lost the drops of blood, she had become weak and powerless. So now when she wanted to mount her horse again, the one that was called Falada, the waiting–maid said: "Falada is more suitable for me, and my nag will do for you," and the princess had to be content with that. Then the waiting–maid, with many hard words, bade the princess exchange her royal apparel for her own shabby clothes; and at length she was compelled to swear by the clear sky above her, that she would not say one word of this to anyone at the royal court, and if she had not taken this oath she would have been killed on the spot. But Falada saw all this, and observed it well.

The waiting–maid now mounted Falada, and the true bride the bad horse, and thus they travelled onwards, until at length they entered the royal palace. There were great rejoicings over her arrival, and the prince sprang forward to meet her, lifted the waiting–maid from her horse, and thought she was his consort. She was conducted upstairs, but the real princess was left standing below. Then the old King looked out of the window and saw her standing in the courtyard, and noticed how dainty and delicate and beautiful she was, and instantly went to the royal apartment, and asked the bride about the girl she had with her who was standing down below in the courtyard, and who she was.

"I picked her up on my way for a companion; give the girl something to work at, that she may not stand idle," the bride said. But the old King had no work for her, and knew of none, so he said: "I have a little boy who tends the geese, she may help him." The boy was called Conrad, and the true bride had to help him to tend the geese. Soon afterwards the false bride said to the young King: "Dearest husband, I beg you to do me a favour."

He answered: "I will do so most willingly."

"Then send for the knacker, and have the head of the horse on which I rode here cut off, for it vexed me on the way." In reality, she was afraid that the horse might tell how she had behaved to the King's daughter. Then she succeeded in making the King promise that it should be done, and the faithful Falada was to die; this came to the ears of the real princess, and she secretly promised to pay the knacker a piece of gold if he would perform a small service for her. There was a great dark–looking gateway in the town, through which morning and evening she had to pass with the geese: would he be so good as to nail up Falada's head on it, so that she might see him again, more than once. The knacker's man promised to do that, and cut off the head, and nailed it fast beneath the dark gateway.

Early in the morning, when she and Conrad drove out their flock beneath this gateway, she said in passing:

"Alas, Falada, hanging there!"

Then the head answered:

"Alas, young Queen, how ill you fare!
If this your mother knew,
Her heart would break in two."

Then they went still further out of the town, and drove their geese into the country. And when they had come to the meadow, she sat down and unbound her hair which was like pure gold, and Conrad saw it and delighted in its brightness, and wanted to pluck out a few hairs. Then she said:

"Blow, blow, thou gentle wind, I say,
Blow Conrad's little hat away,
And make him chase it here and there,
Until I have braided all my hair,
And bound it up again."

And there came such a violent wind that it blew Conrad's hat far away across country, and he was forced to run after it. When he came back, she had finished combing her hair and was putting it up again, and he could not get any of it. Then Conrad was angry, and would not speak to her, and thus they watched the geese until the evening, and then they went home.

Next day when they were driving the geese out through the dark gateway, the maiden said:

"Alas, Falada, hanging there!"

Falada answered:

"Alas, young Queen, how ill you fare!
If this your mother knew,
Her heart would break in two."

And she sat down again in the field and began to comb out her hair, and Conrad ran and tried to clutch it, so she said in haste:

"Blow, blow, thou gentle wind, I say,
Blow Conrad's little hat away,
And make him chase it here and there,
Until I have braided all my hair,
And bound it up again."

Then the wind blew, and blew his little hat off his head and far away, and Conrad was forced to run after it, and when he came back, her hair had been put up a long time, and he could get none of it, and so they looked after their geese till evening came.

But in the evening after they had got home, Conrad went to the old King, and said: "I won't tend the geese with that girl any longer!"

"Why not?" inquired the aged King. "Oh, because she vexes me the whole day long." Then the aged King commanded him to relate what it was that she did to him. And Conrad said: "In the morning when we pass beneath the dark gateway with the flock, there is a horse's head on the wall, and she says to it:

' Alas, Falada, hanging there!'

"And the head replies:

' Alas, young Queen, how ill you fare!
If this your mother knew,
Her heart would break in two.'"

And Conrad went on to relate what happened on the goose pasture, and how when there he had to chase his hat.

The aged King commanded him to drive his flock out again next day, and as soon as morning came, he placed himself behind the dark gateway, and heard how the maiden spoke to the head of Falada, and then he too went into the country, and hid himself in the thicket in the meadow.

There he soon saw with his own eyes the goose-girl and the goose-boy bringing their flock, and how after a while she sat down and unplaited her hair, which shone with radiance. And soon she said:

"Blow, blow, thou gentle wind, I say,
Blow Conrad's little hat away,
And make him chase it here and there,
Until I have braided all my hair,
And bound it up again."

Then came a blast of wind and carried off Conrad's hat, so that he had to run far away, while the maiden quietly went on combing and plaiting her hair, all of which the King observed. Then, quite unseen, he went away, and when the goose-girl came home in the evening, he called her aside, and asked why she did all these things. "I may not tell that, and I dare not lament my sorrows to any human being, for I have sworn not to do so by the heaven which is above me; if I had not done that, I should have lost my life." He urged her and left her no peace, but he could draw nothing from her. Then said he: "If you will not tell me anything, tell your sorrows to the iron-stove there," and he went away. Then she crept into the iron-stove, and began to weep and lament, and emptied her whole heart, and said: "Here am I deserted by the whole world, and yet I am a King's daughter, and a false waiting-maid has by force brought me to such a pass that I have been compelled to put off my royal apparel, and she has taken my place with my bridegroom, and I have to perform menial service as a goose-girl. If this my mother knew, her heart would break in two."

The aged King, however, was standing outside by the pipe of the stove, and was listening to what she said, and heard it. Then he came back again, and bade her come out of the stove. And royal garments were placed on her, and it was marvellous how beautiful she was! The aged King summoned his son, and revealed to him that he had got the false bride who was only a waiting-maid, but that the true one was standing there, as the former goose-girl. The young King rejoiced with all his heart when he saw her beauty and youth, and a great feast was made ready to which all the people and all good friends were invited. At the head of the table sat the bridegroom with the King's daughter at one side of him, and the waiting-maid on the other, but the waiting-maid was blinded, and did not recognize the princess in her dazzling array. When they had eaten and drunk, and were merry, the aged King asked the waiting-maid as a riddle, what punishment a person deserved who had behaved in such and such a way to her master, and at the same time related the whole story, and asked what sentence such a person merited. Then the false bride said: "She deserves no better fate than to be stripped entirely naked, and put in a barrel which is studded inside with pointed nails, and two white horses should be harnessed to it, which will drag her along through one street after another, till she is dead."

"It is you," said the aged King, "and you have pronounced your own sentence, and thus shall it be done unto you." And when the sentence had been carried out, the young King married his true bride, and both of them reigned over their kingdom in peace and happiness.

The Journey to the Sun

A Slovak folk tale

There once lived a kitchen boy at the court of a king. Though he was only of humble birth, he was a good-looking lad, and if you had dressed him up in a nobleman's clothes, I do not think you would have found a finer-looking lad in the whole country.

Now the king had a daughter who was a little younger than the kitchen boy. The two children were good friends as children often are when growing up together, and there was not a day when they did not play with each other. As they got older, it seemed only natural to them to go hand in hand walking in the royal garden. All this, of course, hardly pleased the king's counsellors. They put their heads together and exclaimed in horror: "The king's only daughter and a kitchen boy!"

At first the old king let their murmuring go in one ear and out the other. But as the mutterings and whisperings went on and on, he became irritated with the matter and gave orders to have the kitchen boy sent away. But oh dear, the little princess began to weep bitterly. As soon as anyone even touched the kitchen boy she began to wail most pitifully. The old king could not listen to her crying very long and every time he simply gave in, saying: "Oh well, she's only a child, in time she will have more sense."

So things went on as before. The children continued to spend hours together and walk with each other in the garden and no one dared to prevent them. As time passed, they ceased to be children, but their joy in each other continued. Now their friendship began to blossom and grow deeper every day, and every day became more beautiful and intimate.

The young princess was growing up and soon she was old enough to marry. From all sides came suitors, all of them kings' sons, but she wanted none of them. When one had gone, another even prouder came. Indeed she could have had ten on each finger! She could have chosen among them as you might choose pears from a fruit-stall. But as they pressed their claims before the throne, the dear little king's daughter only thought of how she could escape and, as soon as she could, she slipped away and was never anywhere else to be found than with her dear kitchen boy. Whenever her father asked if any of the stately suitors pleased her, she would always answer frank and free: "Dear Father, I can only say I like our kitchen boy the best, and if you wish me to marry, let me marry him!"

At first the king pretended not to hear, but what is too much to bear is too much, and in the end he was thoroughly vexed, and no wonder. So many kings' sons to choose from, and all she wanted was the kitchen boy! He called his counsellors to him and set them the question what was to be done. They said at once that he should have the kitchen boy put to death, and that would be the end of the matter. But the good old king thought it was quite wrong just to kill off the poor lad without more ado.

"Well, Your Majesty," said the wisest of the counsellors, "if you consider that an injustice, let us send the kitchen boy well provisioned on a journey which is so long that he will never come back from it even if he were to take a hundred years. Let us send him to the sun to ask it why it rises higher and higher every day till noon, and then after noon goes down and down and warms everything less and less."

"That is truly wise counsel," all the counsellors agreed, and even the king thought that his daughter would soon forget the kitchen boy when he was off on his journey to the sun and she could no longer see him.

So they summoned the youth at once, gave him new clothes, money for the journey and sent him off to the sun to bring back the answers. The king's daughter bade him farewell with tears, and he set off with a heavy heart. No one could tell him, indeed no one could even offer a vague suggestion to him which way he should go. But he was led by his own nose: he did not go eastward towards the sunrise but westward in the direction of the sunset.

On and on he went, through dense forests, along rough paths, until after wandering for a long time he came into a country where a very mighty but blind king reigned. This king heard about the kitchen boy, whence he came and whither he was going, and he sent for him at once, for he sorely needed advice which could only be given to him by the sun.

So the kitchen boy came to the king. And the dear old king, who wanted to hear it with his own ears, asked him: "My son, are you really going to the sun?"

"Yes, indeed I am," answered the youth boldly.

"Well, when you get to the sun ask how it is that I who am so powerful a king, am blinded in my old age. If you succeed in that I will leave you half my kingdom."

"Oh, I'll do that for you all right. Why shouldn't I once I've got there," promised the kitchen boy. Then the king gave him money and what else he needed for the journey.

So the youth continued on his journey to the sun. He went through dense forests, through desert valleys, where no human voice was heard and where no trace of humans was to be found, until he came to the edge of the sea.

The sea was broad and deep. His direction was neither to the right nor to the left for the sun was resting straight ahead on the horizon. But how was he to cross over the great waters? He walked up and down the shore and thought what was to be done. And while he was thus walking and thinking a great fish came up to him and the fish was half in the water and half out of the water. Its belly was like the belly of other fishes, but its back was sparkling like a glowing coal, and that came from the shining of the sun.

"How have you come hither, young man?" the fish asked him. "And where are you going to? What do you want here?"

"Where am I going to? What do I want? I should like to be over there beyond the sea, for — well — I'm going to the sun to ask him some questions."

"To the sun?" asked the fish in surprise. "Is it true what you are saying? For I too can only be helped by the sun. Can you ask the sun why I who am such a great and heavy fish can never rest at the bottom of the water like other fishes? Will you ask that?"

"Indeed I will," said the kitchen boy. "But how can I do that when I am here and the sun is at the other side of the sea?"

"I can carry you across, just you sit on my back."

Full of joy the kitchen boy jumped on to the broad back of the fish who carried him quickly to the other side.

"Make sure that you come back this way. I'll be waiting for you," called the fish after the youth who was hurrying away.

On went the kitchen boy through the empty desert where not even a bird or butterfly, not to mention a human being, was to be seen. Now he could not be far from the end of the world, for the sun was descending close to the earth near him. He ran towards it as long as he had breath.

As the kitchen boy arrived at the end of the world, he found the sun was just resting in his mother's lap. The kitchen boy bowed politely and they greeted him. The boy began to speak and they listened.

The boy asked: "Dear sun, tell me for my master's sake how it is that you climb higher and higher till noon, making everything hotter and hotter, and from noon onwards while you are going down you grow weaker and weaker?"

Then the sun answered him: "Well, little brother, just ask your master how it is that from his birth onwards he grows stronger and stronger, but then in old age becomes bowed down and weak. It is the same with me. Every morning my mother gives birth to me as a strong newly born child, and every evening she takes me on to her lap as a weak old man."

Then the kitchen boy asked why the old king had become blind in his old age while before he had had such good keen eyes.

"Yes," the sun replied. "Why did everything grow dark round him? He became blind because he had become arrogant! He wished to make himself the equal of God so he had a glass sky built with gilded stars so that he could sit on his throne high above the world and rule it all. He ought to bow humbly down to earth before God and shatter his glass sky, and then he will see as he used to."

"And the fish, why can he not rest at the bottom of the water like other fishes?"

"That is because he has not yet eaten any human flesh. But do not tell him that until you have crossed the sea and you have gone a good bit inland from the shore."

The kitchen boy thanked the sun for this good advice and wanted to leave. But the sun kept him back. He gave him a suit so fine that it could be put into a nutshell. And it was — guess what! — it was a sun–suit.

Now the kitchen boy started on his way back and soon he came to the sea. The fish at once began to ask him to tell him quickly what the sun had revealed to him. But the boy said he could not tell him anything until he had landed on the other shore. He sat down upon the back of fish and they shot through the water so that the waves splashed up behind them. As soon as they landed on the other side the boy jumped like a shot from the fish's back on to the shore and fled inland. When he had run a good way he turned round and called: "You will never rest on the bottom of the water until you have eaten human flesh."

As if a hundred devils had entered into him, the fish fell into a rage. He thrashed the sea so hard with his tail that the water flooded over on to the land and soon reached up to the kitchen boy's belt. But luckily the water was still not deep enough for the fish to reach him.

"If the Devil did not catch me that time, he will never catch me," said the kitchen boy with a sigh of relief, hastening on in the direction of the rising sun. After a time he came to the court of the blind king who greeted him impatiently: "Well, my son? Do you have the answer? Do you know why I have grown blind?"

"You became blind because you grew arrogant and wished to make yourself equal with God. If you bow down humbly to the earth before

God and let the sky of glass be smashed the world will become bright around you again and you will see as you did before."

The king obeyed. He smashed the glass–sky above him and he bowed down humbly to the earth. His eyes grew bright again and it seemed to him as if he had been led out of the grave into daylight. Right away he gave half his kingdom to the kitchen boy.

Now our kitchen boy was a king like the others, even so he did not stop for a moment, but hurried on towards home. And it was good that he hurried, for if he had been later by one hour all would have been lost.

Already from afar he could hear all the bells in his home town ringing. "What is happening here?" he asked the people crowding in the streets.

"It is the wedding of the king's daughter," they told him. It was a wonder that no one laughed at him for his ignorance as all the sparrows on the roof were chattering about it.

Quickly he considered what to do. He took out of his pocket the nut-shell and from the nutshell the sun–suit. This he put on and went straight to the church where the doors stood open in readiness for the wedding, and sat down in the first pew in front of the altar.

After a while the brightly dressed procession of wedding guests came in. As they caught sight of the rich guest in the front pew, they whispered to each other: "Who is that? What kind of a person is that?"

But no one recognized him, and no one knew where he came from. They all admired his splendid appearance and indeed they thought he was so rich and handsome that he put the young bridegroom in the shade.

Then the bridesmaids brought the bride to the altar. But she did not need to ask who was sitting in the foremost pew. She slipped out of the arms of the bridesmaids and clung to her beloved kitchen boy. Nor would she leave him for anything in the world, and not for any price would she hear about being married to the other one.

At once the king suspended the ceremony and called the kitchen boy to appear before his throne. When the lad in his sun–suit stepped before the throne, he related from beginning to end all that had happened to him.

"And what about our question for the sun? Do you have an answer?" asked the king anxiously.

"Yes, I do," replied the kitchen boy. "Every morning the sun–child is born as a fresh baby, and every evening his mother takes him back on to her lap as an old man, just as you grew into strength as a youth but must now decline into old age."

"Yes, indeed, I grew from childhood into the strength of manhood and now I have become old and my strength is in decline. But you, my children, are in the morning of your life and your powers are still

207

increasing," the king said. And with that he solemnly gave them his blessing and bestowed on them the rule of his kingdom.

The joyful lad then took his dear princess by the arm and led her to the altar. And so they were married with great rejoicing and, soon after the wedding–feast was ended, a splendid coronation was held to mark the beginning of the rule of the new king and queen.

Maria Roseta

A Spanish folk tale

There was once a young king who was still unmarried. He very much wanted to find a wife, and day and night he thought what the princess should be like to whom he should give his hand. After much thought, he decided that the best thing would be if she were a good dancer for, he said to himself: "If one day we should be hard pressed and have to escape through the window, she must be very light of foot to be able to jump down."

So he had it proclaimed throughout the country that he wished to marry; but that the girl who would marry him must first perform a task. He announced that he would set up a bed all of roses on the square in front of his palace, and the girl who could jump over this bed without touching a rose or a leaf should become queen.

As you may imagine, at this challenge simply thousands of girls came along, old and young, rich and poor, beautiful and ugly, good and bad; and they all tried to jump over the bed of roses. From all ends of the world they came, and this went on for months but no one succeeded in jumping over the bed without disturbing a rose or a leaf. The whole town came every day to the king's palace to enjoy the spectacle, and they never could have enough, for there was always something to laugh at whenever a maiden jumped too short. The poor girls who wished to become the king's bride had to undergo a lot of mockery.

One day it so happened that there came along a beautiful young widow who, young as she was, had lost her husband when she was already with child. Now this girl was so quick on her feet and so light, she took a long run and jumped with a mighty leap right over the bed. And, believe it or not, she did not even skim a rose or a leaf. Hardly had she landed than she hurried away through the crowd standing around, and however much they tried to catch her she escaped, ran home, shut the door with seven bolts and seven locks and never went out except to church on Sundays.

At first the king was delighted when he saw that at last a girl had appeared who could jump over the bed so gracefully: and when the girl ran away, he sent his servants out to bring her to him. But the servants searched here and they searched there, but nowhere could they find the light–footed jumper, nor could they find anyone who could tell them where she lived.

Then the king said: "She was the only one who knew how to jump; she is the one who will have my hand, and I shall marry no one else. One day I'll find her and know who she is."

It so happened that, when her time came, the young widow gave birth to a girl whom she called Maria Roseta. The baby was very beautiful and lovely, even more beautiful than her mother was. Years passed and the mother sent her child to school, and she was the best and most industrious pupil among all those in the class.

One day the king went past the school, looked in through the window and, seeing the girls, thought he must go in and see if his lovely jumping girl was there. When he had gone into the schoolroom, every one of them had to tell him a story, sing him a song and ask him a riddle, and the king was exceptionally pleased with them all, so that he promised them to come again and bring them each a golden chain. Maria Roseta was specially pleased as she thought the king was a fine handsome fellow, and when she came home she told her mother everything that had happened.

But her mother said to her: "When the king comes again to give you a golden chain, tell him that you do not need one, because I will give you one which is much more beautiful and valuable than his. And when he asks you how that is to be, then answer him:

> I am Maria Roseta.
> My father was a rosebush,
> my mother is a rose.
> My home is in the rose–street.
> In the rose–bed I flower alone."

After a few days the king came to the school again and with him were many servants carrying the golden chains. And the king began to give out the golden chains one to each girl. When he came to Maria Roseta she said that she did not want a chain, for she had a more beautiful one from her mother. The king was surprised and asked her who she was, and where she got the chain from. And Maria Roseta replied:

> "I am Maria Roseta.
> My father was a rosebush,
> my mother is a rose.
> My home is in the rose–street.
> In the rose–bed I flower alone."

The king was so surprised by this answer that he went back to the palace with the chain which he had intended to give to Maria Roseta.

After a number of days the king went back to the school, and once again all the girls had to tell him a story, sing him a song and ask him a riddle. This time too the king was very pleased with the girls and he promised to bring each of them a golden pin–cushion. Maria Roseta told her mother about the king's visit and his promise. Then her mother gave her a golden pin–cushion which was even more beautiful than the one which the king would bring. She told her daughter to answer the king as before.

Once again after a few days, the king came to the school with his retinue and gave to each of the girls a golden pin–cushion. When he came to Maria Roseta she refused to have one and showed her own pin-cushion which was indeed more beautiful than the one which the king was offering.

Then the king was angry and asked her where she had got the pin-cushion from, who she was and where she lived. She answered him:

> "I am Maria Roseta.
> My father was a rosebush,
> my mother is a rose.
> My home is in the rose–street.
> In the rose–bed I flower alone."

The king was quite perplexed by all this and turned his back a little bit crossly upon the school and went back to the palace with the golden pin-cushion that Maria Roseta had refused.

Some days later, the king went once again to the school, and once again the girls had to tell him stories, sing him songs, and ask him riddles. The king was pleased with everything, and promised to bring each of them a golden needle–case. Maria Roseta hurried home and told all this to her mother. But her mother brought her a golden needle–case that was more beautiful than the one which the king had promised the girls. Then she told Maria Roseta to answer the king as she had done the previous times.

After some days the king went back to the school, convinced that the girls would never have seen such beautiful needle–cases as those which he was bringing. Once again he gave one to each girl in turn, but when he came to Maria Roseta she already had one which was more beautiful. Extremely vexed, he asked her where she had got it from, what her name was and where she lived. Maria Roseta answered:

"I am Maria Roseta.
My father was a rosebush,
my mother is a rose.
My home is in the rose–street.
In the rose–bed I flower alone."

Then the king flew into such a rage that, as he stormed out of the school, he threw the needle–case at her head and all the needles stuck in her hair. The poor girl spent all morning pulling the needles out. But one needle stuck so hard that she could not get hold of it. So she set off home with the needle in her hair. On her way, she met an old woman who was a wicked witch. Without thinking of any harm, Maria Roseta begged the old woman to pull the needle out of her hair. But the witch thrust the needle deep into her head, and immediately Maria Roseta was turned into a dove.

When the poor girl realized that she had become a dove, she did not know what to do. She flew back to her home where her mother did not recognize her. Finally, in despair, she set off for the king's palace where she flew into the king's hall and sat on the back of his chair. He liked the beautiful dove so much that he allowed her to stay there and even sit on his shoulder and eat from his plate.

In this way many months went by. Often the king thought of getting married, but he still hoped that the girl who had jumped over the bed of roses would one day be found. But as she never appeared, his prospects of ever getting married seemed hopeless.

One day the oldest of his wise men came to the king and said: "Your Majesty, it is time that you sought a wife, for if you die without an heir it will cost us much strife and trouble after your death."

Then the king decided that he should follow this good advice, and because he had not found a suitable girl in his own country, he called for the captain of his ship and commanded him to sail into the neighbouring kingdom.

The captain got his ship ready and the next morning the king with seven of his wisest advisers went on board, and they set sail. But the ship would not move one hand's breadth. Then the captain asked the king and his followers whether they had forgotten anything. They all thought of this and that but they could not think of anything that had been forgotten.

At last the king clapped his hand to his head and said, "I'm the one who's forgotten something. I promised I would ask my dove if she wanted to come with us."

"Then go, my lord king," said the captain, "and ask her, for if you don't the ship won't move from this spot."

The king ran as fast as he could back to the palace, found his dove and asked her whether she would go with him or whether he should bring her something back from his journey.

Then the dove sang a plaintiff song and the king asked his wise men what it could mean. And the wisest of his wise men said: "She is singing:

> ' Fetch a piece of the stone called heartbreak,
> that brings with it laughter and tears,
> and a strand of hair that flowers
> with the promise of life or death.' "

The king promised to bring her what she desired, and hastened back to his ship. The captain weighed anchor again, raised the sail, and at once the wind blew merrily so that the ship shot like an arrow over the sea and soon reached the land of beautiful maidens. The king with his seven wise men left the ship and went on land to visit all the maidens desirous of marriage. These all came in dozens, in hundreds, indeed in their thousands, but none of them pleased the king. No matter how beautiful and lovely they were, no matter how clever and courteous, the king's heart remained cold and would not kindle towards any of them.

In this way the king and his faithful followers travelled through seven countries with twice as beautiful maidens and even more beautiful maidens, but all was in vain, for none of them pleased the king. In the end the seven wise men decided there was nothing else to be done but to return home. But when they wanted to sail away the ship would not move from the spot.

Then the captain spoke: "Is there perhaps someone amongst us who has forgotten something?"

Then the king remembered — and perhaps you can, too — what he had promised the dove before he had set off on his travels. So he went on land again and tried all the shops that were there, asking for the stone called heartbreak and for the flowering strand of hair. But he could not find them anywhere.

The king went on looking until evening, and he grew tired and sad for now he thought he would have to go back to his kingdom without keeping his promise. But as he was about to return to his ship, an old beggar–woman stopped him and asked for alms. The king generously gave her money.

Then the old woman asked him: "Lord, why do you look so sad?"

"Dear grandmother, I am looking for something which I cannot find."

"What is it, then?" asked the old woman.

"Listen to me, dear grandmother," said the king. "Perhaps you can tell me where I can find this:

> A piece of the stone called heartbreak,
> that brings with it laughter and tears,
> and a strand of hair that flowers
> with the promise of life or death."

The old woman said: "If that is all you want, I can tell you. Travel towards the south for seven hours and you will find two high mountains. On the top of one of those mountains there lies a white stone. This stone is made of the tears of a girl who is weeping for her dead bridegroom. She has wept so long and so bitterly that her tears have turned to stone. That is the stone called heartbreak.

"If you climb the other mountain you will find on top a strand of woman's hair, and it is the only one in the whole world that flowers with the promise of life or death."

Then the king was full of joy and the very next day he set off for those mountains. Sure enough he found the stone called heartbreak as well as the flowering strand of hair. He took them both and returned to his ship. Quickly they weighed anchor, set the sails, and sped back to the king's own kingdom.

There all the people were waiting with the greatest impatience, for they all wished to see the princess that the king was to have brought with him, but to their great astonishment he came back still alone and unbetrothed.

Now it so happened that the king who was very devout, arose every morning with the dawn in order to go to church with his servants. He had one servant who was a terrible sleepyhead and never could get up early in the morning. One day this fellow slept in even longer than usual and woke only after the king had left the palace with his other followers. Quickly the fellow got up, dressed himself and started to run through the corridors. But as he was dashing along, he heard a sad voice crying:

> "O stone called heartbreak
> that brings laughter and tears,
> why do you not end my sorrows?
> O strand of hair that flowers,
> where is your promise of death?"

The servant stopped in astonishment and listened to the voice. Only when it had ceased its sad cries did he go on. He reached the church right at the end as the missal was being closed. The king noticed the servant come in so late and was very annoyed. He went to him and upbraided him, but the servant begged for forgiveness and told the king about the sad voice that had held him listening to its lament. The king only half believed him and thought it was just an excuse.

Next morning the sleepyhead woke up again too late, and found himself alone in the palace after all the others had left. He dashed through the corridors and, when he got to the same place as before, he heard the voice crying again the same words in the same way.

The servant could not go on but had to stay until he had heard everything. So he reached the church only at the end of the mass and the king ticked him off severely. The servant tried to excuse himself and related again what had happened to him on the way.

The king then decided to find out for himself if the man was speaking the truth or not. The next morning he sent all his servants at the appointed time to church, but he remained alone in the palace.

Sure enough, when all was quiet, he heard the sad voice crying:

> "O stone called heartbreak
> that brings laughter and tears,
> why do you not end my sorrows?
> O strand of hair that flowers,
> where is your promise of death?"

The king could not stop listening to the sad voice till it had ended. He realized that it was coming from his own rooms and he hurried along there and found the dove, still with tears in her eyes, for it was she who had spoken.

Then the king asked her: "What is the matter, my little dove, that you wish to die?"

And the dove spoke to him in a sweet voice: "Oh my lord king, if only you knew my misfortunes. My mother was a young widow who jumped over a bed of roses without disturbing a leaf or a flower and should have been your bride. But she was already with child and soon afterwards I was born, and when I grew bigger I went to school. One day you came and promised each girl a golden chain and other fine things. My mother did not want me to have your gifts, and gave me even more beautiful presents than yours. Then you grew angry and threw your needle–case at me. A wicked witch thrust one of the needles into my head and changed me into a dove. I came into your palace to be near you and for many years I have stayed by your side, unable to tell you that I love you dearly. I never even returned home until this very week. There I found my poor mother dead and lying in her bed with no one to bury her. And my grief was so great the needle broke within me and I found that I could speak again."

When the king heard this story, he felt that his own heart would break with sorrow. He took the dove tenderly on to his lap and carefully looked for the needle in her head. When he found it, he drew out the pieces with great care and immediately the dove was changed back into a lovely girl. She was so beautiful, so graceful and charming that the king had never seen any girl her equal. He fell instantly in love and asked her at once whether she would marry him. The girl said she would but that first she must bury her mother. Then they both went together to the house in the rose–street and there the poor mother lay dead upon the bed, but as fresh and rosy as she had been in life. So they went and buried her, and when they had mourned for three days, they sent out invitations for their wedding which was a splendid affair. And thereafter the king and his bride, Maria Roseta, lived happily and had many many children.

The Swan Prince

Jeanna Oterdahl

His name was Botvid and he was fifteen years old. He was the poor orphaned son of a knight. He had no castle or sword. His noble desire to serve the highest and to help the weakest was all that he possessed.

On Christmas Eve, Botvid was walking through a birch wood. The sun was just setting. In the west the sky was like a faint red sea on which golden ships were sailing to foreign lands. The hoar–frost on the birch–trees and the snow on the ground mirrored all the colours of the sky.

Botvid stood still, entranced. He could not tell which was more beautiful, the sky or the earth. Then above his head he heard a loud noise; it was three white swans flying towards him from the east. The young lad stretched out both his arms towards them, calling: "Take me with you! Oh, take me with you!"

The birds came swooping down near him. The foremost swan which was bigger and whiter than the others bent down his head so that Botvid could look into his eyes. In its eyes he saw an unimaginably great sorrow and he felt a great love for the royal bird.

From the swan's breast, blood trickled and one of the drops of blood fell into Botvid's open hand. The drop burned like fire, but was transformed immediately into a sparkling ruby. Then the swan rose again and gave out a long drawn–out woeful cry. Its powerful wings beat the air as it continued on its way followed by the other swans.

The lad watched the swans until they disappeared in the evening twilight.

He went on his way and it was quite dark when he knocked at the door of a castle that stood grey and lonely at the edge of the forest. Here there lived an old knight alone with his hounds and falcons. The knight received him hospitably. He was pleased by the courteousness of the young lad and he was happy not to have to be alone on that Christmas Eve.

"Where do you come from, lad, and what is the purpose of your journey?" he asked.

Then Botvid told him that he had seen a beautiful white swan and that he had felt a great love for this swan. He showed his host the shining jewel.

The old man took the stone in his hand and let it sparkle in the light of the fire.

"It is a drop of the enchanted prince's blood," he said. "Long ago, when I was as young as you are now, I saw him too. Every year on Christmas Eve he comes in the hope that he will be released from his enchantment. I, too, once had such a stone."

"The enchanted prince?" asked Botvid as he felt the wing–beats of the adventure brushing his cheeks. "I shall go and free him."

"I wanted to do that, too," said the old man, "but I did not succeed nor did any of the others who tried."

"Why not?" asked the lad.

"I was afraid," replied the knight. "Remember, child, people often fail because they are afraid."

Botvid looked even more surprised, because the knight did not look as if he knew what fear was.

"I shall remember that," he said.

The following morning, the first day of Christmas, after hearing early morning mass with the old knight in the nearby church, Botvid started his quest for the enchanted prince.

He asked everywhere after the three white swans, but no one had seen them or even heard of them. As darkness was falling he came to the cave of a hermit. There he asked for a night's lodging and whether he could warm himself by the fire.

The hermit liked the lad's frankness and asked: "Where do you come from, and why are you journeying?"

Botvid brought out the drop of blood turned to stone and told the hermit about the bleeding swan with the sad eyes and the cry full of fear. The old man took the ruby in his hand and suddenly a few tears trickled down his weathered cheeks.

"My jewel sparkled just like this one," he said. "I, too, once tried to free the enchanted prince, but I did not succeed, no more than all the others who have tried."

"Why not?" asked Botvid.

"Because I doubted," answered the hermit. "Remember, child, that people fail because of doubt."

"I shall remember," said the lad without understanding exactly what the hermit meant. After spending the night with the hermit, he went on his way to seek the prince who had been turned into a swan. Everywhere he asked about the three white birds, but no one knew anything about them.

Towards evening he came to a monastery and asked for lodging. After

Botvid had shared the Christmas meal of salt fish and rice pudding with the brethren, the abbot came and spoke to him. He liked the gentle character of the lad and he asked: "Where do you come from and what is the object of your journey?"

The lad showed him the blood–red jewel and told about his meeting with the three white swans on Christmas Eve. The old abbot took the ruby in his hand and held it up to the light.

"It is the same stone," he said, "the very same stone. I, too, wanted to break the spell, but I failed just as all the others did."

"Why?" asked Botvid.

"Because I was not able to forget myself," answered the old man. "Child, remember, that people can often fail because of that."

Botvid looked at him with his eyes wide open, because the abbot did not look as if he belonged to those who think a lot about them-selves.

"I shall remember," he said, and the next morning he set out again to look for the swan prince.

For a long time he wandered on his quest. Sometimes he could not go any further for weariness, and often he was on the point of losing heart. But as soon as he looked at the blood–red ruby, his weariness and his despair vanished as if by magic. Then he remembered the beseeching eyes of the swan and its woeful cry and he felt that nothing in the world could prevent him from releasing the enchanted prince.

"How handsome he must be as a human being when he is so beautiful as a swan," he would say to himself.

One evening, Botvid came to a forest of black fir–trees that were taller than any firs that he had ever seen. The wind blew through the branches with a sound of fear and longing. Deeper in the forest glimmered the walls of a white palace, and Botvid realized that he had reached the dwelling–place of the white swan. A voice seemed to whisper to him the three golden words which he had heard from the three old men: "Fear not! Doubt not! Forget yourself!" Botvid repeated them softly and took the ruby in his hand in order to draw strength from its lustre. Then he noticed that with the ruby in his hand he could understand the language of the birds. Two blackbirds each sat in the top of a fir–tree and one of them said: "Today is the day when the prince changes his shape. Today he will get back his human form for one hour."

"Today his rescuer should come," sang the other. "This is the day when the enchantment can be broken."

"Look, his rescuer approaches," rejoiced the first blackbird. "I see a youth with a shining forehead making his way through the trees."

"But he is still small and young," answered the other. "How can he achieve what no one else could?"

Then Botvid raised his hand to make a vow, and the ruby shone between his fingers.

"I shall do it," he exclaimed. "I feel that I have been chosen."

Startled, the two blackbirds flew up and disappeared among the fir-trees.

Botvid went on his way through the forest and came to the palace. Three wild swans had alighted on the steps, and at the same moment that the lad saw them they cast off their coat of feathers and three young men stood before him. One was of more slender and graceful build than the others and when Botvid went up to him, he recognized in his eyes the look of the bleeding swan. "The prince!" thought Botvid and knelt before him, for he felt the presence of the very highest and best, the one that he had set out to serve. The prince stretched out his hands.

"Welcome," he said. "I can see by your eyes that you have come to save me. Many have tried, but no one has succeeded. That is all that I am allowed to tell you."

Never in his life had Botvid heard a voice with such a sorrowful gentle sound, and he was ready to do everything to break the spell.

"I shall give my heart's blood for your sake," he said with shining eyes.

The prince smiled sadly.

Now the prince's two companions gave Botvid a sword and shield. They clad him in armour and helmet. Botvid felt his strength increase and he waited with loudly beating heart for the monster that should come charging along and was to be overcome. But there came no monster; no dragon came. Instead he was surrounded by an unearthly twilight. The prince and his servants vanished, the white palace seemed to be swallowed up by the earth and the twilight melted into night.

Botvid stood alone in the deathly still darkness. He did not know how long he had been standing there when he heard footsteps behind him. Something slipped past him noiselessly and then went by him again. Botvid felt the air round him was filled with an evil presence. Sometimes the thing was behind him, sometimes in front of him. Terrified, he swung his sword wildly but struck nothing. The thing came close up to him and he struck out but hit nothing for there was nothing that he could touch. Now the earth started to shake and the air trembled. He felt the thing slipping right beneath his armour and touching him with cold formless hands. He broke out in a sweat of fear and shook like a leaf. His sword slipped from his powerless hands and with a cry of terror he sank to the ground, overcome by fear.

Night turned to dawning and the dawning to day. Botvid saw that the prince on the steps had collapsed. The highest, that he had wanted to serve, was now the weakest, which he had always wished to help. Fear left him. He wanted to cast himself upon his knees to ask for forgiveness, but in a moment the prince and his servants were changed back into three white swans, who rose into the air with a plaintive cry and disappeared.

"The hour is past," sang the blackbirds. "The hour is past."

But Botvid held the ruby aloft and saw the sun sparkling in the blood-red depths.

"The hour will come again," he said and then he went out into the world to learn how to overcome fear.

After a year had gone by, Botvid came again to the palace. The two blackbirds sang still in the forest, telling of the breaking of the spell, and the prince and his two servants again cast off their feathers as Botvid approached.

"Welcome," said the prince. "Only two before you have returned for a second attempt to free me. That is all that I am allowed to tell you."

The sorrowful voice penetrated even more deeply into the lad's soul than it had before.

"Nothing is too much," he said and his eyes shone more ardently than ever; but the prince's smile was sadder than the first time. The servants came forward, and clad Botvid in armour and helmet and gave him a sword and shield to his hand. The day gave way to twilight, and the twilight turned to night. All the evil powers of fear cast themselves upon Botvid. They made the ground shake and the air tremble. They grasped his neck with formless hands twice as strongly as the first time. This time however he did not try to use his sword. He stood calmly and through the dark night and the fear he saw the sad look of the prince, whose pain he wished to change to joy. Then slowly the spirits of fear withdrew and again it became bright day. Botvid was filled with joy for he thought that the prince was now freed. But when the servants had unarmed him and he approached the prince to kneel before him, he saw that the prince's face was changed. Nothing remained of the noble dignity and the patient sadness. The prince's eyes had become cold and hard. His mouth had twisted to a mocking laugh and evil words came from his lips. Botvid remained standing in front of him, dumb with amazement. Had not the prince yearned for his release, and had not he, Botvid, withstood the ordeal?

But before Botvid's eyes the prince's features changed even more. He now looked like a loathsome animal and Botvid felt his whole being stiffen with revulsion.

"No!" he cried, overcome by doubt and covering his face with his hands, "You are not who I thought you were. Why did I ever try to free you?" And as he stared at the twisted face, he shivered with horror.

But gradually the prince recovered his usual features and again Botvid saw the sad eyes and he realized that he had failed for the second time. Even before he could ask for forgiveness, the three white swans rose above the tops of the trees and disappeared with a woeful cry.

But Botvid looked through his tears at the shining ruby and made a vow to conquer doubt the next time.

A year later he came back again and everything was as before. The prince held out his hand to him and bade him welcome.

"Before you there was only one who came back for a third attempt to free me," he said, "But he failed. I may not say more."

Botvid who thought that nothing worse could happen to him than what he had already experienced, laughed confidently, saying: "There is nothing that cannot be overcome."

Once again he was clad in full armour and the powers of fear fell upon him in the darkness, three times as strong, but he triumphed over them. After that the prince became the ghastly being this time twice as repulsive. But through the distorted face Botvid saw as through a veil the true being of the prince, and behind the terrifying voice he heard the real voice of the prince. Not for one moment did he allow doubt to enter his mind and then the prince resumed his true shape.

Botvid's heart bounded with joy. "Now the ordeal is over," he thought to himself. "The prince is free and I may stay with him always as his friend and servant." But before he had time to bend his knee before the prince and swear fealty to him, the prince said: "Now you shall die," and handed him a sword.

Botvid drew back and his eyes grew round with terror. "Die?" he stammered. "Now, just when my life is about to begin?"

"You promised to give your heart's blood," went on the prince while he came nearer. "Do you not remember?"

"No, not my life," cried Botvid. "My life is all that I possess!" And his whole life beckoned him — love, heroic deeds, honour.

"Not my life, not my life!" he cried in a loud voice. "A man may say such a thing, but never do it!"

Then the sword fell from the prince's hand and as a white swan he rose above the treetops with his two servants. From his breast there fell a rain of ruby–red drops and the cry of the bird was so full of sorrow that Botvid threw himself upon the ground and wept.

"He has failed!" called the blackbirds. "Three times he has failed. He will never come back again."

But when Botvid stood up again with the ruby firmly clasped in his closed fist, he was resolved to go out into the world and learn to forget himself.

Many years passed before he thought he was ready to return to the fir-wood. But as he came near to the palace, the blackbirds recognized him.

"Look, look," they sang, "the rescuer is coming. The conqueror of fear, the master of doubt has come back to overcome himself."

Botvid bowed his head humbly and spoke no proud words now.

When he arrived before the prince, Botvid knelt down and kissed his hand. "Try me once more, Lord," he said.

The prince bade him rise to his feet and looked at him. "No one, no one has ever come back for the fourth time. Why have you come back after all that you have endured?"

"Lord," answered Botvid, "How could I ever forget you! What is life to me if I cannot serve you?"

Now he withstood the first and the second ordeal, and neither fear nor doubt could shake his courage or his faith.

Finally the prince drew the shining sword again and handed it to him. "Now you must die," he said and Botvid took the weapon from him.

"Now I can die!" And he looked at the one whom he would free and at the two who should be freed with him and at the white coats of swan–feathers which were no longer to be fetters and prisons.

Then he raised the sword, thrust it into his breast and fell to the ground. A ruby–red stream of blood spread out over the grass.

The prince bent over him and drew the weapon out. Then he laid his hand upon the wound, which closed and healed in a moment. Botvid stood up with all his strength and youth restored. He looked deep into the prince's eyes with his own fearless glance and no longer saw sorrow but joy shining there. The prince held out his hand to him.

"I thank you, my rescuer," he said.

And the blackbirds sang of the loyalty that knows no bounds and of the love that conquers everything.

The Fire-Flower

Maja Muntz-Koundoury

By the banks of a broad Russian river lay a large village. Green meadows and fruitful fields with rich black earth stretched to the horizon. Life was good in that prosperous village and each house kept its pot full of shining coins hidden under the floor. But the richest of all was the miller. He owned a fine mill and had an even finer daughter. Every lad from far around had fallen in love with fair Vasilisa and dreamed of her golden plaits and her eyes as blue as cornflowers. But the rich miller was haughty and found no one good enough for his daughter. He did not know, however, that the girl had already given her heart away to the handsomest lad in the village. He was Ivan, the village shepherd, an orphan without home or money, but with eyes which shone like stars and a smile warmer than a sunbeam. Had he been rich, Ivan could have taken any girl for a wife. And indeed some of them would have married him without money. But his whole attention was fixed upon the miller's daughter and hers on him.

Every evening they would meet on the other side of the river where the tall trees of the forest were reflected in the water. But the future looked dark for them, for never could Vasilisa marry without her parents' blessing. And before that would be given a miracle must happen, so they thought. To help their prayers, they had lit innumerable candles before the stern eyes of the icon in the village church, but without success.

Like all Russians, the inhabitants of the village liked to keep the festivals and observe the old customs handed down to them from their forefathers. Thus it was the custom on St John's Day, the twenty-fourth of June, to gather together on the meadow outside the village and light the St John's fire. The older ones took with them titbits to eat and *kvass*, a sweet-sour fermented drink. The girls wore wreaths of flowers which they had plaited themselves and the lads put on their red Sunday shirts. And of course they had their balalaikas and their harmonicas. The flames of the bonfire flickered joyfully and the whole meadow was filled with dance-music, songs, cheers and laughter. On one side flowed the river where the girls stealthily threw their wreaths of flowers into the water. If the wreath was swiftly caught by the current, there would soon be a wedding. But if the wreath got snagged anywhere, or what was worse if it sank ...!

With boundless energy the girls and the lads danced their dances round the fire and couples in love boldly jumped hand in hand over the flames. But in the end they did grow tired and they lay down on the ground near where an old blind beggar was sitting. He had appeared at the festival and no one knew where he had come from. A wanderer often knows wonderful stories so the crowd pressed round him, saying: "Come, grandfather, tell us a story."

The old man lifted up his head to the dark sky where the first stars had appeared and said: "No, tonight I won't tell you a story, but something that is really true. Now just listen:

"Today is St John's Day and old wise men say that miracles can happen on this night. In the thickest part of the forest there is a ravine where the giant ferns grow, and there the fire–flower will blossom three times tonight. It gives out a light that penetrates right through the earth. Somewhere under the roots of the ferns there lies hidden a treasure: gold, silver and sparkling jewels bigger than any man has ever seen. When the fire–flower blossoms, the treasure becomes visible and the brave man who dares to pluck the flower can take possession of the treasure and be rich for the rest of his life. But, oh how great are the dangers!"

The old beggar fell silent and stared with his unseeing eyes in front of him. The grown–ups and the children sitting round him were silent. Suddenly someone laughed. It was the avaricious miller, his voice ringing sharply through the stillness: "So, lads, there is a fine chance for the bravest among you. I know that many of you are dreaming of marrying my daughter. Well now, whoever comes to me with that treasure shall be my son–in–law!"

Two young men jumped up. A rich peasant's son, rough and idle, whose suit had been repeatedly rejected by Vasilisa, and Ivan the young fair–haired shepherd.

"I'll go and get the treasure," cried the peasant's son brashly. "Neither God nor the Devil shall keep me back!"

Ivan did not speak, but only looked at the fair face of his lass. The blind beggar shook his grey head and muttered: "God be with us."

He crossed himself and many imitated him. But not the rich peasant's son. He was known to favour sitting in the inn on Sundays rather than in the church.

Night fell. The fires had nearly burnt out and slowly the villagers were turning their steps towards home. The last of the songs and a single harmonica still sounded over the meadow. At last only the two young lads remained and, hidden behind a large oak–tree, Vasilisa.

The peasant's son looked at the shepherd contemptuously and sneered in a whisper: "You impertinent lout, do you dare look at my bride? My men will beat you to death!"

With great strides he strode towards the river. He was going to get the treasure and make proud Vasilisa his own, that is if the old man had spoken the truth.

Now only the shepherd and the girl were left standing in the meadow. Vasilisa threw her arms round Ivan and begged him urgently not to go into the dark forest. In one way or another God would help them. But he shook his head laughing. This was such a good chance of winning her!

"Pray for me, my darling," he said, "then God will protect me."

In the meantime it had grown completely dark. The moon had disappeared behind thick clouds and a strong wind blew the smouldering ashes of the St John's fire over the meadow. The young lad brought his lass home to the great mill and whispered to her once more: "Pray for me."

Then he jumped into his boat and rowed over the river. The storm died down as quickly as it had arisen and the girl watched him go until he sprang ashore on the other side. Then she quickly went to her room and knelt down before her little picture of Mary. In the aromatic oil the wick burned day and night and sent forth a pale rosy light through the glass. The glass hung on a little golden chain in front of the face of the icon and the calm eyes in the stern face of the saint looked down on the praying girl.

Meanwhile the peasant's son had crossed the river and entered the wood. Everything was quite still among the tall trees and the thick undergrowth. The pale light of the moon shone in occasional patches upon the forest floor. Sometimes a crackling sounded in the grass and the youth quickly grasped the knife in his belt. But he saw nothing and walked on further. Over a little open patch hundreds of fireflies danced. They crept into his clothes and over his hair. "Cursed beasts!" he cried, and tried to brush them off but he did not succeed. Cursing he struck at them and all at once they flew away. It grew darker and quieter in the forest. An owl hooted three times.

The peasant's son had now penetrated deep into the wilderness and he saw the ravine where the big ferns grew. Again the owl hooted and his heart was filled with fear. A light flitted behind the trees, dark shadows glided over his head. But all was eerily still. An oppressive damp warmth rose from the ravine.

"I must wait here," he muttered. He was nervous and at the same time he was annoyed with himself for being so strangely afraid.

"Old wives' tales!" he mumbled and sat down on the grass. But suddenly he jumped up when a thick green snake slid past him. Aghast he stared at the horrible red eyes and the horns on its flat head. It vanished, but now other eyes appeared, flaming green and pale yellow. He was surrounded by invisible beings and dared not move. He broke out in a sweat. Somewhere in the distance the wind moaned but in the forest round him it was deathly quiet. Suddenly a cock crew. A light appeared in the heart of a gigantic fern and grew and formed a chalice. The fire-flower, a flower of flaming tongues!

As if bewitched, the youth stood watching. "It is true after all," he whispered in surprise. He dared to move one step towards the plant and, in the same moment, a howling gust of wind shot through the dark forest, trees fell with a crash, torn off branches hurtled down around his ears and from behind the bushes pitch-black devils crept towards him, howling like hungry wolves, their ghastly red tongues spitting fire. Thunder-claps rolled over the groaning forest and green bats flitted out of the trees and clutched at the peasant lad's hair. A vile and crooked witch on her broomstick fell like a black cat on to his shoulders and scourged him with a whip of serpents.

Half-mad with fear the once so arrogant youth tried to pray, or even just to make the sign of the cross. But his hand cramped together in a fist and from his lips there came only curses. Desperately he tried to force his way towards the shining flower but again and again the burning chalice escaped him. Cursing God and all the saints he lunged at the flower. His feet slipped and thrashing out in a frenzy he fell into the ravine. At the same moment the ghosts and the fire-flower vanished and all became quite still. The light of the moon broke through the clouds and glided tremblingly over a human hand that was still clutching desperately at the air ...

After a while footsteps sounded. It was Ivan, the young shepherd. After crossing the river he had entered the forest. He had walked on calmly beneath the tall trees. He knew this part of the forest well for he had often gone there after stray sheep. Motionless the trunks rose up all round him. When he reached the open glade, hundreds of fireflies were dancing their summer dance. They flew round his head and came down into his hair.

"Oh, how lovely," murmured the young man and took one of them

carefully in his hand. "Creature of God," he said softly to the shining insect, "you, too, are a little fire. Show me the way to the wonderful fire-flower."

Now all the fireflies formed themselves into a long line and like a moving cord of light flew on before him. "That is a good sign," he thought happily and he followed, feeling encouraged. In this way he came to the edge of the ravine which was surrounded by the thickest forest that he had ever seen. All at once he heard a cock crow. At the same moment something began to glow in the biggest of the ferns. And slowly a shining chalice opened: the fire-flower.

The youth was filled with awe and wonder. He looked and looked ... until he had the feeling of being taken up in the golden glow. Then he remembered the treasure and he took a hesitant step towards the flower. A loud clap of thunder made him jump back in a fright. Lightning forked in the dark air. A raging storm plunged raging on to the tall trees and huge branches crashed round the head of the shepherd lad who trembled with fear. In horror he looked about and saw from all sides ghastly forms closing in towards him. Pitch-black devils with fiery red tongues and tails like serpents; repulsive beasts, half-pigs half-dwarfs. Thin slimy arms appeared out of the ravine and clutched him. Witches in the trees howled like wolves and shrieked: "The flower is ours, ours, ours!"

The youth felt himself drawn irresistibly towards the ravine and with his last strength raised his arms to the skies and cried: "Great God, help me!" And far from him, kneeling in front of her holy icon, Vasilisa was praying: "Dear God, help him!"

As if by magic the storm died down and the devilish forms vanished. The treacherous arms slipped from his body and freed he stood up. And there the fire-flower was shining and lighting up all the surroundings with its golden light. Reverently Ivan made the sign of the cross and plucked the wonderful flower. Then suddenly there came a sound in the trees like distant music. It was as if his eyes and ears were opened for the first time. His gaze penetrated deep into the earth and the earth revealed her secrets to him. He heard the grass growing and understood the language of the birds. "John," he whispered, "The St John's fires have been burning, this is the night of St John." Then he saw beneath the biggest fern a sparkling treasure buried. He grasped the spade which he had brought with him, opened the earth and brought out a great pot filled with gold, silver, and glistening jewels.

The flower in his hand was extinguished like a candle, but the youth felt as if all its light and warmth had flowed into his heart. He gathered up the treasure in his arms and walked home, thanking God. The first rays of the sun accompanied him and high in the air the larks sang joyfully.

Never before in the village had they celebrated a festival so joyfully as on the wedding–day of the fair–haired shepherd's lad and the miller's daughter, Vasilisa.

Faithful John

Brothers Grimm

There was once upon a time an old king who was ill, and thought to himself: "I am lying on what must be my deathbed." Then said he: "Tell Faithful John to come to me."

Faithful John was his favourite servant, and was so called, because he had for his whole life long been so true to him. When therefore he came beside the bed, the King said to him: "Most faithful John, I feel my end approaching, and have no anxiety except about my son. He is still of tender age, and cannot always know how to guide himself. If you do not promise me to teach him everything that he ought to know, and to be his foster–father, I cannot close my eyes in peace."

Then answered Faithful John: "I will not forsake him, and will serve him with fidelity, even if it should cost me my life."

At this, the old King said: "Now I die in comfort and peace." Then he added: "After my death, you shall show him the whole castle: all the chambers, halls, and vaults, and all the treasures which lie therein, but the last chamber in the long gallery, in which is the picture of the princess of the Golden Dwelling, shall you not show. If he sees that picture, he will fall violently in love with her, and will drop down in a swoon, and go through great danger for her sake, therefore you must protect him from that."

And when Faithful John had once more given his promise to the old King about this, the King said no more, but laid his head on his pillow, and died.

When the old King had been carried to his grave, Faithful John told the young King all that he had promised his father on his deathbed, and said: "This will I assuredly keep, and will be faithful to you as I have been faithful to him, even if it should cost me my life."

When the mourning was over, Faithful John said to him: "It is now time that you should see your inheritance. I will show you your father's palace."

Then he took him about everywhere, up and down, and let him see all the riches, and the magnificent apartments, only there was one room

231

which he did not open, that in which hung the dangerous picture. The picture, however, was so placed that when the door was opened you looked straight on it, and it was so admirably painted that it seemed to breathe and live, and there was nothing more charming or more beautiful in the whole world. The young king noticed, however, that Faithful John always walked past this one door, and said: "Why do you never open this one for me?"

"There is something within it," he replied, "which would terrify you."

But the King answered: "I have seen all the palace, and I want to know what is in this room also," and he went and tried to break open the door by force.

Then Faithful John held him back and said: "I promised your father before his death that you should not see that which is in this chamber, it might bring the greatest misfortune on you and on me."

"Ah, no," replied the young King, "if I do not go in, it will be my certain destruction. I should have no rest day or night until I had seen it with my own eyes. I shall not leave the place now until you have un-locked the door."

Then Faithful John saw that there was no help for it now, and with a heavy heart and many sighs, sought out the key from the great bunch. When he had opened the door, he went in first, and thought by standing before him he could hide the portrait so that the King should not see it in front of him. But what good was this? The King stood on tip-toe and saw it over his shoulder. And when he saw the portrait of the maiden, which was so magnificent and shone with gold and precious stones, he fell fainting to the ground.

Faithful John took him up, carried him to his bed, and sorrowfully thought: "The misfortune has befallen us, Lord God, what will be the end of it?" Then he strengthened him with wine, until he came to himself again.

The first words the King said were: "Ah, the beautiful portrait! whose is it?"

"That is the princess of the Golden Dwelling," answered Faithful John.

Then the King continued: "My love for her is so great, that if all the leaves on all the trees were tongues, they could not declare it. I will give my life to win her. You are my most faithful John, you must help me."

The faithful servant considered within himself for a long time how to set about the matter, for it was difficult even to obtain a sight of the King's daughter. At length he thought of a way, and said to the King: "Everything which she has about her is of gold — tables, chairs, dishes, glasses, bowls, and household furniture. Among your treasures are five tons of gold; let one of the goldsmiths of the kingdom fashion these into all manner of vessels and utensils, into all kinds of birds, wild beasts and strange animals, such as may please her, and we will go there with them and try our luck."

The King ordered all the goldsmiths to be brought to him, and they had to work night and day until at last the most splendid things were prepared. When everything was stowed on board a ship, Faithful John put on the dress of a merchant, and the King was forced to do the same in order to make himself quite unrecognizable. Then they sailed across the sea, and sailed on until they came to the town wherein dwelt the princess of the Golden Dwelling.

Faithful John bade the King stay behind on the ship, and wait for him. "Perhaps I shall bring the princess with me," said he, "therefore see that everything is in order; have the golden vessels set out and the whole ship decorated."

Then he gathered together in his apron all kinds of golden things, went on shore and walked straight to the royal palace. When he entered the courtyard of the palace, a beautiful girl was standing there by the well with two golden buckets in her hand, drawing water with them. And when she was just turning round to carry away the sparkling water she saw the stranger, and asked who he was.

So he answered: "I am a merchant," and opened his apron, and let her look in.

Then she cried: "Oh, what beautiful golden things!" and put her pails down and looked at the golden wares one after the other. Then said the girl: "The princess must see these, she has such great pleasure in golden things, that she will buy all you have."

She took him by the hand and led him upstairs, for she was the waiting-maid. When the King's daughter saw the wares, she was quite delighted and said: "They are so beautifully worked, that I will buy them all from you."

But Faithful John said: "I am only the servant of a rich merchant. The things I have here are not to be compared with those my master has in his ship. They are the most beautiful and valuable things that have ever been made in gold."

When she wanted to have everything brought up to her, he said: "There are so many of them that it would take a great many days to do that, and so many rooms would be required to exhibit them, that your house is not big enough."

Then her curiosity and longing were still more excited, until at last she said: "Conduct me to the ship, I will go there myself, and behold the treasures of your master."

At this Faithful John was quite delighted, and led her to the ship, and when the King saw her, he perceived that her beauty was even greater than the picture had represented it to be, and thought no other than that his heart would burst in twain. Then she boarded the ship, and the King led her within. Faithful John, however, remained with the helmsman, and ordered the ship to be pushed off, saying: "Set all sail, till it fly like a bird in the air."

Within, the King showed her the golden vessels, every one of them, also the wild beasts and strange animals. Many hours went by whilst she was seeing everything, and in her delight she did not observe that the ship was sailing away. After she had looked at the last, she thanked the merchant and wanted to go home, but when she came to the side of the ship, she saw that it was on the high seas far from land, and hurrying onwards with all sail set.

"Ah," cried she in her alarm, "I am betrayed! I am carried away and have fallen into the power of a merchant — I would rather die!"

The King, however, seized her hand, and said: "I am not a merchant. I am a king, and of no meaner origin than you are, and if I have carried you away with subtlety, that has come to pass because of my exceeding great love for you. The first time that I looked on your portrait, I fell fainting to the ground."

When the princess of the Golden Dwelling heard this, she was comforted, and her heart was drawn to him, so that she willingly consented to be his wife.

It so happened, while they were sailing onwards over the deep sea, that Faithful John, who was sitting on the fore part of the vessel, making music, saw three ravens in the air, which came flying towards them. At this he stopped playing and listened to what they were saying to each other, for that he well understood.

One cried: "Oh, there he is carrying home the princess of the Golden Dwelling."

"Yes," replied the second, "but he has not got her yet."

Said the third: "But he has got her, she is sitting beside him in the ship."

Then the first began again, and cried: "What good will that do him? When they reach land a chestnut horse will leap forward to meet him, and the prince will want to mount it, but if he does that, it will run away with him, and rise up into the air, and he will never see his maiden more."

Spoke the second: "But is there no escape?"

"Oh, yes, if someone else mounts it swiftly, and takes out the pistol which he will find in its holster, and shoots the horse dead, the young King is saved. But who knows that? And whosoever does know it, and tells it to him, will be turned to stone from the toe to the knee."

Then said the second: "I know more than that; even if the horse be killed, the young King will still not keep his bride. When they go into the castle together, a wrought bridal garment will be lying there in a dish, and looking as if it were woven of gold and silver; it is, however, nothing but sulphur and pitch, and if he put it on, it will burn him to the very bone and marrow."

Said the third: "Is there no escape at all?"

"Oh, yes," replied the second, "if any one with gloves on seizes the garment and throws it into the fire and burns it, the young King will be saved. But what good will that do? Whosoever knows it and tells it to him, half his body will become stone from the knee to the heart."

Then said the third: "I know still more; even if the bridal garment be burnt, the young King will still not have his bride. After the wedding, when the dancing begins and the young Queen is dancing, she will sud‐ denly turn pale and fall down as if dead, and if some one does not lift her up and draw three drops of blood from her right breast and spit them out again, she will die. But if any one who knows that were to declare it, he would become stone from the crown of his head to the sole of his foot."

When the ravens had spoken of this together, they flew onwards, and Faithful John had well understood everything, but from that time forth he became quiet and sad, for if he concealed what he had heard from his master, the latter would be unfortunate, and if he disclosed it to him, he himself must sacrifice his life. At length, however, he said to himself: "I will save my master, even if it bring destruction on myself."

When therefore they came to shore, all happened as had been foretold by the ravens, and a magnificent chestnut horse sprang forward. "Good," said the King, "he shall carry me to my palace," and was about to mount it when Faithful John got before him, jumped quickly on it, drew the pistol out of the holster, and shot the horse.

Then the other attendants of the King, who were not very fond of Faithful John, cried: "How shameful to kill the beautiful animal, that was to have carried the King to his palace!"

But the King said: "Hold your peace and leave him alone, he is my most faithful John.

Who knows what good may come of this!" They went into the palace, and in the hall there stood a dish, and therein lay the bridal garment looking no otherwise than as if it were made of gold and silver. The young king went towards it and was about to take hold of it, but Faithful John pushed him away, seized it with gloves on, carried it quickly to the fire and burnt it. The other attendants again began to murmur, and said: "Behold, now he is even burning the King's bridal garment!"

But the young King said: "Who knows what good he may have done, leave him alone, he is my most faithful John."

And now the wedding was solemnized: the dance began, and the bride also took part in it; then Faithful John was watchful and looked into her face, and suddenly she turned pale and fell to the ground as if she were dead. On this he ran hastily to her, lifted her up and bore her into a chamber — then he laid her down, and knelt and sucked the three drops of blood from her right breast, and spat them out. Immediately she breathed again and recovered herself, but the young King had seen this, and being ignorant why Faithful John had done it, was angry and cried: "Throw him into a dungeon."

Next morning Faithful John was condemned, and led to the gallows, and when he stood on high, and was about to be executed, he said: "Every one who has to die is permitted before his end to make one last speech; may I, too, claim the right?"

"Yes," answered the King, "it shall be granted unto you."

Then said Faithful John: "I am unjustly condemned, and have always been true to you," and he related how he had hearkened to the conversation of the ravens when on the sea, and how he had been obliged to do all these things in order to save his master.

Then cried the King: "Oh, my most faithful John. Pardon, pardon — bring him down." But as Faithful John spoke the last word he had fallen down lifeless and become a stone.

Thereupon the King and the Queen suffered great anguish, and the King said: "Ah, how ill I have requited great fidelity!" and ordered the stone figure to be taken up and placed in his bedroom beside his bed. And as often as he looked on it he wept and said: "Ah, if I could bring you to life again, my most faithful John."

Some time passed and the Queen bore twins, two sons who grew fast and were her delight. Once when the Queen was at church and the father was sitting with his two children playing beside him, he looked at the stone figure again, sighed, and full of grief he said: "Ah, if I could but bring you to life again, my most faithful John."

Then the stone began to speak and said: "You can bring me to life again if you will use for that purpose what is dearest to you."

Then cried the King: "I will give everything I have in the world for you."

The stone continued: "If you will cut off the heads of your two children with your own hand, and sprinkle me with their blood, I shall be restored to life."

The King was terrified when he heard that he himself must kill his dearest children, but he thought of Faithful John's great fidelity, and how he had died for him, drew his sword, and with his own hand cut off the children's heads. And when he had smeared the stone with their blood, life returned to it, and Faithful John stood once more safe and healthy before him.

He said to the King: "Your truth shall not go unrewarded," and took the heads of the children, put them on again, and rubbed the wounds with their blood, at which they became whole again immediately, and jumped about, and went on playing as if nothing had happened.

Then the King was full of joy, and when he saw the Queen coming he hid Faithful John and the two children in a great cupboard. When she entered, he said to her: "Have you been praying in the church?"

"Yes," answered she, "but I have constantly been thinking of Faithful John and what misfortune has befallen him through us." Then said he: "Dear wife, we can give him his life again, but it will cost us our two little sons, whom we must sacrifice."

The Queen turned pale, and her heart was full of terror, but she said: "We owe it to him, for his great fidelity."

Then the King was rejoiced that she thought as he had thought, and went and opened the cupboard, and brought forth Faithful John and the children, and said: "God be praised, he is delivered, and we have our little sons again also," and told her how everything had occurred. Then they dwelt together in much happiness until their death.

Sources and acknowledgments

Thanks are due to the following authors and publishers for permission to reprint copyright material in this collection.

"The Entry into Jerusalem," from the Gospel of Matthew (20:1–11) translated by Kalmia Bittleston, Floris Books, 1988.

"Jesus Washes His Disciples' Feet," from the Gospel of John (13:1–20) translated by Kalmia Bittleston, Floris Books, 1984.

"Robin Redbreast," "Saint Veronica" from *Christ Legends* by Selma Lagerlöf, translated by Velma Swanston Howard, Floris Books, 1984.

"The Student," translated by Ronald Wilks in *The Fiancée and other stories,* 1986, by permission of Penguin Books.

"The Juniper Tree," "The Donkey," "The Crystal Ball," "The Six Swans," "The Goose-Girl," and "Faithful John," from *Grimm's Fairy Tales,* 1978, by permission of Routledge and Kegan Paul.

"The Three Hares" translated by Donald Maclean from *Jonas* 16, 1977.

"The Saint and the Mountain Spirit" translated by Donald Maclean from *De Christen-gemeenschap* 1966, 21:2.

"The Barge-Master's Easter" translated by Polly Lawson from *Vijftien Paasverhalen,* J.N. Voorhoeve, The Hague.

"The Candle," "The Two Old Men" from *Master and Man, and other parables,* in the Everyman Library edition, J.M. Dent, 1982.

"The Easter Grace" translated by Polly Lawson from *Die Ostergnade,* Bruno Schwabe, Basel.

"The Resurrection" from the Gospel of Luke (24:1–12) translated by Kalmia Bittleston, Floris Books, 1990.

"Kira Kiralina," "Guracasca" translated by Donald Maclean from *Jorga der Tapfere,* Freies Geistesleben, Stuttgart, 1969.

"Koschey the Deathless," "The Water of Life" from *Russian Fairy Tales* translated by Norbert Guterman, Pantheon Books, 1973.

"The Devil and the Ploughman" translated by Polly Lawson from *Sämtliche Werke,* München, 1969.

"Sister Amelia" translated by Donald Maclean from *Beim Schicksal zu Gast,* Urachhaus, Stuttgart, 1986.

"Offerus the Giant" translated by Polly Lawson from *Kindheitslegenden,* Freies Geistesleben, Stuttgart, 1983.

"Busy Lizzy of Clausthal" translated by Donald Maclean.

"The Hidden Icon" translated by Polly Lawson from *Zwischen Traum und Tag,* Verlag Hans H. Sörensen, Berlin.

"Pentecost" from the New English Bible.

"The Journey to the Sun" translated by Donald Maclean from *Sonnenmärchen. Slavische Volksmärchen,* Hausbücher Verlag, Vienna.

"The Fire-Flower" translated by Polly Lawson from *Het hele jaar rond,* Lemniscaat, Rotterdam, 1983.